LAKE LIFE

Also by Tanya Boteju

Kings, Queens, and In-Betweens

Bruised

Messy Perfect

Allyship as Action: 7 Ways to Advocate for Others

TANYA BOTEJU

Lake Life

Quill Tree Books
An *Imprint of* HarperCollins*Publishers*

HarperCollins Children's Books, a division of HarperCollins Publishers, 195 Broadway, New York, NY 10007

HarperCollins Publishers, Macken House, 39/40 Mayor Street Upper, Dublin 1, D01 C9W8, Ireland

Quill Tree Books is an imprint of HarperCollins Publishers.

Lake Life

harpercollins.com

Library of Congress Control Number: 2025950355
ISBN 978-0-06-335854-6

Typography by David Dewitt
26 27 28 29 30 LBC 5 4 3 2 1
First Edition

To Jennifer, who built me a cabin with her own hands
so I can write in peace and look up to the trees.

AUTHOR'S NOTE

This book started out as a light, rom-com-esque summer read, and I think it's still that. But when I discovered there would be an environmental activism piece to the story, and how important the land itself would be to the characters, I knew it was necessary to include at least some aspects of Indigeneity, given that Indigenous peoples are the original caretakers of the land and their knowledge is essential to keeping the land and all its beings cared for. I didn't want to mess that part up, but I know that including these pieces will invite criticism—there are so many ways to write about Indigeneity poorly as a non-Indigenous person. I'm grateful to my expert reader for her helpful insights and the handful of trusted friends and colleagues who offered their feedback, as well. Any remaining missteps are my own, and I'm open to the criticism and additional learning that will surely come.

And, as always, I'm thankful for this land I live on and for the Indigenous wisdom that is so generously shared by Indigenous storytellers. In particular, I am deeply grateful to Robin Wall

Kimmerer for her literary gem *Braiding Sweetgrass: Indigenous Wisdom, Scientific Knowledge, and the Teachings of Plants* for its inspiration and guidance around reciprocity with and gratitude for the land. Everyone on the planet should read it. We need all the good medicine we can give and receive if we're to continue living on this planet.

Thank you also to the Yellowhead Institute for their magnificent course Land Back, which gave me so many insights into Indigenous efforts to resist colonial impacts on the land. I highly recommend this learning.

ONE

Maya

The lock for the cabin has always been sticky, but not *this* sticky. I've been jiggling the key for at least a minute, twisting it to the right, then to the left, but can't get it to turn. After another few seconds, I stop, slide my backpack off my shoulders, and stare up at the dusky sky.

If I don't take a few breaths, I'll lose it.

I take the breaths, lose it anyway, and kick the door.

"Mom! This dumb lock is stuck again!"

From the road, my mom whisper-shouts, "Maya, stop yelling. Everyone in Spruce Lake will hear you!" She appears at the top of the stairs that lead down to the cabin, duffel bag in one hand, grocery bags in the other. Dad appears behind her with his own handfuls of luggage and supplies.

"Well!" I continue to yell. "How am I supposed to open it?"

My mom and dad exchange a look that I know means *How long will it be like this?* And honestly, I'd love to know the answer, too. How long will I feel like nothing is working out the way it's supposed to? Like everything is just sticky and stuck and wrong?

I glare at them and their knowing looks as they approach the door.

My mom puts the duffel bag down and holds her hand out to me. "Give it," she says.

I slap the key into her hand with a huff and step back.

She opens the door, no problem, like she's been doing it most of her life. Which she has. She's trying to hide the smile on her face, but I see it and roll my eyes.

"Whatever," I mumble, picking up her duffel and my backpack and barging through the doorway into the cabin's living room.

Cedar, fresh laundry, dust.

The cabin's smells should bring me back to every summer I've spent here, but they only bring me back to last summer, which was also the worst summer. Smells that once held sun-dried towels and late-night nachos, comfort and laughter, only jolt me into embarrassment and loss.

If things were up to me, I would have just stayed home this summer. Continued to pine away in private. Maybe landed a summer job and made a dent in my TBR list. But nothing is up to me, apparently. My parents decided that I shouldn't be home alone for two months, that *they* weren't about to give up our regular summer at Spruce Lake, and that the only way for me to feel better was to be here.

They seem hell-bent on bringing me back to fun and familiarity, and it's exhausting.

They don't understand how heartache works. Why would they?

I watch them now, giggling like kids in the kitchen as they put away the groceries. Already acting like they always do when they get here—like no time has passed since they met in Spruce Lake over twenty years ago and fell in love and got married and had me and then continued to be as enamored and annoying as ever.

I dump Mom's duffel in the middle of the living room and head to "Maya's bunker," as we've always called it, both because it's always had bunk beds, even though I'm an only child, and because it's my little fort in the cabin. As soon as I enter, I know right away that Uncle Diamond—who lives here year-round—has set it up for me. Maybe he was trying to lessen the distress he knew I'd feel.

The fan is on to keep the room cool in the early July heat, a fresh towel is on the side table, a candle (unlit now) has been burning, leaving the faintest hint of vanilla, and the bottom bunk is made up. On the light green bedspread is a foil-wrapped chocolate shaped like a ladybug. A note sits beneath it.

I immediately see the ladybug zoos my best friend, Rashida, and I used to build when we were kids—when we would name each bug and make little enclosures out of branches and rocks and then let them go one by one while singing made-up songs about freedom.

A year ago, a memory like that would have made me smile. Now I pick up the note with dread.

Welcome back, nerd. xx Rashida

My chest clenches and my eyes water.

How the hell am I supposed to do this? See Rashida after getting everything between us so wrong and telling her how I feel?

Felt?

Feel. Definitely feel. As hard as I've been trying not to feel.

"Maya, can you please grab the rest of the stuff from the car and unpack? Dad and I are going to head over to Jasper's and say hi to Diamond." Mom appears at my bedroom door. "Unless you want to join?"

Her face is hopeful, but I definitely do *not* want to join them at Jasper's, the pub that Uncle Diamond and his boyfriend, Jasper, run together. Half the town will be there, and everyone is probably as embarrassed for me as I am. I don't have the energy to act like I'm happy to be here or to see them.

"*No thanks,*" I snap, hoping my tone conveys just how much torture they're putting me through.

Her eyes widen for a moment, but she sucks in her lips, probably holding back whatever she wants to say. That's fine with me. I'm sick of the two of them trying to make me feel better about being wholly rejected by the girl I've been in love with for as long as I've been capable of being in love.

"Okay, well, there's that leftover pasta we brought and lots of veggie dogs and stuff in the fridge if you get hungry. Not sure what time we'll be home. Feel free to come by later if you change your mind."

"I won't."

I know I'm being extra stubborn. I get that I'm fulfilling the role of moody teenager in a made-for-TV movie. But I don't care. I just don't.

My mom sighs. "I love you. This summer will be better than

you think. I promise." She gives me that poor-little-thing look and turns to go. Moments later, I hear her and my dad leave, the front door banging shut because that's the only way it'll close properly after years of expanding and contracting with the weather.

I drop the ladybug and note in the drawer of the bedside table, hoping some of these feelings will get closed up in the dark with them, and unload the rest of our stuff from the car. But I don't put any of it away. Why should I have to do all the grunt work? They're the ones who wanted to come, not me.

Take that, parents.

I grab the towel and a bathing suit from my room and head to the lake to try to clear my mind.

The dock groans and tilts like it always has. The same deck chairs sprawl beneath the canopy we set up every summer. Spiderwebs cling to corners like they do every morning. Even these familiarities feel somehow different, though.

I try not to glance over at Rashida's cabin, right next door. She's not home, thankfully. I know this because if she were, she'd have come by to say hi.

Or maybe not. Maybe she's dreading seeing me the same way I'm dreading seeing her.

But avoiding her and our friendship is virtually impossible here. Even as I stand at the edge of the dock and look out, my eyes land on the tiny island across from our cabin that Rashida and I claimed for "our own" when we were nine and could actually make it out there by ourselves in a canoe.

We'd named it Cutie Beach, but when we told Diamond about

our land claim and naming, he'd patiently explained that the land already belonged to the Quw'utsun people and asked us to consider calling it something more meaningful if we wanted a special name just for ourselves.

So we did some research like the little nerds we were and discovered that the original people here got their name from a Hul'q'umi'num word meaning "warm land." We decided on Sun Island instead—because the small beach there did warm through with the afternoon and evening sun in the summer.

Rashida and I have spent a lot of time out on that island, even creating a "Kitchen Stadium" out of logs and rocks for when we'd make ourselves fancy meals—cheese and crackers, blueberries and plums. At night, we'd float off the beach on our backs and stare up at the sky—stars here are unlike anything you can see in the city. We'd submerge our ears in the water so that all we could hear was a hollow liquid sound and our own breathing.

My eyes grow wet, and I have to blink and shift my sight line to the water in front of me.

The first dip is always the hardest. After a full minute, I finally work up the will to jump in, feetfirst, nose pinched between my thumb and pointer finger.

The water is even colder than I expected, so I front crawl a few times back and forth between my dock and the Morrises' floating dock a couple of cabins down, trying to warm my body up. The only time I ever swim is during my summers here, so I'm a little out of breath. I tread water and dip my nose beneath the surface, peering over the water like an alligator. A couple of

Jet Skis zoom by, sending a few waves my way, and I hear Rashida's voice in my head: "Goddamn Jet Skis with their goddamn obnoxious drivers and their goddamn noise."

She isn't a fan.

Rashida has lived here her whole life, year-round, and her family has owned their cabin next door for two generations. My grandparents built our cabin, and Uncle Diamond lives here all year, as well, but my parents and I are summer Spruce Lakers.

That didn't stop Rashida and me from being best friends our whole lives, though. Even when I'm back in Greenview on the mainland during the school year, Rashida and I talk or message almost every day.

But not this past year. I haven't seen or talked to her since last summer. I couldn't. I needed some distance from her and my embarrassment. I didn't have a clue what to say to her, anyway.

"Sorry I read our whole relationship wrong"?

"Sorry I've made the relationship we *did* have completely awkward now"?

"Sorry I still want to be your girlfriend even though you just want friendship"?

Ugh.

I pull myself up the ladder and start to towel off, but just as I'm about to head back inside, a motorboat rounds the piece of land that juts out past Rashida's cabin and my own. Three people are in the boat, and one is Rashida—and she's looking right at me as she steers toward my dock.

TWO

Gabe

What the shit is this?

I scan the tiny bedroom. A twin bed (*twin?!*) adorned with a bright yellow quilt. Forest-green area rug on wood flooring. Flower- and tree-patterned . . . everything.

A window looks out onto a bunch of trees bordering the property, a series of glass jars sitting along the sill with stuff growing out of them—their roots long and squiggly and on full display in the water like gross little tentacles. A small desk with a stool that probably won't even fit one of my ass cheeks sits in a corner.

This? Instead of my own bedroom, which is at least twelve times the size and has a gigantic en suite bathroom, sliding glass doors that go out onto a long balcony, and not a goddamn flower in sight?

"Everything look okay?" a pert voice says behind me.

I swivel to find Canva—*what kind of name is Canva?*—the owner of these spectacularly underwhelming accommodations that I have to call home for an entire summer, thanks to my mother.

"Yeah, sure," I lie. "A little smaller than I thought it'd be." I bet my mom chose this place on purpose. A small, boring B and B in a small, boring town to keep me out of trouble. Away from my friends. With no convenient transportation to anywhere worthwhile. Close enough to where she's working all summer one town away at her big corporate job, but far enough she doesn't have to deal with me.

She'd told me my accommodations would be "lovely" and "quaint." When I'd asked if I could at least just stay at the hotel she was in, twenty minutes away, she said I'd be too much of a distraction. That *this* tiny hellhole might teach me to "slow down a little" and "focus on something other than parties and nonsense."

Such bullshit.

Canva's smile falters, and I realize I better turn on some charm if I have to live with this woman all summer. "It's nice, though. I love the decor," I lie again—a gift I have—and Canva beams. She's about four inches shorter than I am, Black, looks like she runs marathons, with her wiry, tight muscles, and has a shaved head. Her quick, jerky movements remind me of a squirrel.

"Thank you! I wanted it to feel like the outdoors, but *in*doors, you know?" She shoves past me into the room. "Now, that closet there has extra towels, sheets, and blankets. Grab whatever you need. Leave any laundry you want done in that basket by Friday night, and I'll do it on the weekend."

She looks around but doesn't stop talking as I try to get the thought of her handling my G-strings out of my mind.

"But you wash your own dishes, clean your room, keep common spaces tidy, etc. Anything on the top shelf of the fridge is yours to use, and simple breakfast items will be available from seven a.m. to nine thirty a.m. every day. Oh, and your bathroom is just at the end of the hall. You can drink the water here, but just try and conserve what you use. The first *R* is for *reduce*, after all!"

"Right," I say, wishing the first *R* was for *rye whiskey* instead and I could get a giant shot of it, stat.

Canva goes on for another five minutes, sharing about her many house rules around noise, recycling, common area use, and the chickens who apparently live right outside my window.

"Our chickens are a lively bunch—I wish I could say they're quiet, but they do get a little rowdy in the mornings when they're laying, like they're trying to outdo each other or something." She chuckles with something like affection. "I put some earplugs in the side table, just in case you like to sleep in."

Super.

Finally, she says good night, even though it's only eight thirty, and I'm left staring at these ugly flowers around me. I take out my phone. I only have two bars, but I send a quick text to my mom to let her know I'm here, as per her instructions. I'm supposed to message her every morning and every night, like that will prove I'm not being the little shit she expects me to be.

After a minute with no reply, I pop into my socials to see all the fun I'm missing. It takes about five seconds for that to get too depressing, so I throw the phone on the desk and try to unpack instead. I end up leaving my suitcase on the floor, though, because there's nowhere to actually put anything in this room.

I fall back onto the bed. The ceiling is low and all wood, which is meant to be cozy, I guess, but right now it just adds to the claustrophobia I'm starting to feel.

Christ. How am I supposed to spend two months in a place like this?

When my mom told me she wanted me staying here over the summer, I outright laughed. Leave my sweet house and friends in a proper city like Piedmont to spend a summer in a place like this?

But seeing my mom's face fall at my reaction, I quickly sobered.

"Wait—you're serious?" I asked.

"Yes, Gabe. I'm serious. If I can't follow through on this, do you really think Omni is just going to let me—their first female VP—continue on? My job is quite literally on the line, and I don't want to be worrying about you and what you're getting up to at home alone with your friends while I'm there. I think you've caused enough problems for me, haven't you?" She frowned and crossed her arms, and I hated the pinch her look caused in my chest.

"Problems" meant I was just a little jerk who only cared about myself and partied my life away. It meant I'd torn a hole through my family with all my irresponsible actions and "lack of commitment to anything real."

Because that's what I did. My other mom—Meems, I called

her—left a couple of months ago because she didn't know what to do with me. She was a stay-at-home parent for most of my life, and she couldn't do it anymore. 'Cause I'm a little shit. She called me that once—"You're an ungrateful little shit"—after I forgot to tell her I'd be staying over at a friend's place and she'd been up all night, worrying.

After Meems left, Mom just dove even more into her work, and I dove into being an even bigger dick. Because why the hell not? If one mom can just leave and the other can ignore me, why should I bother trying to be someone I'm not? So I just leaned into all the mayhem that at least gave me something to do.

Until I started to notice some of that defeat and disappointment creep into Mom's eyes, too, and it freaked me the hell out. If this mom left, as well, I didn't know what I'd do. I barely passed high school. I didn't really have any talents or prospects. I liked my house. I didn't want to lose another mom.

So I tried to scale back Party Gabe and make the slow, painful journey to Good Gabe. The pathway from one to the other has been like that old-timey video game where it's just two bars on either side of the screen, hitting a ball back and forth, but sometimes the ball gets hit a certain way and it suddenly speeds up and flings in unpredictable directions.

I felt like that, trying to be this other Gabe. Like I kind of bounced back and forth, slowly making my way from one Gabe to the next, but all of a sudden something would set me off, and I'd catapult off the screen and back to my old, shitty self.

I finally just gave up trying, I guess.

Logistically, though, I had no choice but to accept my mom's conditions for this summer. It was either this or figure out somewhere else to live and pay for it myself, she'd said, which would be hard to do, since all of my money comes from my mom and the idea of getting and sticking to some crap job isn't on my menu.

So here I am, lying in this squishy room in a weird little town by myself for the next two months.

But I don't have to be happy about it.

My phone buzzes. I sit up and cross the two feet to the desk to check it.

Mother-Figure: Glad to hear you arrived safely. Things are incredibly busy here. Might not be able to get back to you right away, but call my assistant if there's an emergency.

Mother-Figure: But please, Gabe, no emergencies.

Mother-Figure: And don't go overboard with the credit card.

My mom's messages cause competing reactions in my body. One is a hot, swarming anger that I'm all too familiar with. The other is that goddamn pinch that makes me want to rip out my chest.

THREE

Maya

My stomach feels like I've ingested too much lake water, even though I haven't. I wish I'd gone inside sooner so I was fully clothed the first time Rashida saw me instead of wearing this crappy one-piece bathing suit that's been sitting in a drawer for the past year and whose elastic crackled as I stretched it over my body earlier.

She waves with one hand, the other on the wheel as she draws nearer. The two people behind her wave, too, and I recognize them as Casey and Jocelyn, two members of the Spruce Lake Eco Alliance (SLEA)—the group Diamond and my mom and dad started four years ago to protect Spruce Lake from over-development and pollution.

My whole body contracts. I'm not ready for this. For seeing her. For others to witness me seeing her. For whatever my mouth is about to say or not say, given how tight and disoriented my body is right now.

I manage to wave back, barely, keeping my towel wrapped tightly around me like a shield. "Hi," I say, trying to muster something other than the ache I feel.

"Hey," she replies, but her eyes don't quite meet mine as she turns off the engine several feet away, letting the boat glide in alongside the dock like the expert boat person she is. I keep my own eyes on the three small black silhouettes of trees Rashida and I painted on the boat's hull a few years ago.

Casey leans over and loops a rope around the mooring cleat on the dock as I just stand there, watching. I should have offered to do that, but the thought of losing my towel as I maneuvered the rope is too much to bear.

Rashida stands from her seat in the fading light and climbs out of the boat. She's wearing her usual cut-off jean shorts, a tank top that says "Water is life" on it, and small silver hoop earrings. Her hair has changed—last summer she wore it in two puffy ponytails, but now she has long braids and a green handkerchief over them. And though she hasn't grown any taller, I can't help but notice some curves that weren't there last summer. Everything about her seems more mature, more attractive. Like the universe is taunting me with what I can't have.

She comes in for a hug, but tentatively. She's not a tentative person, by any means, but she must be as uncertain about us as I am, now that I've gone and rearranged our entire relationship. But there's no way we *can't* hug right now. We're Maya and Rashida.

When our arms wrap around each other, though, my heart stumbles—from new feelings of uncertainty and from older, more yearning feelings for the way it used to be, which now just feel complicated and confusing.

Damn. Get it together, Maya. I try to rearrange my face to resemble "perfectly fine" as I pull back and we let our arms fall from each other. I don't miss the sideways glances that Casey and Jocelyn give each other. I guess I should get used to those kinds of looks this summer, given that I'm sure every single person in Spruce Lake knows about my epic rejection.

"When'd you get here?" Rashida asks, her voice as tentative as her hug.

I can already tell she's going to try to bypass the mortifying moment between us from last summer when I expressed my stupid feelings and she barely hesitated to tell me she didn't feel the same way.

You're my best friend, Maya. We're perfect the way we are.

I can't think of a more imperfect moment than that one.

But this one isn't too far behind.

I try to keep my own tone light, mainly for the benefit of Casey and Jocelyn, who don't need to witness some kind of Maya meltdown. "We got in about half an hour ago. Needed to cool off and stretch out from sitting in the car."

"Nothing like a little nature to rejuvenate!" Jocelyn says, grinning at me.

I smile in response, even though I just want to crawl into my bunk bed for the next two months.

I look back to Rish and try to act like a human being. "Just finished a shift?"

"Yup. Then picked up these two." She indicates Jocelyn and Casey.

"How's Jan?" I ask. Jan is Rashida's boss at Need Something?, which is a fishing, gardening, and a-million-other-things store down the road.

"As cranky as ever."

"Glad to hear it."

"Yeah . . ."

A couple of seconds pass, and I hate this awkwardness. I try, "Thanks for the ladybug."

She gives me a small smile. "No probs, bobs. I've been really looking forward to seeing you."

I crinkle my nose and sniff. A drop of water runs down the side of my face. "Um. Me too." I mean this in some way, despite the fifty-pound weight on my heart. Despite the fact that I don't want to be here at all. But it's impossible turning off the way I feel about her. Have always felt about her.

"You were really looking forward to seeing yourself?" Casey pipes up.

I shake my head but smile. "Funny."

Casey grins and flicks their hair. "I know I am."

Jocelyn calls out, "Rashida, we should probably get going."

"Oh, right. Yeah," Rashida says, and her face becomes uncertain. "Um, would you . . . want to come with us?"

"Me?" I say, before thinking.

A corner of her mouth lifts. "No, all the other people on your dock."

Instead of smiling back, though, my mouth says, "For what?"

"We're doing a loop of the lake, trying to drum up support and donations for SLEA!" Casey says.

I can't imagine getting into a boat to do something normal with Rashida right now. "Oh. Uh. Can we do it another time? I'm kind of beat."

A crinkle appears on her brow. "Oh . . . okay. Would you want to hang out tomorrow? Have breakfast on Sun Island maybe?"

Hard to answer. I *do* want to hang out. I want it to be just like it was before, when it felt like we were in the tightest, best bubble and no one could ever pop it. But it popped last summer, and Rashida was the one to stick the pin in. Now there's no promise of something else. We're just Rashida and Maya, BFFs. Not the best friends who are really in love with each other that I'd conjured up in my head, apparently from nothing.

But how could it be nothing?

"I might sleep in a little—maybe later?"

Her brow crinkles some more, and her shoulders drop a smidge. She shifts her gaze across the lake for a moment, then back to me. She's about to say something else but seems to remember Casey and Jocelyn are here. She glances at them. They glance at each other and then at me. Casey tries for a half grin and sends me awkward finger guns. They must feel the weird tension as much as I do.

"Totally," Rashida finally says. "I finish my shift at two. I'll text you or something?"

"Okay."

"Cool. See ya."

She climbs back into the boat and starts the engine again.

I release the rope from the dock and throw it to Jocelyn. "Good luck on your mission," I say, hoping I don't sound as off-kilter as I feel.

FOUR

Gabe

When I wake up the next day, it's not by choice. I forgot to put in the earplugs Canva left, and the chickens are having a party outside my window—clucking away like it's 1999.

What the hell.

I groan, thrash around in bed for another hour, and then finally muddle my way through my mid-morning stupor. I don't usually wake up until noon most days. After finishing high school last year, I mainly kept up a very active social life, seeing a couple of guys on and off, and plodded my way through two online courses Meems and Mom had forced me to take in order to continue living "under their roof." It was one of the few things they agreed on.

I've missed breakfast according to the schedule that's posted on the bedroom door, and I realize I'm starving. I throw on my favorite red bikini, a pair of frayed designer jean shorts, and a crop top. Just because I'm here under duress doesn't mean I can't look good and get a tan.

I listen at the door to make sure Canva isn't lurking. I don't have the energy to deal with that woman's zest for life at the moment.

Hearing nothing except the damn chickens, I poke my head out, tiptoe to the bathroom, do my business, then check out the fridge to see what the "top shelf" of food I'm allowed to have entails. All I see are a bunch of sauces—tahini, tamari, sriracha—some hummus, sprouts, almond milk, and a bunch of other stuff I wouldn't touch with a ten-foot pole.

But then I hear the chicken party outside. Where there are chickens, there must be eggs, right? And I know how to cook eggs. I may be a rich kid, but no one *cooks* for me . . . at least not since after Meems left.

I exit the kitchen door and round the house to where the chickens are still having their little rager inside their chicken cage or whatever it's called. There are only six of them, but they're noisy as hell. One side of the enclosure has a little hut thing, and I bet that's where the eggs are. I unlatch the door and slip in so the chickens don't escape. They squawk up a storm around me like I'm trying to murder them.

"Keep yer feathers on, drumsticks," I say, making my way to the hut. It stinks in here. I hold my breath and duck my head inside the opening to the hut. Bingo. Two brown eggs lie side by side on a bed of straw. I reach over and grab them both. Chickens lay eggs every day, right?

As I pull my head back out, I feel a poke at the back of my

calf. Then another one. I turn to find three chickens at my feet, pecking at me.

"You little turds. What's the deal?" They keep jabbing at me and clucking.

I shuffle my way back to the door, but more chickens join the fight for who-the-fuck-knows-what. "Hey! Assholes! Isn't this what you're here for? Making eggs?"

One black-and-tan chicken flies up and flaps its wings at my arm. *Since when do chickens fly?* I shoo it away and flee to the exit. But as I try to bang the door shut after me, the little jerk squeezes out and keeps trying to peck at me.

"Jesus! What is your problem!" I yell, while also trying to get my hands on him . . . her? I guess?

But out of nowhere, two thin brown arms reach out and grab the little insurrectionist firmly around the body, and the flapping stops, thank Christ.

"Her problem is that she doesn't know you, so she's stressed out."

A small Black boy is standing in front of me with a suddenly very calm chicken in his hands, judgment all over his baby face. He's wearing sneakers, long purple swim shorts, a lime-green tank top, and a matching lime green headband around a sweet fade.

Impressive look, but who the hell is this? Canva didn't mention a kid.

I'm stunned for a moment and then realize my mouth is open. I close it. "Oh" is all I can muster.

"Auntie's gonna be so mad," the boy says as he turns to put the chicken back in its cage.

Just in case this kid is thinking of snitching on me, I try, "Well, maybe we can agree that this was just an honest mistake and you and I can share these eggs as a truce?"

He latches the door and faces me. "Um." He points to my hands.

I look down and realize that, in my frenzied escape from the stressed-out chickens, I squashed the eggs. Both of my hands are a sticky, disgusting mess, and I can feel the yolks turning gummy between my fingers, which makes me want to hurl.

"Ugh. Gross."

He cocks an eyebrow at me like a cynical old man. "You know there're flaps at the back of the coop so you can get the eggs without going in, right?"

Of course there are. "No. Did not know that. Not exactly a chicken expert."

He shrugs. "There's a hose over there. I won't tell, *this* time."

I'm relieved at both the hose and the second part, until he says, "*But.*"

"But what?" I say.

"But you owe me."

What the hell? This kid looks to be about eight years old, and he's blackmailing me? "Owe you what?"

He doesn't hesitate. "Candy, duh."

Hmm. Well, at least he still blackmails like a kid.

"Fine. Let me wash up properly, and you can show me where to get this candy." Maybe there'll be some proper food, too.

The little rotter beams. I roll my eyes.

When I go inside to properly wash my hands and check my legs for open wounds from tiny beaks, I also call my mom. If this morning is any indicator of what the summer is going to be like, I'm out.

Wonder of wonders, she actually picks up.

"Gabe?"

"Hey."

"Is this important? I'm in the middle of a hundred things."

Oh yeah? A hundred *things? Really?*

"Yeah, it's important. I can't stay here."

"What do you mean?"

"I mean I literally just got attacked by wildlife"—they were *live* chickens and acting *wild*, after all—"and this B and B is crap, and so is this town. I want to go home."

Her sigh is monumental. "Gabe. Don't be ridiculous. You haven't even been there a whole day yet."

"But—"

"I really wish you could show a little fortitude sometimes, you know? Commit to something for more than half a second?"

This is a common refrain from both my moms. And, okay, it's not *un*true—I have a hard time focusing and sticking with things. But maybe that's just because I get bored easily, okay? Maybe I'm just built for something else?

But I'm not letting her win this one. "I commit to things! I finished that dumb course you made me do this year."

"Oh, you mean the one you barely passed? Like all the courses you did in high school?"

School just didn't work for me, *okay*?

She continues, "You're not leaving. Stick it out or find a job. Those are your choices. This could be a good opportunity for you to make some meaningful friendships. Or—who knows? Maybe you'll even meet someone nice, Gabe. I'd love to see you get a little grounded this summer. Join a group. Find something useful to do. Prove to me you're not just going to waste all the privileges you've been given."

"I—"

"And I do *not* want to hear from you again about leaving, understood?"

Fuck you.

"Great. Cool. Good chat, Mom. Talk soon. Kiss kiss."

I hang up before she can hear the wobble rising up my throat, grab my bag, and head out the door to my little blackmailer.

FIVE

Maya

"One made-with-love breakfast, to order," Uncle Diamond says as he lays breakfast out on the kitchen table, his chubby, sweet yellow lab, Prince (as in, "and the Revolution," because he has a tuft of the cutest swirly fur atop his head), following his every step. I didn't see Diamond until this morning because he usually has the closing shift at the pub, and Jasper's is literally the only place in Spruce Lake that's open past nine o'clock.

I'm glad we didn't run into each other last night, though. After seeing Rashida, all I wanted to do was shower and head to bed, which is what I did. Unfortunately, the twisting sensations in my stomach wouldn't settle and I couldn't fall asleep for another two hours, even though I was dead tired.

So it was a rude awakening this morning when I heard Rashida's front door slam early, her French bulldog–pit bull mix, Poppy, yip a few times, and her electric scooter pull away from the gravel outside her cabin. She's always been an earlier riser than me. Even when we were little and had sleepovers at each other's cabins, she'd be the one jumping down from my top bunk and pouncing on me to wake me up. As we got older, she'd let me sleep and busy herself with a morning swim or by walking Poppy. When I finally dragged myself out of bed, she'd have a second breakfast with me.

Just one of the many things I thought showed how in step we were—like two people destined to work inside each other's rhythms and patterns.

After Rashida zipped off on her scooter and my parents woke me again an hour later as they got ready for a morning hike, I gave up on sleeping in but only managed to make it to the couch before flopping back down and curling up again.

The door to the cabin opened two hours later, and Prince bounded in, thumping his tail and lapping at my sleepy face with an exuberant tongue. Diamond followed, gave me a big hug, and coaxed me into the land of the living with smells of his famous stuffed French toast—pears and Brie and maple syrup. My stomach growls now as he sets it before me.

"I'm so glad you're here, Maya," he adds.

"Thanks, D," I mumble, and accept a side squeeze from him before he sits down.

My parents, returned from their hike and sitting flushed and vibrant next to him, exchange a look that clearly says, *Thank God for Diamond.*

I want to roll my eyes, but I *do* love Diamond to bits.

I refer to him as my uncle now, though I used to call him auntie and he had a different name. I just call him D, and most people just call him Diamond.

We have a lot in common—not just because he's queer, but because we both like to cook and fix things up. He's taught me most of what I know about baking and home improvement—everything with his own brand of "less waste" mentality. Use what you have before buying more. Don't throw something out until it's unusable.

There's a lot of backstory with Diamond in this family, but the basics are this: My grandparents weren't okay with Diamond's queerness or gender fluidity, so they left the cabin entirely to my mom after they both died, even though she's younger. But Mom was like, "Screw that," and built a large addition onto the side of the cabin so Diamond could live there year-round without ever having to share with us. He takes care of the place and uses the whole cabin when we aren't here, though.

He could be bitter about his parents, but he's not. Hopefully he'll rub off on me. Maybe I won't always resent this crappy plot twist that life has thrown at me, either.

I try to be a little less bitter now. "Thanks for breakfast, too," I say, even though it's almost noon. "I forgot to eat last night," I add, picking up my fork.

Diamond pours some syrup on my French toast, then passes the jug to my mom. The amber liquid glistens on my plate. "Yeah, these two"—he indicates my mom and dad—"said you were pooped. Did you at least get a dip in the lake before hitting your pillow?"

"Yeah."

"Did you see Rashida?" Diamond asks next. His tone is casual, but I can tell by the way he's not looking at me that the question isn't.

"Oh, yes, did you?" my dad adds, not casual at all, because he can't help it—as though I can just move on like nothing happened.

"Yes" is all I say.

Prince sniffs at Diamond's plate, and D gives the dog's snout a light tap, sending Prince back to his bed, grumbling.

"I saw her on your beach at Sun Island yesterday, tidying up your little kitchen. She couldn't wait to see you," he says, but then winces, and I know my mom has probably kicked him beneath the table.

Ugh.

I ignore them both and change the subject. "How're the protests going, D?"

He lights up. He loves this stuff. I mean, he doesn't love that he has to protest things, but he loves standing up for things he cares about. And he's good at it. Most of what Rish and I know about protesting and activism we learned from him, Jan, and my parents.

"Pretty good, I think," he says. "Kind of two steps forward, one step back, you know? Rish has been amazing. She's really taken on more responsibility with SLEA this past year."

My stomach turns at all these mentions of Rashida. Why can't they see that this is hard enough as it is without them trying to push us back to what we used to be? I want more than friendship with her, and I always will. And I'm irritated that these three people in front of me—who have witnessed more than anyone else how close Rashida and I have been—don't get that.

"Well, good for Rashida," I say, a clear edge to my voice as I press the side of my fork through the French toast with malice.

Diamond and my parents are silent for a few moments while I hack away at my breakfast.

"Sorry, honey," my dad offers. "We know this is hard for you."

"Right. Sorry, hon," D adds. When I don't say anything, he coughs and says, "More to the point, we've got a big fight on our hands, if you didn't know. This company, Lux Corp, is planning on razing over ten acres of Tipper Park for their new development. We could use all the help we can get this summer, if you're game."

This summer? Really? Jumping back into SLEA would mean working closely with Rashida, and part of me actually wants this—to be around her, to convince her how perfect we are for each other. But another part of me knows how painful that will be, too, and D should realize that, since he knows how hard I crashed and burned last summer.

When I continue my silent protest, he adds, "Wait—how about this? Why don't you help me with our SLEA *planning*, at least? We have some great protest action ideas, and I'm sure you do, too. Rashida and I are meeting at the pub tomorrow to chat—"

"Diamond." My mom's tone is reprimanding.

"Sorry, sorry!" Diamond exclaims, covering his face with his hands. "Sorry, Maya."

This whole conversation is twisting me into knots. I drop my fork on my plate, creating a clatter, and stand up. Prince scrambles to his feet with my sudden movement. "Can you all just lay off, already?"

My mom's eyebrows rise. Diamond leans back in his chair and scratches at his neatly trimmed salt-and-pepper beard. His skin becomes an even darker, richer brown in the summer months. Mine gets darker, too, but we've always joked that I'm more latte and he and my mom are espresso. Dad's just steamed milk or something.

I eye Diamond up now as he runs his fingers through his curly hair and sweeps it back into the small, low ponytail he's worn as long as I've known him, wrapping it tight with the hair tie that's always on his wrist.

He does this—uses slow, deliberate actions while he contemplates. He and Rashida are so different in this way. Where Diamond takes his time, weighing his thoughts and options, Rashida usually jumps in with both feet. I don't know how they work so well together on SLEA stuff, but somehow they do.

The silence makes me feel awkward now, as I just stand here. I fold my arms across my chest. Unfold them. Look away. Look back at my half-eaten breakfast.

"Honey," my dad begins, "maybe it will help for you to put your energy toward something more than just mo—"

My mom curls her fingers around his wrist to stop him from telling me I'm moping around, but it's too late. The word sends me over the edge.

"I'm not *moping*! Maybe I'm just sick of people acting like nothing's wrong!" I yell, slipping on my flip-flops and grabbing a ball cap without looking at any of them. In a lower voice, I add, "None of you get it." I'm out the door in seconds, walking away from this cabin, away from Rashida's cabin next door, and to the only spot I can think of that might bring me a little peace and quiet around here.

SIX

Gabe

So the little candy-craving rotter—Blu is his name—led me into what he called "the village" and to a café named Tree Top that is also a corner store that is also a bookstore that is also a gas station that is also a sushi restaurant on weekends, apparently. He made me buy him an obscene amount of candy and then disappeared like some little forest gnome into the surrounding woods.

I grab a corner booth, away from a bunch of old guys sitting at the counter back-slapping and telling animated stories, and even farther away from a group of tweens huddled around a table playing cards and giggling over every little thing. Maybe I should be trying to make friends like my mom wants me to, but after my run-in with the chickens and that pissy phone call with my mom, I really don't feel like it. And besides, the people I've met here so far have been annoying.

The menu is limited, but I'm starving and ready to eat anything, as long as it has meat in it and not just some janky tofu. I order a Club House with fries, and I'm not gonna lie—it's probably one of the best sandwiches I've ever eaten. Finally, one good thing.

As I'm eating, a woman enters the café, and everyone who's here calls out a greeting to her. She waves them off, grumbling, "Yeah, yeah," in response, and everyone just laughs or smiles back. I gather from the greetings that her name is Jan, and I am instantly mesmerized.

She is wearing: a plaid shirt with the sleeves cut off, what very well could be pajama pants that end mid-calf, and purple Crocs. Her long gray and black hair is pulled back in a low ponytail, her tanned arms are sinewy as hell, and she has wrinkles galore.

I'm stunned that anyone would leave the house dressed like this, and she catches me staring as she walks by my table.

"What're you gapin' at?" she says, stopping beside me.

I have to blink and swallow before I can respond. "Nothing. Or. Your shirt? I like the . . . plaid."

She checks out her own shirt, gives me a skeptical look, and scoffs. "Yeah. Sure."

I think the conversation is done and she'll move on, but then she says, "Summer visitor?"

"Yup."

"You fish?"

"Pardon?"

"Did I say something confusing?"

In my head, I cackle, because this woman is amusing as hell. Maybe I'm drawn more to prickliness than I am to perky optimism (cough, cough, Canva). But outwardly, I say, "No, not confusing—but do I look like I fish?" I give myself a once-over, my ample chest fully accentuated by the tight white crop top I have on.

Her eyes don't leave my face, however. "Anyone can fish."

"Well, I don't."

"Maybe you should learn."

"No, thanks."

We stare at each other for a few moments. "So . . . obviously *you* fish?" I ask, because I don't love prolonged silences.

"Yep."

"For . . . fun?"

"I like it. But I do it for food."

"Right. Like, living off the land and whatnot."

"Yeah. And whatnot." She eyes me up. "If you need camping or fishing supplies—and *whatnot*—you should come by my store."

"Oh, I won't be camping."

"Why not?"

"*Why* is the better question."

She plunks herself down at my table, and I raise my eyebrows in anticipation.

"Ya know this place is famous for its natural beauty, right?" she says.

"Is it?"

"Have you looked around much?"

"Well, I just got here yesterday, so no. But also, I'm not really a nature girl. Sorry."

"You're not a 'nature girl'? What does that mean?"

I dip a fry in ketchup and swirl it around. "It means I like my air-conditioned, bug-free house and running water."

She leans back against the bench seat. "Huh."

"Huh?"

She leans forward again and points a gnarly finger into the tabletop. "You're saying you've come to one of the most beautiful places on the West Coast, and you don't wanna spend any time in the trees or mountains or water?"

I shrug. "I might sunbathe on the beach, maybe go for a swim. Does that count?"

"That's a start. But if yer gonna be here, I suggest you get acquainted with the land and the people."

"Wellll . . . I'm getting acquainted with *you*, aren't I?"

"Are ya?"

"Y-yes?" I'm trying hard not to crack up, but it's a challenge.

"You haven't even asked my name yet."

"Neither have you."

"Well?"

"Well what?"

She sighs and wipes a hand down her face. "What the hell's yer name?"

"Oh. Gabe. What the hell's yours?"

"Jan Joseph. Quw'utsun Tribe. My people are Hul'q'umi'num. What about you? Who're your people?"

That's a great question, Jan Joseph. "Oh . . . uh . . . I mean, I guess my moms? Karen and Tracy Martin? We're not . . . My moms are just . . . white."

"You can be white and have ancestry, connections to places, ya know."

"Sure. But I think my moms are just . . . um . . . of European descent or whatever."

In truth, my extended family stops at my moms, and I've never really felt connected to any place. My bedroom, maybe. I fucking love my bed. But I'd rather see lots of places, do lots of things. I don't need to be stuck to someplace. I definitely don't need to be "one with the land" or whatever. Sounds uncomfortable and dirty to me.

Jan's eyebrow is pointy as hell as she continues to scrutinize me. "Right. Well, my people have lived here forever, and I'm telling you—get outside. See some things, all right? We work real hard around here to keep this place clean and beautiful. You might like it if you give it a chance."

She's so firm, I can't help but nod. "Right. Got it. I'll . . . try that," I say, even though I'm pretty sure I won't.

"And like I said, you need anything, come by my store."

"What's your store called?"

"Need Something?"

I look around, then at the half-eaten sandwich in front of me, then back at her. "I don't think so, but thanks."

"No, dammit. The store's called Need Something?"

"Oh. Neat name." *Kind of a weird name, if you ask me.* "Where is it?"

"Down by the dock. Just ask someone."

"I am. Asking. You." I lean back against the banquette seating and cross my arms. This is fun.

She rolls her eyes. "Everything's around everything else around here. You'll figure it out."

You'd be surprised, I think. Figuring things out isn't exactly my forte.

"How long you gracin' us with yer presence?" she asks.

"Alllll summer, ma'am."

"Call me 'ma'am' again and see what happens."

I raise an eyebrow at her. "Yes, ma'am."

She scoffs and wipes a hand down her face again, but I think I see the tiniest quirk of her lips. It's hard to tell, what with all the wrinkles.

My own lips quirk into a smile I can't help. I feel like we're well on our way to being besties.

She considers me for a second. "Well, Gabe. Eat yer damn sandwich. Cold fries're garbage."

And then she's gone from my table, headed to the back of the store.

I twist around in my seat to watch her march away, hoping this won't be the last I see of those pajama pants.

SEVEN

Maya

My walk may have started out as a desperate escape from D, my parents, the cabin, and my frustration, but as soon as I enter the forest, my desperation turns into something less reactive and more assuring. There are a lot of things that are going to make this summer hard, but the forest isn't one of them. My body welcomes the shady path and quiet. I can feel my heartbeat slowing and some of the tension leaving my shoulders. I wish I could bottle up a tiny bit of this and just carry it around with me for whenever I need it. Being away from here this past year was a necessity, and coming back is confusing and painful, but I missed the forest.

Before I can get to the spot where I leave the trail toward my own special place, though, I hear a collection of voices coming from the opposite direction and then see a group of people I know well walking down the path.

Ugh. Del Curry and his little band of misfits—Shannon, Rae, and Kaz.

I did *not* want to run into anyone else right now, let alone one of the most annoying people in Spruce Lake. Del Curry isn't a bad guy, but he's also not known for his tact.

"Maya, Maya, pants on fiya!" he calls out now, displaying said tactlessness.

The others call out, as well, waving hello.

I give them a little wave back. "Hey, all," I say as we come together on the trail.

It's a true testament to how tied people are to the land in Spruce Lake that even the biggest partiers and maybe also the laziest people in town, like this group, still hike on a regular basis. Right now, all four are in their regular clothes—track pants or jean shorts, tanks or T-shirts, and kicks—but here they are, sweating it out on the trail.

"When'd you get back?" Shannon asks.

"Just yesterday."

"Had any ice cream yet?" Del asks, smirking. Rae instantly elbows him, but he's also trying to hide a smile, I can tell. Kaz covers her mouth while Shannon just rolls her eyes.

Christ. That didn't take long.

Del's seemingly innocuous question is actually a thinly veiled dig at me for my epic misfire last summer.

"Super funny, Del," I say, trying not to show just how hard his teasing hits.

"No, but seriously"—and his face goes fake serious—"you seen Rashida yet? Is it weird? Like—"

"Del, Jesus," Shannon interrupts.

"What? Don't pretend y'all don't wanna know, too. I'm just the only one willing to ask."

"You're the only one who's rude enough to ask, dummy," Shannon says.

I'm somewhat thankful for Shannon's intervention, but more so, I'm angry that I can't even escape from my pathetic attempt at love here, in the forest.

"Ignore him, Maya," Shannon continues. "I'm sure there's someone else out there for you."

Ugh. She's trying to make me feel better, but this just feels like a personal hell. I don't *want* anyone else. I want Rashida.

When I finally got up the courage to show Rashida exactly how I felt—like, actually *say* it out loud, instead of what I thought was an unsaid understanding between us—I decided I wanted to make a bold romantic gesture. Something to show her just how big my feelings were—are—for her. Something that would echo the way my mom proposed to my dad.

My mom and dad's marriage proposal is a famous story in Spruce Lake. Two years after they met and fell in love here, she tied a ring to her fishing lure and when she and my dad took our rowboat out to fish in their favorite spot by a little outcrop of land nearby, she waited until my dad wasn't looking and cast her line. Then she faked a bite a few minutes later.

Of course, my dad was instantly suspicious, because the line wasn't taut at all and my mom's not the greatest actor, but when she pretended to struggle with this "big catch," laughing the whole time, he played along, and they pulled in the line together. At the end of it was a small cedar box in a plastic bag securely attached to the lure.

She even got down on one knee like a total nerd.

Diamond and several of their friends were lurking onshore with a fancy camera to capture the moment and a big sign that said "Good catch!" on it. As soon as my dad said yes and he and my mom kissed, everyone jumped out from behind the trees, held up the sign, and cheered their hearts out.

The whole thing sounded goofy as heck.

But I'd be lying if I said I wasn't entirely enamored with this story from the moment I heard it at age seven when Dad replayed the whole thing for me and Rashida on the dock one evening.

I'd been thinking about all the ways I could finally tell Rashida how I felt about her since I was thirteen, and I thought my finalized plan would be just as romantic and epic as my mom's gesture.

I set about pulling together some of Rashida's and my favorite elements of Spruce Lake, garnering the help of our favorite people, and created what I thought was the perfect idea.

A sunset backdrop.

A small paddleboat decorated with lights and cedar boughs and the prettiest Nootka roses.

A playlist of our favorite songs.

A short speech delivered from the boat to Rish as she stood on her dock—my "Top 10 Maya and Rashida Moments," ending with this one, when I finally got to tell her how I felt about her.

Dozens of people would witness this new, romantic moment in

Spruce Lake's timeline—see Rashida climb into the boat, see us share the most perfect kiss. Because people in Spruce Lake *knew* Rashida and I were meant to be. They wanted this almost as much as we did. They'd be telling this story as long as we would.

Instead, Rashida's face grew more and more uncomfortable, her eyes glancing around us to the others watching, her hands twisting in front of her as she stood there, listening to me make a giant ass of myself. And then, when I was finally done, it took her a good ten seconds to get out the words: "Maya . . . this is all so . . . sweet. But I don't think I feel the same way. I mean, I love you, obviously. But . . . you're my best friend, Maya. We're perfect the way we are."

And then I turned into a blubbery, snotty mess as I turned off the music and started paddling away, every single moment I thought would follow this one trailing away behind me in the ripples of the boat's path and disappearing into the lake.

So this light teasing from Del just brings back that exact scene and all the loss that came with it, and reminds me that everyone here in Spruce Lake is going to be thinking about that moment whenever they see me now, too. Because of course, in a town this small, it only took a day or two before all of Spruce Lake knew what happened.

My chest is tight with heartache. "I . . . need to . . . go," I say, ignoring Shannon's attempts at encouragement and Del's eager questions. "See you later," I get out as I walk around them and down the trail, trying not to listen as Shannon and the others admonish Del, but with some measure of laughter in their voices.

Because what happened was funny and cringe-worthy in their eyes, and I can't blame them for seeing it that way, even if that moment is filled with so much more than embarrassment for me. Loss, heartbreak, disappointment boil away in my chest when I think about it. Maybe some anger, too—at myself for being such a fool, but at others, as well, for reminding me at every turn that I am.

EIGHT

Gabe

When I'm finished with my sandwich, I feel both full and groggy. Behind the café, a narrow pathway opens up into the woods, and a sign next to it says "Beach access this way."

I think of that feisty old gal Jan's suggestions to check out more of this place, but I wasn't kidding—I am not a fan of nature. Meems always tried to get us to go camping, but neither Mom nor I was interested—especially after the one and only camping trip we *did* take that ended in stinging nettle wounds for my mother and a Very Awful Experience with an outhouse for me.

Bugs. Dirt. Dirty people. Outhouses (or worse—*holes in the ground?!*). I might find all of these things in the woods right now. But when I turn to look around "the village," I see nowhere and no one I want to interact with (besides Jan, who stomped out of the café long ago), and I'm not about to go back to Canva's and the bitchy chickens.

Besides, I *do* need a tan.

So off I go down the path, mentally preparing myself to pee in a bush if I absolutely need to, but willing my body to refuse any urges to poop until I'm back within indoor toilet range.

As I maneuver farther into the trees, the urge to see what my friends are up to is too strong to withstand, so I check my phone. The signal is weak, but I manage to load my Instagram feed at least, and the first photo that pops up is of my so-called best friends, Maggie and Aysa—so-called because can you really call people you mostly just party with best friends? People who basically just want to hang with you because you have a pool and parentless house and plenty of booze? They're on either side of Jake, one of the two guys I'm dating. Or *was* dating before I told him I was going to be away all summer and he moved on before I'd even started packing my suitcase.

I'm not sure when I veered into being the kind of girl who cared more about partying than about much else. Maybe I was a little bored growing up? Like, I was an only child, and Mom was already working her butt off to move up the ranks in whatever job she had, so she wasn't home a lot. Meems, on the other hand, was with me, but I always got the sense that she was a little . . . resentful maybe? Or distant? Like maybe I was never what she really wanted?

She seemed to have this whole other side to her that was super adventurous, and I guess raising a kid wasn't as fulfilling as she'd hoped—especially one like me that didn't take to her kind of adventure (the kind that included mountains and river rapids and ticks), because she basically tapped out by the time I was eleven or twelve, or at least that's how it felt. She started to leave me to my own devices more and more as she joined these outdoor groups and made friends with people who appreciated the same things she did.

Maybe it didn't help that I'd linked up with some of the popular kids at school, or that my hormones started raging a little early. Maybe it wasn't all that fun to deal with a kid who got all boy-obsessed and snarky. Maybe it was me who started pulling away first and she was just tired of everyone underappreciating her.

Whatever the progression of events and feelings and detachments, by the time I was sixteen, I was basically a nightmare for both my parents. Coming home whenever, barely passing my classes, being a complete asshole. Mom just plunged further into her work, and Meems spent more and more time with her outdoorsy friends. They started fighting more, too. Over me, mostly. What to do with me, whose fault it was that I am the way I am.

Meems finally had it. I caught the tail end of their last fight after coming home late and not completely sober. It was after one in the morning, and they were in their bedroom with the door closed. They weren't yelling—they rarely yelled—but their voices always carried this cold edge toward each other at that point that was somehow way worse than yelling.

From where I was eavesdropping just outside their door, I could hear whispers of "she's out of control" and "none of you appreciate me" and then thumps and shuffling, and Mom asking, "What the hell are you doing?"

I knew what the hell Meems was doing. She was packing. She was going to open this door any moment with a suitcase and probably a backpack, and she was going to look at me with the kind of disappointment I'd caught in her eyes more and more these past few years.

I'd saved her the trouble by shuffling to my room so we wouldn't have to face each other at all. Then I listened at my door, a part of me hoping I'd hear her approach my room to see if I was there, to at least let me know she was leaving before she actually left.

But all I heard were footsteps down the hall and the front door closing.

She didn't even try to reach out to me after that. She came by at some point when both Mom and I were out to pick up some more of her things, left a vague note saying she was going somewhere she was appreciated, and that was that.

I stare at the photo on my phone. Aysa is making a sideways peace sign and has her tongue out, which isn't unusual for her. Maggie is licking the side of Jake's face, which is . . . whatever. The photo is a selfie, and I can see they're all dressed for the beach. They haven't even tagged me in a cheeky, "hey, look at how much fun we're having without you" kind of way. They're just having fun. Without thinking of me at all.

Well, good for fucking you.

I try to swipe up past the photo to something that won't bum me out, but the feed won't load.

I try again. Nothing.

I look up and let out a feral groan.

All I see above me are trees with small bits of blue poking through. Then I look back at the path and realize I'm probably not headed toward the water anymore because everything has gotten bushier and darker. It's taken me approximately three minutes to get lost.

Great work, Gabe. Meems would be so proud.

I try using my phone to figure out where I am, but in addition to Instagram not loading, neither will Google Maps, and besides, I suck at directions and maps almost as much as I suck at camping and making my parents happy.

I keep wandering for what feels like forever (but is probably about twenty minutes), until out of nowhere, a pond shaped kind of like a jellybean appears in front of me, sunlight breaking through the trees and shining off its surface like I'm in some kind of goddamn nature poem or something.

It takes a second before I notice the green hammock tied up between two trees just behind the pond. The hammock looks a little tired, but also sturdy and clean enough, and the sun is hitting it like a spotlight, so even though I know I'm going to get gobbled up by mosquitoes, this seems like a sign. Besides, this twenty-minute hike has been exhausting, and I could use a break.

My crop top, jean shorts, and flip-flops are off in seconds, and I throw them on top of some kind of box that looks too old and too dirty for me to want to see what's inside of it.

After six very awkward attempts to get into the hammock, I finally get my butt balanced and am able to lie back and soak up some heat. I push my sunglasses back to the top of my head and rest my hands on the canvas beside me to try to get an even tan. If I was sure some rando wasn't going to stumble in here, I'd whip off my bikini top, too, but I keep it on for now.

With the sun beating down on me and bird sounds and shit, I actually feel a little relaxed for the first time since getting to this place. I close my eyes and try not to think about my absent moms, my asshole friends, or about how hard it is to be better than I actually am.

NINE

Maya

After leaving behind Del and the others, I walk until I find the spot where I always leave the trail and head toward Jellybean Pond—that's what I call it anyway, because that's what it looks like. I found the pond when I was twelve after bushwhacking through the woods with my dad. His plan was to leave me out here and see if I could find my way back on my own. And it turned out to be a good idea, eventually—my sense of direction is excellent now.

But in the moment, I was flustered and got a little turned around. Then I got angry and resentful like any twelve-year-old would, so I decided to teach my dad a lesson and just sit in the woods until he got scared and came to find me.

The spot I chose was Jellybean Pond, and the water, trees, and blue sky poking through had such a calming effect on me, I decided I didn't need to freak anyone out and instead made my way out of the woods just fine.

My dad was so proud of me. He and my mom were seated out on the dock when I got back, holding hands between their chairs, the sun shining down and the lake glistening just beyond them like some kind of magazine cover for lovers and lake life. When I announced my triumphant return, my dad winked at my mom and said, "See, Hessy? I knew she could do it."

I frown now, thinking about how many moments between my parents I thought I'd be repeating myself, with Rashida. Us holding hands on the dock, watching the sun disappear behind the mountains. Us snuggled under a blanket in my mom's old canoe, searching for shooting stars. Us on the porch swing in the morning, stealing kisses over coffee.

I shake my head, mad at myself for still wanting these things—at her for not seeing what I see.

I need to get to my spot. After finding it back when I was twelve, I set up a hammock (that I named Ruth, after one of my favorite characters in my favorite book, *Fried Green Tomatoes*) and stashed a couple of important items in a waterproof box next to the pond.

It was the only place in Spruce Lake I'd kept for myself—Rish knew I had a spot, but she didn't know where it was, and she seemed to get why I needed it. I've always liked a bit more alone time than her. But I'd imagined sharing it with her at some point—after we were officially together. I would bring her here, and it would be like magic, revealing this place to her that had been just for me, but was now for us.

Except.

A half-naked white girl is lying on Ruth right now, her eyes closed, one bare foot propped over the edge of the canvas. Her bright red bikini pops off her light skin and very full, very curvy body. She has dark brown hair that sprawls around her face, and even from where I'm standing, maybe fifteen feet away, I can see she has several piercings in at least one ear. One hand is visible where it loosely grips the edge of the hammock, and both her fingernails and toenails are painted a bright red that matches her bathing suit. A tiny tattoo I can't quite make out sits just above her hip bone.

I'll admit, it's not a terrible sight, but . . . that's *my* hammock.

Who are you, and what are you doing on Ruth?

I'm perplexed. After a morning of annoying, painful conversations, my instinct is to creep away, silent and unseen.

But . . . this is my place. My special place. And I really need it right now.

"Um," I say, genius that I am.

The girl doesn't move.

I take two steps forward. "Excuse me," I try, a little louder.

Nothing.

"PARDON ME."

Finally, her eyes pop open, and she sits up with a start, which you just don't want to do in a hammock. She loses her balance and flops out of Ruth onto the—lucky for her—soft forest floor beneath.

Only *she* doesn't see how lucky she is. "What the actual *fuck*?" she yells from where she's lying on her stomach, propped up on her elbows. She finds me with her glare, and part of me wants to just run away, but another part of me is *very* defensive of this place.

"Oops. Sorry. I just—I—this is kind of my spot."

She scrambles to her feet and brushes off nonexistent dirt like she's being attacked by it or something. Not exactly one with nature, it seems.

"*Your* spot? Like, you *own* it or something?"

She's gorgeous, but I can also tell she's a jerk, and I find the whole package a little jarring. I'm also in no mood for her attitude.

"Well . . . no. But I set up that hammock that your practically bare butt was on, and I've been coming here for years for peace and quiet."

"My butt is not *bare*."

"I said *practically*."

We stare at each other for a moment or two.

"You could've been less *abrupt*," she says.

"I tried to be, but you weren't responding."

"Right—*because I was sleeping*." She rolls her eyes like she actually has a reason to. "I should have known this spot was too good to be true."

She moves to get her clothes from on top of my stash box. I watch as she pulls on her jean shorts and crop top, trying very hard not to notice her butt cheeks still visible beneath the hem of her shorts, or her soft-looking stomach, or the cleavage rising above her shirt.

I'm obviously failing at not noticing.

She catches me, and my cheeks get hot. A smirk lifts her lips, and my cheeks grow even hotter.

She taps her flip-flop against the lid of the box. "What's in here?"

I shrug. "Just a blanket and book."

"What book? Something dirty?"

Funny enough, when I was younger and first read *Fried Green Tomatoes*, I *did* think I was getting away with something. It was the first time I'd read a book with a romance between two women, and I thought Idgie and Ruth were badass. I always keep a copy of it in the stash box.

"What? No. Maybe that's the kind of stuff *you* read," I say, knowing I sound juvenile.

"And? Nothin' wrong with a little of *that* kind of dirt." She's still smirking as she walks toward me.

I roll my eyes now, losing patience for this cocky girl already.

"So this is your secret spot, huh?" she says, when she stops a foot in front of me.

"Yeah. It is."

She places her palms backward against her hips, which only thrusts out her chest more. She's definitely not shy. "Why d'you need a secret spot?"

To get the hell away from rejection and my annoying family and everyone's pity, I think, but instead say, "Who *doesn't* need a spot to call their own?"

She studies me for a moment. Then she shrugs. "I don't."

"But you liked *this* spot."

"I need a tan. The sun was there." She turns a little sheepish. "And maybe I couldn't find the beach."

My eyebrows lift a little at this admission. "You're new here, then?"

"*Obviously*. Do I look like I'm *from* here?"

This needles me. "Do *I*?" I ask, and immediately regret it as she eyes me up and down and cocks an eyebrow at me. "Whatever," I say. "Are you visiting?"

"Unfortunately," she says.

"Okayyyy . . . ?" I wait for her to say more, but she doesn't. I really don't want to stand here while this girl judges me, and so I decide the only way to get her out of here is to take her to where she was going. At least she doesn't know anything about me or last summer, and her judgment is reserved for this moment, not any previous ones. "Do you want me to show you where the beach is?"

She looks surprised by my offer. "What about your 'peace and quiet'?"

I shrug. "The beach isn't that far. I can come back. Call it small-town hospitality." Then, hospitably, I add, "My name is Maya, by the way."

She considers me, her eyes narrowing. But then she shrugs and says, "Sure. Why not?" like she's doing *me* a favor. "I'm Gabe."

We walk for a minute in silence through a shortcut to the beach. Well, almost in silence. Gabe curses under her breath at least four times as she lurches through foliage behind me.

"Is this really the way to the beach?"

"It's a shortcut."

"Can we take the long cut?"

"This is way faster," I say, meaning, *I can drop you off and get back to some peace and quiet faster.* Feeling a little spiteful, I add,

"Although the beach isn't that far. And the regular path is pretty clear. Not sure how anyone can get lost on the way."

She scoffs. "Thanks for pointing that out. So much for small-town hospitality, I guess?" she says.

"I'm taking you there, aren't I?"

"Sure. I might die from thorn punctures and a branch to the gut, but your generosity is noted."

I roll my eyes again and immediately think of Rashida. She'd find this girl aggravating as hell and would say something sharp and witty about her. Then we'd laugh and push through the foliage with no trouble at all, because that's just the way it is with us.

Gabe stumbles and bumps into me, interrupting my pesky thoughts. She grabs my arm to keep her balance, cursing again.

"All right there?" I ask, a tiny bit amused by this ridiculous girl. Something about her complete incongruity with this place is actually kind of refreshing. Maybe it's just nice meeting someone who knows nothing about me or my embarrassment.

She drops her hands from my arm and narrows her eyes at me. "Enjoying this, are you?"

I shrug and keep walking, unable to keep the smile off my lips.

TEN

Gabe

"So . . . this is . . . it?" I ask. We're standing at the edge where the grass from the playground meets the so-called sand of the dingiest little beach I've ever seen.

Okay, it's not *dingy* exactly. But it's *tiny* and full of pebbles and definitely not what I was picturing.

Plus, there's a playground adjacent to the beach and, like, *a thousand* little kids are playing and screaming and generally being disgusting right behind us.

She side-eyes me. "Sorry it's not Mexico or whatever."

"It's not even *close* to Mexico."

"Well, we're literally nowhere close to Mexico, so I guess that makes sense, doesn't it?"

"True," I concede, hitching my bag farther up my shoulder. I'm not gonna lie, her snark actually makes me feel a little more at ease. "Is this the only beach around here?"

"The only public one."

"Are the private ones any better?"

"Depends on what you mean by better."

"I *mean*, do they have actual sand? And no kids? And, like, reclining beach chairs or something?"

"Some do, but unless you know someone with lakefront property, you're stuck with this one."

"Do *you* have lakefront property?" I'm just being a brat. It's in my nature. But I also want to see what she says. She's acting all snippy, but she's also been eyeing me up like she can't help it, and I'm not averse to being admired by people who aren't creeps.

She hesitates and rubs her nose. "Oh, um, I do . . . but . . ."

"LOL, relax." I push her arm. "I'm not asking to come over, weirdo." I watch three kids run past us. "I can make this work," I say, although part of me wants to head back to the hammock.

"Okay, well, enjoy," she mumbles, and abruptly turns to go.

"Unless you want to hang out?" I ask, for no good reason whatsoever. Or maybe I just like the attention this girl's been giving me.

She pauses and seems as surprised as I am at my invitation. "Oh. Uh . . ." She looks around and plays with the old-school friendship bracelet on her wrist.

"Never mind," I interrupt, because hell if I'm going to be rejected by this chick. "Go be one with nature or whatever." I take a step onto the pebbles.

"I can hang out."

My eyebrows pop up, but I play it chill. "Cool. Come on, then."

We find a spot a little ways from the nearest family, and I

realize I didn't bring a towel or anything with me. I whip off my shorts and top and lie down on those instead. They don't do much to protect me from the pebbles, but it's better than nothing. I place my bag behind me and lie back with my head on it.

Maya sits next to me, looking out at the water with her knees folded in. I'm behind her a bit and shield my eyes from the sun to give her a proper once-over. She's wearing a scrappy gray T-shirt and neon-yellow running shorts, worn canvas boat shoes that she's kicked off, and a trucker hat. Lakeside chic, I guess. Her skin's a light shade of brown, and her hair is almost black. It's tied back in a low pony beneath her hat. She's got full lips I'd kill for and hella long eyelashes.

She bites her lower lip now, and I wonder if she's nervous to be here with me. I wouldn't mind if she was. It's fun to intimidate people.

I ease into some talk about Spruce Lake by asking her about the pub, since it seemed like the only place open at night.

She glances over at me but shifts her eyes back to the lake as she says, "Jasper's? It's actually owned by a guy named Jasper, but he and my uncle Diamond run it together. They're also together together."

I cock an eye at her. "Like, they're gay? Here?"

She looks down at me, sees my skepticism, and rolls her eyes. "Because all small towns are full of homophobic jerks, you mean?"

"Well, if the shoe fits . . ."

"It's not like that here. Half the town is queer or genderqueer or has been or will be, probably. Maybe it's something in the water."

I snicker at that. "That's cool. Are you?"

"Am I what?"

I smirk. "'Queer or genderqueer or have been or will be'?"

I'm flirting. I know I'm flirting. Which is weird, since this girl is not my usual type, but then, I flirt with lots of people—the guy at the corner store, the hot chick who gives me my mani-pedi. I even toyed with the annoying but very built dude who drops off our groceries.

I guess I just can't help it. That's probably what Meems and Mom would say, anyway. Just built to waste my time and energy on superficial crap. My stomach dips at the thought, but Maya blushes at my question, which gives me some satisfaction.

"Yeah. I like girls," she says, glancing at me.

I watch her for a moment. She seems completely okay with this part of herself, which is surprising, because she's a little awkward in other ways.

"So how does a queer girl find other queer girls in this town?" I ask.

She scrunches her nose and looks out at the lake. It's kind of cute, in a nerdy way. "Everyone knows everyone, so it's hard *not* to find other queers. My best friend is queer, and we figured that out years ago." She frowns for a moment, sniffs. "Most people are just who they are around here, so you don't have to look too hard."

This surprises the hell out of me, but I'm not about to admit it. "Huh," I say. "So . . . is your best friend *just* a friend?"

I watch her swallow back something.

"Yeah, we're just friends."

The way she says this, it's clear there's subtext, and I wanna know what it is, 'cause I'm nosy like that. "You're lying."

She looks at me and frowns. "What? No I'm not."

"Well, you're not telling the whole truth. I'm excellent at reading bullshit, you see."

She scoffs, but I can see her brain get busy, and I nudge her along. "How about this? I'll guess, and you tell me if I'm on the right track?" She keeps frowning, but I forge ahead.

"You're friends but have hooked up?"

Her frown deepens.

"No. Okay. You're friends, but you want more?"

Her jaw tightens instantly. *Bingo.*

"And you haven't told her yet?"

Her eyes water, and her chin crumples.

Oh, damn. "You *did* tell her. But . . . ?"

She wipes at her eyes and doesn't say anything for a beat.

Man, she's got it bad.

"But she just wants to be friends."

"Ugh. That sucks, dude. Sorry." I mean, I assume it sucks. I'm usually the one doing the rejecting when it comes to dating, but I sure as hell know what other kinds of rejection feel like. "Are you still trying to get with her?" I ask.

She looks at me again. "*Get* with her?"

"Yeah, like, are you gonna try to win her over or whatever?"

She stares at my mouth like she's contemplating my question carefully. "I'd like to, but I have no idea how. We've been friends forever, and I really thought she felt the same way as I did."

Jesus. This all sounds so *wholesome*. Best friends. Small town. Pining away for someone you genuinely care about. My mom would probably love this. Nice people. Meaningful relationships. Resentment starts to creep in, but then my devious brain interrupts and I get an idea. Why not cash in on some of this wholesomeness and have a little fun while I'm at it?

"It's simple," I say. "To win her over, I mean."

Her eyebrows rise, then deepen into another frown. "It is?"

"Yeah. You just need to make her jealous. Make her see what she's missing." I'm a pro at these kinds of games. And I can also see a winning situation for me here, too.

Maya rolls her eyes. "Great plan."

"It *is* a great plan. Don't you think if you're such close friends, and you started showing interest in someone else, she'd get jealous?"

She seems to think about this, but then shakes her head. "And who exactly would I be showing interest in? She already knows everyone I know here."

"Everyone but one person." I grin.

More frowning. "You?"

"Me." I push myself up on my elbow. "Like, what if—and hear me out—you and I hang out and pretend we're into each other and just see what she does?" I watch her for a second, then add, "I mean, do you have a better plan?"

Her hand moves to the pebbles beside her and starts playing with them. "What do you mean—like . . . fake-date?" she asks, looking at her hand, not at me.

I shrug. "Sure. Let's call it fake-dating. Fun, right?"

"I don't know. I'm not sure anyone will buy it, including her. Everyone around here knows how I feel about her. That's the other crappy part. I can't even regroup and figure out what to do because everyone either keeps reminding me of my rejection last summer or trying to get me to move on."

"Even better!"

Her face twists in confusion. "What?"

"Think about it—if you started dating someone else, wouldn't those people get off your back, too? You'll prove to them that you can actually nab a girl *and* that you've moved on from this other chick. It's a win-win, dude."

Honestly, I'm pulling this out of my ass right now, but the more I say, the more I think my idea could work—for this lovesick chick *and* for me. Like, this could be seriously entertaining—better than hiking or climbing trees or whatever Jan had in mind for me—but also, this fake stuff *could* help with my mom, too.

What if she thought I was legit dating someone—a nice, small-town girl who is *clearly* the committed type, nonetheless? I've never been in an actual relationship with anyone. My mom might think I've turned a corner.

And bonus—Maya is so swoony over this other chick, there's no threat of messy emotional stuff, either.

Maya glances at me now. "I . . . don't know."

"But you gotta admit—it's a great plan, right?"

She shrugs and doesn't reply. I'm about to needle her a bit more, but her phone lights up on the sand beside her. She doesn't notice, so I say, "Your secret lover is texting you."

She frowns. "What?"

"Your phone, weirdo."

Her eyes flick to her phone. "Oh." She picks it up and reads the message. Her lips tighten, and she drops the phone back beside her.

"That was her, wasn't it?" I ask.

She nods.

"So?"

"So what?"

"So do we have a deal?"

Her nose does that scrunchy thing again and she still looks unsure, but then she blurts, "How do you feel about karaoke?"

ELEVEN

Maya

Gabe frowns and lifts her sunglasses. “Pardon?”

I guess my question came out of left field, but her fake-dating idea—though ridiculous on the one hand—makes me wonder what it would be like to show up someplace familiar with this very *un*familiar girl. If I might surprise—or at least distract—people out of their pity for me. Maybe make Rashida a little jealous, too, like Gabe said. The first thing that came to mind was karaoke night at Jasper’s.

“Karaoke,” I say. “There’s a weekly fundraiser at the pub. I’ll take you, if you want. I’m not saying yes to fake-dating, though. But I’m not saying no, either. Maybe we could just see what happens?” I try a smile.

A smirk and peaked eyebrow appear. “Well, my karaoke game *is* pretty sick.”

"Oh yeah?" I say.

She lowers her glasses again, saying, "Get ready to have your mind blown."

I shake my head at her and laugh. *So cocky.* "Consider me ready," I say. But my nerves stir again. Now that she's agreed to come to karaoke—which most of the town attends because karaoke nights are fundraisers for SLEA—I'm not sure I'm ready at all. I don't know anything about this girl. On the one hand, she makes me nervous, and she seems a little pushy and maybe selfish and superficial.

On the other hand, I also find her kind of a relief? She's not all wrapped up in Spruce Lake and is so completely *different* from everyone else I know here. And even though I don't know how she got me to tell her about Rashida, once I did, her reaction was refreshing in a way, as well—just a straight up "that sucks, now let's do something about it."

Bringing her to karaoke is scary, but the alternative—arriving on my own and facing a bunch of people who feel sorry for me—is much worse.

Gabe and I sit on the beach awhile longer, and she peppers me with questions about Spruce Lake, which I answer as best I can, even though I'm surprised she's asking. But when I ask her about her own life, she gives me vague nonanswers.

Before we know it, though, it's after four o'clock, and a massive growl emits from Gabe's stomach. We both look at her belly and laugh.

"Hungry?" I ask.

"Guess so. Had a sandwich around eleven, but I'd kill right now for a hot dog or something."

I'm vegetarian. So are my parents and Rashida. But I do know where to get a really good hot dog.

Within twenty minutes, we're at Moises Jones's little hot dog stand—which isn't a licensed establishment in any way but just a window Moises Sawzalled out of the side of his cabin. It's *the* place in Spruce Lake to go for hot dogs and corn dogs, though.

Gabe is less snobby about this place than she was about the beach.

"I love this kind of shit," she says, adding a thick strip of mustard to her hot dog. "I have certain standards for some things—beds and accommodations and cars and such—but give me a greasy spoon any day." She grins and takes a huge bite of her hot dog.

Moises has set up a variety of seating around his cabin—logs, camping chairs, a picnic table—and Gabe and I are sitting on a log, side by side. I got a veggie corn dog, which Gabe eyed with suspicion as Moises handed it over.

"How are your accommodations here? Up to your standards?" I imagine her staying at one of the fancier B and Bs on the other side of the lake. Most rentals around here are small and quaint, but we do have a smattering of wealthier folks who've built what Rashida calls "lakeside monstrosities."

Gabe chews and swallows, rolling her eyes as she does. "Let's just say I've had to readjust my standards for the summer."

"Where are you staying?" I ask.

"Owner's name is Canva? You know her?"

"Oh! Yeah. Canva's awesome. And her place is so homey and sweet. She's put a lot of work into making it sustainable, too."

Gabe grimaces. "What you call homey and sweet, I call cramped and inconvenient. My bedroom at home is bigger than her whole ground floor."

She doesn't seem to notice how showy this sounds. "Wow. Sounds fancy. What does your family do?" I wonder if she's one of those wealthier people Rashida can't stand.

She shrugs, dismissive again as soon as I ask about her, and says, "Honestly, I don't even know. My mom's in finance or something. Boring."

"Is she here, too, or . . . ?"

"Nah. She's got work in Miller's Bay and dumped me here to keep me out of trouble." She takes another bite and looks away. There's a tinge of something—sad? resentful?—in her voice, I think.

"Trouble?"

I watch as she swallows and turns back to me. A sly smile forms, and she winks. "I'm *very* troublesome, you see."

I have no idea what to say to that, and am just about to ask more about her family when she asks, "You said you have a cabin here?"

"Oh, yeah. My mom's family built it and has owned it for years. It's not fancy, though. Definitely not bigger than your bedroom, it sounds like." I smile so she knows I'm just teasing.

She pushes my arm and grins. "Shut up. Not my fault I'm a queen built for luxury." She gives a royal wave as she pops the rest of the hot dog into her mouth, wiping a smudge of mustard off the corner of her lips with her thumb and adding it to her mouthful.

"You come here every summer, then?" she asks once she's swallowed.

"Yup."

She eyes me up for a moment. "But you don't seem that happy about it."

Either she's perceptive or I'm just too obvious. I shrug. "Just that whole in-love-with-my-best-friend thing that kind of sucks. But my parents really wanted me to come. They're very keen to get me back to my 'old self.'"

"I bet finding a new crush would convince them you're back to your old self." This time she gives me an exaggerated wink and laughs.

I laugh, too, and shake my head. "Having a new crush wouldn't be anything like my old self," I say. "My only crush has ever been on Rashida." As I say this, I'm instantly embarrassed and deflated.

Gabe must be embarrassed at this admission, too, because she swings an arm around my shoulders and gives me a little shake. "Sounds like a good time for some sad-song karaoke, then, am I right? Really lean into all that heartache?" She's grinning and probably joking, but at least she's not trying to *bypass* all the heartache, like my parents and Diamond.

"Should we head over?" she adds.

I check my phone. It's almost five o'clock. Karaoke doesn't start till six. My stomach continues its flip-flopping, but I decide the sooner we get to the pub, the less likely I am to chicken out of this wild idea.

"Sure" comes out of my mouth, but the trepidation stays right where it is in my stomach.

TWELVE

Gabe

"Okay, so what song should we sing?" I ask as Maya and I head over to the pub. I'm actually getting kind of excited about this whole karaoke thing. I wasn't lying—my karaoke game is strong. I can sing. It's one of my very few talents, other than pissing people off and wearing clothes that make me look hot.

I've convinced Maya we should definitely do a duet after she told me that she and Rashida always sing together at these karaoke nights. What better way to see if we can make Rashida jealous?

"Oh, uh . . . What are your usual songs?" she asks now.

"Power ballads, baby," I say, grinning.

"Okay, well, that might be a bit out of my range."

She's smiling, but I can tell she's extra nervous all of a sudden. "You sure you're down for this? You seem a little freaked out." I try not to sound as exasperated as I am. Like, *let's go*, Maya.

She glances sideways at me and then shakes her head. "No, sorry. I just—lots of people will be there. And everyone—you know—knows about me and Rashida. And Rashida will be there. So things are just . . . complicated."

"All the more reason to blow them away with a sweet duet, right?" I say.

"Yeah . . ."

"Come on—it'll be great. Choose something you're super comfortable with, and I'll run with it."

"Most of the duets I know I used to sing with Rashida. 'I Got You Babe' was our go-to."

Her shoulders hunch over as she says this, and her voice is so pathetic I almost laugh. Sorry, but this is why I don't get mixed up with actual feelings—I never want to look or sound like this.

I manage to control myself, though, 'cause I want this girl to play along with my little plan here. "Okay, well, let's avoid those. How about . . . Oh! I know—'Don't Go Breaking My Heart'?"

She gives me a weird look. "Um . . . might be a little too close to home?"

Oh, Christ. "Right. Okay." I think for a few seconds, searching my brain for a song that will get this sad kid out of her funk. Finally, one comes to me. "I got it. 'Islands in the Stream'? But I get to be Dolly."

I grin at her and am relieved when she smiles back. "I could handle that."

When we walk into the pub, the atmosphere is raucous and

lively. The place is packed, and two big guys are leading the crowd in a group rendition of "The Greatest Love of All."

"That's Dennis and Buddy," Maya tells me, her eyes darting around the bar. "They run the gas station and are huge saps. They like to warm up the crowd before everything gets started. Aren't they cute? Such sweethearts."

Her words tumble out, and she's still nervous, I guess. But she invited me here and agreed to a duet, so we're doing this. Besides, I'm not leaving without a beer.

Some people wave to Maya, and she waves back, tentatively. An older Asian couple approaches from our right, swooping in to give Maya big hugs. They're both shorter than her and look to be in their sixties at least. The woman has a shiny wooden cane, the guy's in a bow tie. Both seem spry and classy as hell.

I watch as Maya receives their enthusiastic hugs, but her smile isn't full, and her eyes are bright with panic.

"Maya!" the woman says, coming out of their hug. "It's so good to see you." She's smiling, but it's one of those "poor little puppy" smiles, and she rubs Maya's arm like she's giving Maya her condolences.

The guy pats Maya on the shoulder. "We're glad you're here, sweetheart. Nothing like a little lake time to heal all wounds, right?"

Oh, Jesus. Maya wasn't kidding. These people aren't subtle.

Maya looks ill, and I feel sorry for her, so I step up and say, "Hey! I'm Gabe. What's up?"

I can tell the woman tries to register if she knows me for a moment before smiling wide and saying, "Hello! I'm Judith Garner, and this is James." James stretches out his hand, and I reciprocate with a firm handshake. "Are you a friend of Maya's?"

I don't know if "friend" is accurate, but for the sake of Maya's dignity, I reply, "Sure am! Maya's been showing me a great time."

In my peripheral vision, I see Maya raise her eyebrows. I add, "She's a real blast." I'm laying it on thick, obviously, but it's all part of the plan. And besides, Maya hasn't been *unpleasant* to hang out with. She got me unlost, found me a good hot dog, and brought me here, at least.

"Oh!" Judith says. "Well, that's lovely to hear."

The surprise in her voice is obvious—guess she expected Maya to be a sad sack over this best friend, which she is. But my little performance seems to have achieved its goal, which just convinces me my fake-dating plan is legit, and I'm hoping Maya sees that, too.

Judging from her expression right now, which is decidedly less panicky and forced, I think she might. I can't help but picture me introducing Maya to my mom, as well. My mom greeting her the way Judith and James just greeted me—with both surprise and delight. Maybe even thinking that I'm capable of something meaningful, even if it's not real.

But when Judith and James say their goodbyes and move on to their table, Maya's face shifts into nauseous again as her eyes look past me and land on something else. I turn to see what it is.

What I see is a super hot Black girl with long braids, ripped arms, and an ass that—while not as perfect as my own—is not too bad.

This must be the infamous bestie.

She's busy at a table near the stage, chatting with some people while simultaneously arranging a few items.

I turn back to Maya, who still looks ill—all my hard work to buff her up to Judith and James lost, apparently. "That's her, huh?"

Her eyes flit to me and then away across the room. She swallows, sighs, and scratches her nose. "Yeah."

Fer fuck's sake. Patience is not my strong suit. Never has been. "Well, it's now or never, Maya. Let's do this duet, get some people off your back, and just have some fun, all right?"

She hunches up her shoulders, takes a deep breath, and finally says, "Okay."

It's not the most convincing "okay," but I'll take it over wistful looks and sad sighs.

Our agreement comes just in time, because we hear a "Maya!" from behind me, and I turn to see the object of her woeful affections waving to her.

THIRTEEN

Maya

I automatically wave back to Rashida, because it would be weird not to, but my heart falls through my chest. Like Gabe said, though—"It's now or never."

As I lead Gabe through the room, I notice a few people glance my way and wave, but their expressions feel forced. Or maybe I'm just being too sensitive. But maybe not.

Rashida's in her usual spot at the bar, closest to the stage. She likes to be front row for everything. Needs to be all up in whatever business is happening and in control. I'm mostly the opposite—happy to blend into the background, let others do the talking. It was something that felt like a good balance between us before, but now I wonder if it's one of the things that makes her only want to be friends.

She's smiling at me, but like yesterday, her smile is a little tentative. Maybe she's hoping I don't make a fool of myself in front of everyone here, too.

Gabe trails behind as I weave through the crowd. She leans in and whispers, "Wouldn't it send this place into a tizzy if we were holding hands right now?"

I turn to look at her. Her eyebrow is raised into a cheeky peak, and a smirk is forming.

I try a smile, but instead of answering, I say, "Just come on."

By the time we make our way to Rashida, she's surrounded by a group of people signing up to sing. Since this is a fundraiser, everyone is donating five to twenty dollars for each song they perform. Half the pot will go to materials for the protests, and half will go to the best act, as voted on by the audience. But knowing this crowd, any winners will donate their half to the cause anyway—everyone here just wants the water and trees and land to be okay.

"Hey, Maya," Rashida calls out over the group gathered around her and gives me a little wave. "Would you mind helping me with money collection and sign-up? You totally don't have to, but . . ." Some of the people around her glance between us and my stomach is starting to turn again. Before I can answer, though, Rashida registers Gabe next to me, and a tiny wrinkle forms on her brow.

She's about to open her mouth again when Jasper calls out from behind the bar, "Hey, beautiful! I missed ya! Come sit nice and close so I can ogle yer lovely face."

Jasper is a very extravagant gay. He wears his dirty blond hair in a towering pompadour, and his wardrobe is wild with color and patterns. Rarely does he move with subtlety. The romance between him and D is going on five years, and it's as adorable as it is entertaining. Diamond appears from the kitchen now, too, and waves at me. He doesn't give away that there's any unpleasantness between us from this morning, and I'm relieved.

But I have no idea what to do right now. Do I just sit in my usual seat next to Rashida? Help Rashida with the money and introduce her to Gabe? Pretend I didn't practically yell at Diamond this morning?

My decision is made for me as Gabe nudges me in the shoulder and loud-whispers, "That guy wants to ogle your face—get a move on."

"Oh, right . . ." I nudge my way through a couple of people closer to the bar, okay with avoiding Rashida for the moment.

"Hey, Jasper!" I say, trying to act like everything is just fine. I notice that Rashida continues to watch me and Gabe as Jasper practically climbs over the bar to gather me up in a big hug, which is awkward but sweet.

When we part, he says, "How *are* you, my queen?"

"Great!" This isn't true, but I'm trying to break up the crappy energy floating around and inside of me. "How are *you*?"

"Dazzling, as always," he says as he turns his attention to Gabe. "And who is *this* gorgeous creature?"

Gabe actually turns a little bashful at this, which is surprising. "I'm Gabe. Hey."

I notice Diamond's expression remains pleasant, but can also tell he's confused about who Gabe is. Jasper, on the other hand, simply yells, "Gabe the *babe*!" and chuckles. Gabe and I smile at him, then at each other. I wipe the smile off my face when I turn to find Rashida beside me.

"Hey, I'm Rashida," she says to Gabe, and raises a hand in greeting.

Gabe lifts her chin and says, "Hey. Gabe. What's up?"

I try to read their faces. Maybe some tentativeness and curiosity on Rashida's? Or . . . surprise? And Gabe shows the slightest smile, but consideration or scrutiny crosses her eyes.

Rashida asks, "Are you visiting Spruce Lake, Gabe?"

"Sure am. All summer. Maya's giving me a private tour."

Oh. Am I? I *have* already shown her the beach, Moises's place, and now karaoke night.

Rashida's eyebrows lift ever so slightly. "Oh, that's nice. She's a good tour guide." She smiles at me, and I try a smile back but end up looking at my feet instead.

"It's true," Gabe says, and places a hand on my arm. "She's been incredible."

I look up at her, catching Rashida's eyes on Gabe's hand as I do. Gabe's giving me a grin, and I know she's trying to help me out here, like she did with Judith and James. I find that I appreciate it, mostly, and I'm glad she's here. Her breeziness sets me a little more at ease. Maybe she'll work as a good buffer between me and my broken heart—for tonight, at least.

"What've you seen so far, Gabe?" Diamond asks, setting a couple of beers on the bar for Buddy and Dennis, who've finished their warm-up set and gulp thirstily as they wander away.

Gabe's smile is sparkling as she says, "That cute public beach you have, and . . . um . . . a hot dog stand?" She looks to me.

"Moises's," I say, and the others all nod in recognition.

"And here, of course."

I think she's done, but then she adds, "Oh! And this sweet little spot in the woods? By a pond? Maya's set up a hammock there and everything."

Oh.

I notice Rashida's brow wrinkles again at this. She's been taking money as people sign up to sing, but she pauses now. I know exactly what she's thinking.

"Gabe found it, and we ran into each other there," I say, but don't offer anything more. It's my spot. I can do what I want there, right?

Rish rearranges her face and says, "That's . . . amazing you found it, Gabe. Maya's been keeping that place a secret for ages."

"Just lucky, I guess," Gabe says, a hint of cheek in her voice.

Diamond must read some of the tension, because he claps his hands and says, "Well, kids, what can I get you?"

But before I can answer, Gabe pipes up. "We need to sign up for our song first, right, Maya?"

Oh. Right. That was the plan, wasn't it. I can tell everyone who's part of this conversation is thoroughly confused at this point. Not just because I've shown up with this complete stranger, who's apparently seen my very secret, special spot in the woods, but also because we're singing a duct together, which has almost exclusively been a Rashida-and-me thing for as long as we've had karaoke nights.

"Um, actually, I think I might sit this one out, if that's all right?

I think I'm feeling all that sun we got today," I say. It's not *un*true. We did get a lot of sun, and I am *definitely* feeling a bit woozy right now. Just not from the sun.

Gabe's eyes narrow at me. "You sure?"

I'm failing our little test run, I know, but I can't imagine getting up onstage right now. "Yeah. Sorry."

"You're not singing at all tonight?" Rish asks.

"Um, no, I don't think so."

Her face falls a little, and I don't know whether I should be happy or sad about that. Happy that she's disappointed we're not singing together, or sad that I don't feel I *can* sing with her.

There's some awkward silence, but then Gabe says, "Well, duets are always more fun. Why don't you and I sing together, Rashida? I'll even put in"—she rifles around in her shoulder bag and pulls out a purse—"fifty bucks if you do."

My head turns sharply toward her. Her face has shifted into something more brazen, and I wonder what she's up to.

Rashida seems taken aback by this suggestion, too, because she fumbles a bit with her response, but then manages to get out an "um, sure." I guess she doesn't want to turn down fifty dollars for SLEA.

FOURTEEN

Gabe

"Sweet," I say, giving Rashida my easiest smile. To be honest, I'm impressed she took me up on my suggestion. After Maya completely bailed on our plan to sing together, I decided to turn it into an opportunity.

Singing a duet with Rashida could be a great way to show Maya my fake-dating plan is legit. I have no idea if Rashida can sing, but I know *I* can. I plan to blow this whole room of people away, including Maya, while also showing her that I can distract everyone from her drama. I'm really, really good at pulling attention to myself when I need to.

"How about that Sonny and Cher song 'I Got You Babe.' You know it?" I ask, knowing full well she does. I wanna see what Rashida does with this. I'm being a brat, but it's fun.

"Oh, uh . . ." Rashida gets super awkward, which I find

satisfying. Her eyes flit to Maya, who's fascinated with her own shoes at the moment.

Before Rashida can pull some "but that's our song" shit, I add, "Come on. It's a nice easy one, and I don't know a ton of duets. Can we?"

Rashida's eyes land back on me. She sighs. "Yeah, sure. That's cool."

"Super—thanks for making a new kid feel welcome," I say, laying on another coat of bullshit.

"Yeah, no problem," she says, but her eyes are still flicking to Maya.

After Rashida signs us up, a bunch of people crowd around the table to sign up for songs, too.

I use the moment to pull Maya away. "How about that drink?"

"Oh, yeah—sure."

I give Rashida a cheeky wink and call out, "See you onstage, 'babe,'" then place a hand briefly on Maya's arm before leaning back over the bar.

As we wait for Jasper to serve us, Maya angles her head in toward me to say, "I'm only eighteen. And I don't really drink that much."

"It's cool. I'll get you whatever you want. But I'm getting a pitcher, and you're welcome to share if you want. Or not." I just turned nineteen and legal in March, but I've had fake ID since I was fourteen.

"Oh. Okay. I'll start with just a lemonade. Thanks."

Once we get our drinks—Jasper ID-ing me but then serving

me with several flourishes like I've just earned my own personal gay cheerleader—we survey the room to find a spot to sit.

"Any preference?" I ask as Maya waves to a couple who've just walked in.

They've gotta be her parents. The woman is brown, like Maya, and has the same big eyes and lips. The guy is white but tanned, with thick, curly brown hair that's held back with a purple hairband. He's also got a full beard with a mustache. They both look chill and sun-kissed, all fit and outdoorsy. And both have massive smiles on their faces—happy to see their kid, I guess.

I clear my throat to get rid of the tightness that's forming there for no goddamn reason. "Those your parents? Wanna sit with them?" I ask.

Her smile toward them is less enthusiastic, and she turns to me to say, "Oh, no. That's okay. I don't have the energy for their energy right now."

She must still be annoyed at them for making her come here or whatever. "'Kay, if you're sure . . ." I search the packed room and see Canva and that little candy gremlin, Blu, in the corner with a group of people. Canva waves, and Blu pokes his tongue out at me. Little stinker. I make a noncommittal chin lift at them because God help me if I have to sit with Canva and listen to her go on about bean sprouts or whatever all night.

I see a couple of seats at a table with some people around our age. "How about over there?" I say to Maya, indicating with the beer glass in my left hand.

She looks over, and her face shifts to uncertainty. "Oh, that's Del Curry and his crew. He's kind of . . ."

"Kind of what?"

"Well . . . he'll probably tease me about Rashida."

"Oh. Well . . . what if I make sure he doesn't?"

Her eyebrows raise. "How?"

"Just trust me." She has zero reason to trust me, of course.

She seems to consider this for a moment, then her shoulders shrug and she nods. "Okay, sure."

She ignores her parents' questioning looks, and as we make our way to the table, she says, "Thanks for letting me bail on singing tonight. And sorry. You sure you want to sing with Rashida?"

I give her a cheeky smirk. "Girl, I got this."

When we get to the table, I look at a skinny guy sitting against the wall and say, "Hey—can we nab these two seats? I'll even share my beer." I lift the pitcher.

Buddy looks up, and his eyes don't make it past my chest. He grins like a total dork.

Eye roll.

Then he notices Maya and his eyebrows rise to the backward baseball cap he's wearing. "Well, well—Maya, Maya, pants on fiya."

Oh my God. This guy. Maya's rubbing her nose and getting all awkward.

"Okay!" I say, placing the pitcher and glass on the table. "I'm gonna take that as a yes and you're just gonna call Maya by her actual name. Cool?"

The guy looks at me for a second, but then cracks up at my hostility, which I kind of respect.

"For sure, for sure!" he says, folding his hands behind his

head like some kind of mafioso. "I'm Del, that's Shannon, Rae, and Kaz," he says, lifting his chin toward his buddies. "And you are?"

"Gabe, Maya's new friend." I add a wink to suggest more than friends.

The wink must hit the spot, because Del and his friends exchange some glances before Del says, "Welcome to our metropolis, Gabe," and cracks up again.

We sit, and after several minutes of listening to Shannon go on and on about her cats, my phone buzzes from my bag, and I pull it out to see a text from my mom. Hope you're making nice and staying out of trouble, Gabe.

I huff out a bitter laugh to myself and shake my head. Guess she's not too busy to send me annoying messages.

Then I eye up Maya, who's the person I'm supposed to be "making nice" with, but who can't stop glancing over at Rashida.

God. She's really bad at this.

Lucky for her, I can be really good at it. I shift my chair closer to her so our arms are pressed against each other on the table and our bare thighs meet below. I feel her look over at me, but I just top up my beer like nothing's happening. She doesn't move a smidge, which makes me smirk to myself. Plan Get Maya to Fake-Date Me is well underway.

A minute later, the mic comes alive onstage with a thunk and screech.

"Oops, sorry about that, folks," Rashida says, and I don't miss the way her eyes find Maya at this table. But then her demeanor switches to something like circus master. "Okay, everyone! It's time to karrrrr-eeee-o-keee!" she yells into the mic.

As Rashida revs up the crowd, Maya turns to me and says, "She's awesome at this part—rallying people. Years of running protests." The admiration and yearning in her voice is so obvious, I almost roll my eyes.

Rashida goes on about the fundraiser and door prizes, and then introduces the first singers, who are the guys from behind the bar.

"Diamond and Jasper like to go on early in the evening and always make sure they're terrible so everybody else feels at ease," Maya continues to explain. I nod and smile, but I'm actually strategizing my next move.

As Diamond and Jasper take the mics and start their truly horrible (but also kind of adorable) version of "Pump Up the Jam," complete with the *worst* Running Man I have ever seen in my life, Rashida sits back down at the bar. I can see her eyeing us up again, and it's clear to me, even if it isn't to Maya, that this girl is jealous. Whether it's a romantic jealousy or not, I don't care. Whatever I'm doing is working, and I hope Maya sees it, too.

After three more songs and another beer in my belly, Canva and Blu get up to sing a Disney duet, which reminds me I'm supposed to do a duet with Rashida. I plan on killing it while *also* showing Maya I'll be a perfect fake girlfriend.

Attention-getting is my jam, after all—my moms would definitely agree. They used to argue regularly about it. As I sip my beer now, my brain trips into a memory of this time I was sent home from school for acting out in class, and the two of them got into it in the kitchen. I was sitting at the table, arms folded and staring out the window, while they fought.

"She's obviously just trying to get attention—*your* attention, Karen. You could try *giving* her—or hell, *me*—some for a change." Even though I hadn't been looking at them, I could picture the tightness in Meems's face—it was always there by that point.

"That's a real laugh, Tracy," Mom had replied. "Like you're not running off half the time with your woodsy little friends? All of this is my fault?"

They'd gone on like that for a while—arguing about who paid me the least attention while neither of them once looked at me.

I empty my beer glass. Whatever. Maybe I like attention a little too much, but at least I can use my skills tonight to convince this girl my mom would approve of that my plan is a good one.

As if agreeing with me, Del claps at my chugging abilities and says, "Girl's got *skills*."

Encouraged, I grab the now-empty beer pitcher I've been sharing with the others and say, "Refill!" as I get up from the table. Del and his friends cheer, and I wink at Maya, whose expression, I think, is a little surprised, but maybe also amused. That's me—entertaining as hell. And I'm about to prove it to this whole damn crowd.

FIFTEEN

Maya

While Gabe goes to get a refill and Del and the others try to flick quarters into an empty beer glass, I'm left trying to sort out for myself what's happening right now. Gabe seems hell-bent on helping me by distracting everyone else from my humiliation, and I'm not gonna lie—I appreciate it, even if I also feel a little dizzy from this new, very gregarious element to my Spruce Lake life.

I'm also trying to figure out what's up with Rashida. I can't quite read her interactions with Gabe—curious? Uncertain? Maybe even a little jealous?

Gabe appears with her new pitcher of beer and announces, "We're up!" She flits away again, but not without squeezing my bare shoulder, which feels kind of nice—like she's on my side or something.

I watch as Rashida follows Gabe up to the stage. There are two mics, and Gabe grabs one. Rish takes the other, looking like she wants to be anywhere but there.

The song starts. Rish knows "I've Got You Babe" perfectly, given that we've sung it together every summer since we were ten. I thought Gabe said she knew it well, too, but her eyes are glued to the screen and she fumbles through the first few words. Maybe she's too tipsy to focus? But after the first lines, she just goes for it and starts belting out every lyric on the screen, whether it's Sonny's or Cher's. She's a good singer, despite the haphazard approach. Raspy and deep and, well . . . sexy, to be honest.

The crowd doesn't seem to mind this new person singing with Rashida, judging from the smiles and whistles around me. I ignore my parents, though, who are sending inquisitive glances from across the room. I'd be offended by this easy acceptance of Gabe in my place if I wasn't so entertained by her myself and relieved to not be up there.

Onstage, Rish is trying her best to do her thing, but Gabe is demanding a lot of attention. She starts out next to Rashida, staying mostly on track with the lyrics (but only partially in tune with the melody), then kind of drifts offstage with the cordless mic. She makes her way past a couple of tables, trying to look back at the screen but also trying to sing to people. It doesn't really work, but it's kind of funny, and people cheer her on.

Gabe must take this as encouragement because she saunters over to my table and starts singing to *me*. She can't possibly see the lyrics now, so she's just singing words from previous parts of the song in a tune that kind of sounds like the national anthem.

At first, I don't know where to look. I hate that all eyes are on us right now. But watching Gabe belt out her personal rendition of the song, a huge smile on her face, I can't help the smile that takes over my lips. People are hooting and hollering, and she is *feeling* it. She feels it so much that the next thing I know, she steps onto her empty chair, *then onto the table*—almost knocking over my half-full glass of lemonade as she does.

Del and his crew are whooping and whistling, while I'm a mix of amused and worried Gabe is going to fall off the table. This is definitely a first for Spruce Lake karaoke nights, which can get a little rowdy, but fall short of table dancing.

Diamond and Jasper must be a little worried, too, because they come over and—in true gay fashion—smoothly guide Gabe off the table like two cabaret dancers, holding her by the arms and armpits while Gabe, impressively, keeps her arms firm enough for them to bring her down to the floor.

Gabe makes her way back to Rashida to end the song, and I can tell Rish is a little stunned. But the whole thing is actually so fun and charming, and the number receives an explosion of applause and cheers from the crowd. I let out a sigh of relief, and any nervousness I felt disappears into thrill.

Rish has to somehow segue from this remarkable performance to announcing the next singer. When Gabe sits down at our table beside me, Del and his buddies give her high fives, and I lean in to say, "Gabe, that was outrageous."

She takes in my face for a moment, and something unexpected crosses her own. The tiniest frown. But it's gone in an instant. A slick smile replaces it.

"Damn right it was," she says.

I grin and shake my head. She's managed to push aside so much of my anxiety about tonight and fill it with something unexpected and much lighter.

"Let's get out of here," she says.

"Oh—um . . ." I can't help but glance up at Rashida, who's still onstage trying to set up the next singer. I feel weird about leaving her here. But then I realize, she probably won't care that much if I leave. Maybe she'll even be relieved, given how awkward it is between us.

"Come on, Maya," Gabe says, her hand finding my knee. "My little plan is working, and you know it." She winks, squeezes my knee, then stands, grabs her bag, and heads out the exit.

I hesitate, but then I realize she's a little tipsy, it's getting dark out, and she's already been lost once today. I glance over at Rashida again, who's frowning in my direction, and I wonder if Gabe is right. If Rish just needs to see what it would be like if I were with someone else. Maybe then she'll realize that "just friends" won't cut it with us.

Replacing hesitancy with hope, I grab my stuff and am out of my seat in seconds.

I catch up to Gabe as she heads toward nowhere in particular. "Gabe, Canva's place is this way."

She nudges my arm and says, "Come on, fake gf. Don't take me back there. Take me on our first fake date." She gives me a wide grin.

Would it hurt too much to try out this whole fake-dating thing? Even just for a couple of days to see what happens?

"Fine," I say, before I can stop myself.

She arches an eyebrow. "Fine, what?"

"Fine, let's try this little plan of yours. You pretend to be my fake . . . whatever."

"I think the word you're looking for is *girlfriend*. Ever heard of it?" She smirks. "And if we're doing this, let's do it right."

"Meaning?"

"Meaning you take me on some very public, very awesome fake dates around this quaint little town of yours."

The "very public" part sends a wave of nausea through me, but I know she's right—if we're going to try this, it *has* to be public—not just so Rashida witnesses it, but so the rest of Spruce Lake sees that I'm *just fine* and leaves me alone, thank you very much.

"Okay, fair. But," I add, "if things aren't working out as planned, I reserve the right to call things off, no hard feelings. Okay?"

She nods and smirks, like maybe she's impressed with me?

"Deal," she says.

I eye her up for a moment as we walk. "Why are you doing this?" I ask, genuinely unsure why someone like her would want to do something like this with me, or *for* me.

She glances over, but takes a few more steps before answering. "Well, first, I think it could be fun, right?" When I narrow my eyes at her, she shrugs and adds, "And maybe I need a little something out of this, too."

"Oh. Okay. What is it?"

She clears her throat. "At least one of these public fake dates needs to involve my mom."

Not what I thought she was going to say. "Sorry?"

She looks away for a second, then turns back to me and says, "Just—I need my mom to think I've 'settled down' with a nice girl this summer, okay? It's weird, I know. But both my parents think I'm a fuckup, and dating someone like you from a town like this would go a long way to showing my mom I'm not completely hopeless."

Her words strike me as heavy, but she says them matter-of-factly, and her tight jaw signals "beware," so I don't press for more info.

"Um, okay. I can do that, if you think it will help."

"It will. We can send her a few selfies or whatever, too." She waves a hand around flippantly. "Now. I think it's time for you to show me something cool, fake honeybunch." She grins again. "Let's call this a practice date—not public—just to suss out the details." Her head tilts in a challenge.

This also makes sense, and I'll probably need all the practice I can get, given I've never actually been on a date before, even though everything I've ever done with Rashida just felt like one long date to me.

Thinking on my feet is not a strength I have, but I can tell Gabe isn't the patient kind, so I decide on somewhere that's not too far, different from anything she probably gets in the city, and isn't *too* nature-based for her.

"Okay, let's go this way, then," I say, and take her through the forest, but I use a path this time so she doesn't have to wrestle with nature at night. We walk side by side. The moon is full and bright, and I don't even need my phone flashlight to guide us.

"Are you trying to get me into the woods to fake take advantage of me?" she says after a minute or two of slapping at mosquitoes.

"Well, if we're going to fake-date in Spruce Lake, you'll definitely need to learn how to fake a lot of things in the forest."

She lets out a big laugh, sending something skittering into the branches above us. "Oh, *really*?" she says.

I realize too late how my words sounded—especially to this hyper-flirty, very confident girl beside me.

"*Not* what I meant," I say, feeling my cheeks go hot.

She lets out a cackle and shoves me with her shoulder. "Relax, Maya. I'm just hassling you."

But this conversation about fake fooling around urges me to ask, "*Should* we make up some rules or something, though? About—you know—physical stuff in front of others?" I can't believe I'm even saying those words. I'm not exactly the biggest risk taker—that was always Rashida's domain. But here I am, launching into what may be the most bizarre thing I've ever done.

"I like the way you think," Gabe says. "To sell it, we should probably act a *little* like horny teens, right?"

I have to take a deep breath to calm the nerves her words cause. I swallow. "Right."

"Okay—here's what I suggest: hand-holding, pecks on the cheek, arms across shoulders, hands on legs and knees and other casual touches. Nothing involving tits, ass, or cooch, obviously. And no kissing, I'm guessing?"

She's guessing? She rattles off these specifics like she's done this before. "Do you do this . . . often?" I ask.

She laughs. "Fake-date? No. Real date? Yes. I'm a full-blooded babe, Maya. I know what comes with the territory, and I can adapt to this fake-dating situation, all right?"

I try not to think about how much more experienced she probably is than I am, and instead think about the things she's listed. All things I've done with Rashida—but under the label of friendship. Just regular stuff two best friends do to show affection. Of course, none of it felt like friendship to me.

"I think that should be okay. But maybe not too much? I'm not a big PDA girl, and Rashida knows that. She might get suspicious if we're too touchy-feely."

"Got it. How about if I get too 'touchy-feely,' you have a code or something. Like, 'Gabe, I can't handle all your sexiness.' That'll work, right?"

I can practically *feel* her smirk, it's so potent. "How about something more like 'I've got a bit of a headache'?"

She shrugs. "Boring, but okay," she says.

We walk more until we come to one of the three public boat launches around the lake. It's late, and everyone's at karaoke, so I'm pretty sure no one will find us here, which is important, since I'm not supposed to be doing this. But that's the part that I'm hoping will appeal to Gabe—the delinquency of it all. And I'll admit—it gives me a bit of a thrill, too.

Next to this particular launch is the antique and thrift shop Marissa Jacobs runs on her property. Her yard is huge, extending from the beach beside the boat launch up to her house. The garage part is closed right now, but her backyard is just *there*, surrounded by a simple wooden fence. The gate is never locked. It's Spruce Lake.

Marissa's spent years cultivating the store. Tall hedges line wide pathways around the lawn in a maze, and within the maze she's set up wooden booths that hold the antiques and other items. If the weather is bad, she covers everything up with tarps. In the offseason, everything goes into storage.

"A-MAZE-ing Antiques?" Gabe says, squinting in the darkness to read the sign attached to the gate. "You're taking me antique shopping?" Her skepticism is clear, but Marissa's shop is one of a kind. My parents come at least twice a summer, treating it more like a museum than a shop, poking around to see what's new.

When I was younger, Rashida and I would make up stories about where things came from—the pirate Marissa must have fought for these ornate silver binoculars, the forest gnome who must have gifted her that mushroom-shaped teapot. It always felt special to visit here with her.

Those memories make me sad now, so instead of sharing that part, I tell Gabe, "I remember racing around here as a kid—the maze isn't big enough to get completely lost, but once you're inside, it definitely feels like you're part of a secret web of greenery. Bet you don't have anything like it in the city."

She still looks a little weary, but then shrugs. "You're right. I'm pretty sure we do not have an outdoor antique maze shop that looks out onto the water." She pauses and then tilts her head. "That does sound kind of cool, actually."

"You mean, a-*maze*-ing," I say, opening the gate and walking through.

SIXTEEN

Gabe

I'm still skeptical but also curious about what Maya thinks is so special about this place, so I follow her through the gate.

We wander around for a bit, mostly in the dark, though there are twinkle lights here and there. Maya points out a few bits and pieces—a collection of those dashboard dolls that wobble around in grass skirts, something she says is a vintage ink bottle but just looks like a small bong to me, some chunky costume jewelry that's so cheesy it's actually kind of chic. We cringe at the terrifying horde of puppets with china heads and glazed eyes, giving them a wide berth as we circle one end of the maze and almost smack into a statue or something?

"What the hell is this?" I whisper. My body still feels a little loose from the beer and my *breathtaking* karaoke performance, but I'm trying to control my volume, because Maya's right—this maze does seem secret and kind of . . . I don't know . . . rare, I guess.

"It's a scuba suit from who knows when," Maya whispers back. "Nuts how people used to dive in those."

"Nuts how people deep dive at all. The ocean is terrifying."

"The ocean is miraculous."

I roll my eyes. "Sure. Yeah. Sharks and blubbery alien creatures are magical."

She shakes her head at me, and I shrug.

We keep meandering, Maya pointing out this or that, me cracking jokes about each thing and satisfied when she laughs.

I start wondering what she and Rashida are like when they're together, because Rashida didn't seem all that fun to me. Before I can control my mouth—it's not a strength—I ask, "What d'you like so much about this chick Rashida, anyway?"

She's silent for a few moments, her gaze aimed at the ground as we turn a corner of the maze. Then, "We're best friends. She knows everything about me, and I know everything about her. We're just so . . . comfortable."

"Huh. That sounds . . . okay, I guess."

"You guess?"

"Yeah, I mean, if that's your thing. Comfortable sounds a little boring to me? But different strokes for different folks." I nudge her with my arm, hoping to keep things chill.

"So what do *you* look for, then? In a . . . partner?" she asks.

I laugh at her word choice. "I don't. I'm not looking for a 'partner.'"

"Oh." She seems to think about this, then asks, "So . . . you've never had a girlfriend? Or boyfriend? Or . . . ?"

"Nah. Who needs it." Meems's tight features, Mom's cutting tone flash across my brain. But I also wonder what my mom's face will do when she meets Maya. When we roll up holding hands and I give her a peck on the cheek.

"My parents' relationship might say different," Maya says. "They're disgustingly perfect."

"Oh yeah? Like, they never fight or anything?"

"No—I mean, they do, once in a while. But their fights are more like very serious discussions that end in a lot of kissing and giggling."

"Gross."

She looks at me and smiles. "Very."

"But you obviously want that," I add.

Her smile drops. "I mean, who wouldn't?"

I shrug. "Seems pretty rare. Not sure I'm cut out for that kind of stuff, anyway."

"Not cut out for . . . ?"

I grip the strap of my shoulder bag and hitch it up my shoulder. "I dunno. Lovey-dovey stuff. *Romance.*" I use air quotes for that last nonsense word. "My parents weren't exactly the poster children for it."

"They're not together anymore?"

"Nope."

My face must communicate how little I want to continue talking about this, because "Hmm" is all she says.

I must seem like an oddity to her, given her parents and this thing she has with Rashida. But I don't know anyone who's all caught up in being in love or whatever. Seems like a waste of time and energy.

We keep walking down the path, past some old-school lawn mowers. I steal a few glances at Maya, trying to read her expression. She's frowning and chewing on her lower lip. I remind myself of our deal and my role in the whole thing. Maybe she's worried I'm not the person for the job?

"Hey—don't worry—I can fake all kinds of romance for 'the cause'!" I raise a fist like a total dork, hoping it makes her laugh.

She looks at my raised fist like she thinks I'm a dork, too, but a laugh follows, and dork or not, I win.

Building on this win, I decide to fake a little romance now to plant a seed with my mom, too.

"Give me a sec, okay?" I say, pulling out my phone and ignoring all the notifications reminding me of what I'm missing back home. I type in a reply to my mom's earlier text. *Making very nice. Met someone local and she's super sweet. Even won a karaoke contest.*

Okay, that last bit is a lie, but one in service of a greater cause. I can be wholesome. I can date nice girls. I can use proper punctuation and capitalization in a text.

I put my phone away and clap my hands together, feeling a renewed sense of purpose. "Let's go over some other stuff that will sell this whole thing to the people that matter, all right?"

"Oh—yeah, okay."

"First, we should probably know each other's last names."

"Right. Mine's Brady-Jayasinghe."

"Whoa. Wait. Sorry. You're gonna need to say that again for me."

She rolls her eyes. "Repeat after me: Brae-dee." A smile lifts her lips.

I narrow my eyes at her. "Very funny. I admit it—I'm white. I'm not used to saying brown names. I'm sorry for my ignorance."

She grins. "Jye-ah . . ."

"Jye-ah . . ."

"Sing . . ."

"Sing . . ."

"Uh."

"Uh."

"Try it."

"Jye-ah . . . sing . . . uh. Brady-Jayasinghe."

"Correct. A-plus," she says with a half smile.

"Okay. I'll practice, I promise."

"You better. What's yours?"

"Martin. Marrr-tiiin," I say slowly, just to be an ass. "You better practice, too." I wink at her.

"Gabe Martin."

"Maya Brady . . . Jayasinghe."

We smile at each other, pleased with ourselves, I guess.

Arriving at a collection of those old-timey lanterns—the metal ones that require oil or whatever, I ask, "Okay, if we were on a date right now—a real one—what would we be doing?"

She looks at me. Looks at the lanterns. The sky. Frowns.

Jesus. "For instance," I say, too impatient for her to come up with something, "I might come in a little closer to you and lean over like this"—I bend at the waist to take a look at one of the lanterns, my hip bumping lightly against hers in the process—"which would be a great opportunity for you to *also* lean in, right?" I'm looking back at her and curl a finger in a come-here gesture.

"Right. Yes." She leans over, as well.

"Closer, Maya."

Her nose wrinkles for a moment, but she shifts so our faces are only a couple of inches apart.

"Nice. Always go for contact if you can and if they're open to it. Or at least get close." I rise to standing, and so does she.

"Okay."

"Do you wanna try holding hands?" I ask. The last time I held hands with someone was probably in the eighth grade when Cam O'Brien and I went to the school dance together. We lasted that one night. He was boring AF.

"Sure, I guess."

"Don't get too excited."

"Am I supposed to get excited about fake hand-holding?"

"I mean, yes? Fake excited, at least?"

She clasps her hands in front of her and does a stage-whisper squeal. "Eee! I can't wait!"

"Okay, gross," I say, rolling my eyes. "Just give me your goddamn hand."

She does, and we clasp on to each other. I'm a bit taller than her, so I switch positions, placing my hand over hers. We walk a few steps, but something doesn't feel right.

She spreads her fingers and laces them through mine, and that definitely feels a lot better. Hers is soft and a little sweaty, but not unpleasant. The image of me walking up to my mom with my hand in Maya's appears again. Maybe a smile on her face when we do.

"Feels okay, right?" I say, looking at Maya.

She's staring at the ground in front of her, though, and just nods her head.

"What's up?" I ask, hoping she's not going to launch into some sob story about the last time she held hands with Rashida.

"Nothing. This is just . . . kind of weird. Not what I thought this summer would be like."

"Babe, this is gonna be *better* than the summer you expected," I say. "'Cause let's face it—pining away while everyone brings up your . . . you know . . . *situation* . . . did not sound fun."

She nods again. "True."

"Okay"—I squeeze her hand and let go—"I think we nailed close proximity and hand-holding. The only thing left to do is plan out some dates, right?"

We stop walking just inside the entry to the yard. "Yeah. What were you thinking?" she asks.

"I wasn't thinking anything, except the date with my mom. This is kind of your department. Just no sweaty-ass hikes, camping, or hard labor, please."

Her eyes go a little wide. "You know Spruce Lake is known for its natural beauty, right?"

Ugh. This must be a Spruce Lake refrain. "Sure, whatever. But there's gotta be some stuff that's public but that I might actually like?"

She folds her arms and stares at me for a few seconds, thinking. Then her eyes widen again, but this time more from excitement than disbelief. "Tomorrow's Saturday! That means the farmers market is on. It's outdoors, and super busy, and *does* involve tents, but there doesn't have to be any sweat, work, or dirt. Just great food, live music, and tons of cool, artsy stuff. You might even enjoy it. And it's perfect, because Rashida will be there, selling her dad's art."

Sounds like hippie shit to me, but I'm always down for good food. "Yeah, okay. What time?"

SEVENTEEN

Maya

When I get home that night, it's almost midnight and I'm buzzing. This new plan with Gabe, Gabe's karaoke performance, the way Rashida was maybe curious or possibly even jealous of Gabe—set alight some hope that wasn't there this morning or this past year.

And now I at least have some concrete things to focus on, too. Tomorrow Gabe and I start with the farmers market, and then we decided our next date would be on Wednesday and Gabe would see if her mom was available.

I push open the front door to get into my cabin and hear Poppy yapping away inside Rashida's cabin. I do feel a little bad about leaving the pub with Rashida and my parents there, but when I said that to Gabe tonight as I walked her back to Canva's, she said it was an *excellent* "hard to get" move and would just make Rashida want to spend more time with me.

I'm still figuring out how much of Gabe's advice I can trust, but I decide it can't hurt to let Rish wonder what I was doing with Gabe while she was still at karaoke. I've been angry-slash-sad for a year, so a little uncertainty won't kill her.

After a quick shower, I lie in bed, listening to the dock creaking below against the constant ripples of the water. I should be sleepy, but instead I toss and turn, the bed frame echoing the creaks of the dock. I find myself staring out the open window that faces Rashida's bedroom window, which is only about thirty feet away.

I get up now and pad over to it to breathe in some fresh air. Rashida's curtain is open because she's not in bed yet. She's always needed blackout curtains to sleep—any bit of light or noise wakes her up. I know this from the thousands of nights we've slept over in each other's cabins. The million conversations we've had in her dark, dark bedroom or in my room—me on my bottom bunk, her on the top. Me wishing as I got older that I just had a single bed so cuddling was inevitable.

When Rashida's not in here, though, I like to keep the curtains wide open so the moonlight can stream in. I don't mind it.

I hear voices rise above the sound of the water and the creaking of the dock. People are wandering back from the pub. Karaoke night must be finished. I hear D's voice, then Rashida's. Mom and Dad sometimes head over to friends' cabins for after parties. They somehow function on four or five hours of sleep. I don't hear them now, so they must still be out.

I shouldn't listen to D and Rish's conversation, but I do.

I hear D say, "I wish I could lighten your heart, love. Maybe things will feel better in the morning. Try and get some sleep, okay?"

Rashida doesn't say anything, and they're both quiet for a few moments. D is probably giving her one of his exquisite hugs. My heart dips a little. Her heart must be heavy because of me, right? What else could it be? But then I remember that this is exactly what I'm hoping for—not to hurt Rish, I mean, but to get her thinking about what it might be like if we're not "Maya and Rish." A heavy heart is sadness, right? Loss?

The door to D's section of the cabin opens and closes, as does Rashida's. A light goes on in the main room of Rashida's cabin, then I see Poppy race down to the dock for a nighttime pee in the bushes off to the side of the property.

Rashida follows behind Poppy, stopping at the little beach next to the dock. She kicks off her sneakers and immerses her feet in the shallow water.

I know exactly what she's doing right now. She's curling her toes into the soft sand in that spot, feeling it squeeze between them and picturing each tiny speck as the miraculous bits of rocks and minerals they are. Shiny and sharp in their own minuscule worlds, smooth and harmless in ours.

It's one of the things she's always done to calm her body down, which she's needed to do a lot. Her mom and dad argued for most of Rashida's childhood, her mom leaving when Rashida was just seven and living somewhere overseas now. Rish barely ever sees her. Her dad, Winston, is an artist and famous on the West Coast—his art is nature-based and is used for all kinds of conservation efforts. He's away a lot because of it.

Through the fights and abandonment and disinterest, the land has always been Rish's remedy and comfort. The land and me and my family.

When Rashida was younger, Winston would basically entrust her to my parents during the summer, or to folks like Jan and Diamond during the other months. The past couple of years, Rashida didn't really need anyone to look after her, though lots of people are ready to do it whenever she needs them.

So Rashida has the cabin all to herself, and mostly, we loved this. We would play house like her cabin was ours and we'd make childish food together in the kitchen as new teens and fancier meals together as fifteen- and sixteen-year-olds. We'd sit out on her dock and wave over at my mom and dad as they sat on ours like we were two happy couples—neighbors.

I'd be lying if I said I didn't think this was exactly what we were, and what we *would* be for years to come.

My eyes sting, watching her. Wanting to be her person—her one and only person to make things better.

Rashida calls to Poppy and steps out of the water. I duck back away from the window so she won't see me if she looks up here. If this thing is going to work with Gabe, I have to sell it. I can't be seen pining away for her from my window. It doesn't feel great to hide from her, but I tell myself it's "for the cause" and think of Gabe's fist raised in the air like a weirdo. As I crawl back into bed, the image makes me smile, despite all the other feelings churning inside of me.

EIGHTEEN

Gabe

Hummingbirds are *bananas*. Two of them keep flitting around me as I lie on Maya's not-so-secret hammock on Saturday morning. Their tiny wings are so freaking fast—a blur, really—that they sound like bees. One even hovered in front of me for a couple of seconds like it was figuring me out.

I'd been trying to doze off away from the chickens (and I am *extremely* proud of myself for finding Maya's spot without getting lost, thank you very much) after being woken up by my feathery archenemies just like yesterday.

Maya and I agreed to meet at the café at ten thirty and walk over to the farmers market together—holding hands, might I add—and I decided I needed to catch up on my beauty rest if I was going to be seen around town today. I ended up back on this hammock. But then these goddamn, teeny-tiny miracle birds showed up and I couldn't take my eyes off them.

Staring up through the treetops at another blue-sky day now, I guess I can see why Maya likes this spot. I'd still choose my home theater and leather couch over it, but some greenery and water can be nice . . . as long as I don't have to bushwhack or wade through either.

I don't get how people can be so wrapped up in any one place, though. I've lived in the same place my whole life, been to plenty of cool cities, but I sure as hell never felt connected to any of it. None of it seems attached to me, either. Maybe I'm just someone who needs to see a lot, do a lot, meet lots of people.

I feel a prick on my arm and slap at it. I am definitely not tied to these *bugs*, that's for damn sure.

The hummingbirds disappear to whatever magical place they're from, and I finally close my eyes and doze in and out of sleep for a while.

But in my drowsy state, bits and pieces of the day before flit through my mind.

Hot dogs. Singing on tabletops. Cheering and high fives. Silent antique shops.

I'm surprised by how many moments I enjoyed. Do I still think this town is embarrassingly small and limited? One hundred percent. But karaoke felt like a party, I got to get my buzz on, and all those locals thought I was the shit.

And getting things sorted out with Maya about our fake-dating plan was the grand prize. After I sent that text to my mom last night, she replied this morning with Wow, Gabe. Glad to hear.

Not an overwhelmingly positive response, but I can't blame her for being restrained in her excitement. For one, she's not an emotionally expressive person in general, and two, she has no reason to believe I've turned a corner so quickly.

But I plan on following up with some added wholesome details when I check in with her this morning. I'll do that as soon as I'm in town with proper cell service. Now, though, I take a luxurious stretch and realize I'm too awake to keep dozing.

Since I don't have anywhere else to go until I meet Maya in half an hour, I (very carefully) climb out of the hammock and kneel down by the steel box close by. I push aside the leaves and dirt scattered across the lid and pull the box open with some effort. I see a blanket, a pair of neon-pink plastic sunglasses, and a book. *Fried Green Tomatoes.*

Why would anyone fry tomatoes? Or *green* ones for that matter?

I read stuff online sometimes, if I have to, but I don't read a lot of books. They're, like, so *long.*

I've got time to kill, though, and this at least doesn't look like one of those tedious old-timey books with small print and words that don't make sense in the present day. The cover has a tear in it, and a couple of pages are hanging on for dear life. Maya's name is written on the inside cover in what has gotta be preteen printing with its bubble letters and happy faces inside the *a*'s.

I nestle back into the hammock and try to figure out what a fried green tomato is and why anyone would want one.

I'm on page twenty-two and not hating this story, even with all its "down home" goodness, when I realize it's almost time to meet Maya, so I tuck the book into my shoulder bag for later and make my way back through the forest and into town, following the exact route I took to get here so I don't get lost.

When I arrive at the café, I wait outside for Maya. A few people do a double take when they see me, then smile and wave. One guy even points and shouts, "I got *you*, babe!" but it's not a creepy thing—he's grinning like a dork, and it's just kind of sweet.

I guess I made quite the impression last night. Being Entertaining Gabe pays off sometimes. Just not with my parents. But maybe it will now that I got the girl.

Leaning against the building in the shade, I message my mom. Gotta keep this ball rolling, after all.

Gabe: morning

I wait. It takes her a full minute to get back to me.

Mother-Figure: Morning

I try something new to see if it makes a difference.

Gabe: how's work? You good?

Mother-Figure: The usual. Busy.

So no difference, then.

I try something else, just to see whether my inclination is even close to correct.

Gabe: meeting the new girl. We're going to the farmers market

Mother-Figure: Oh?

Gabe: yeah. She's super nice.

I don't think my mom has heard me describe any of my friends, let alone people I'm dating, as "nice."

Mother-Figure: That's refreshing to hear, Gabe.

Okay, not bad, not bad.

Gabe: her name's maya

Gabe: want anything from the market?

Three dots flicker across the screen for a few seconds. Then nothing. Then there they are again. *Not a hard question, Mom.*

Mother-Figure: I'm fine, but thanks.

I think that's the end of it, but then my phone buzzes again.

Mother-Figure: But let me know how things go. I'm glad you're doing nice things with nice people!

Okay. That could have gone worse. I make a mental note to message her with an update tonight, tuck my phone away, and wait for my "nice people" to arrive.

NINETEEN

Maya

I wake up the next morning to the sound of my parents using the blender in the kitchen. When I wander out of my room, they look as chipper as ever. I don't know how they're out until after midnight, up before me the next day, *and* look this fresh and upbeat. Diamond's the same way, so is Rish, and where before I always just wished I was the same as all of them, now I find the whole thing tiring.

"Morning, sunshine!" Dad says over top of the whirring blender.

His zest for life and the blender hurt my head. It's not like I have a hangover or anything, but since I still couldn't sleep after seeing Rashida last night, I sat up in my bunk watching reruns of *The L Word* in the dark—immersing myself in other people's drama instead of in my own. Hoping I wouldn't have to spend years apart from Rashida before we finally ended up together, like

Bette and Tina. It must have been after two a.m. when I finally dozed off.

So I am definitely *not* well rested, nor prepared for my dad's morning-person-ness.

"Hi," I say, making it as far as the couch and flopping down onto it.

The blender finally stops. Dad pours his morning smoothie into three glasses, and I groan because I know he's going to offer one to me and all I really want is toast with loads of sugary peanut butter on it.

"You better not be moaning about this delicious smoothie I just made you," he says.

I sit up as he hands it to me. "Of course not."

"Good." He clinks his glass against mine and sits beside me, leaning one shoulder into the back of the couch. My mom sits on the other side of me with her smoothie.

"Sooooo . . ." Dad says.

I side-eye him. Sigh. Barely mask an eye roll for a trifecta of aggravation. "Yes?" I ask.

"Where'd you disappear to last night?" he asks.

"I walked Gabe home." True. "I was worried about her when she left on her own." Also true.

"Oh, I'm glad to hear that," Mom says. "Was she okay?"

"Yeah—definitely a bit tipsy, but better with some fresh air and walking." And antiques and practice fake-dating.

"That's good," Dad says. "She seems like a lightning rod. What's her story?"

A lightning rod. I nod, thinking, *Accurate.* "She's here for the summer. Her mom's working in Miller's Bay or something."

"Ah." He sips his smoothie, and I know what's coming before he says it. "Everything okay with you and Rashida?"

I sip my own smoothie, the citrus in it causing a twinge at the back of my jaw. I decide that this is as good a time as any to start convincing my parents that all is well and that they and Diamond can leave me alone already. "Yeah. I think so, anyway. She was pretty busy last night. We'll catch up later."

"If you're around tomorrow afternoon, you can catch up then," Dad says.

"Why?"

"SLEA meeting at the pub at two."

"*If* you're interested," my mom adds.

Right. Because tomorrow is Sunday. SLEA meetings take place here or at the pub every Sunday and on Wednesday evenings, if needed. It's been this way for as long as SLEA's been a thing.

As of yesterday, I was a bit nervous about this—about spending so much time with Rashida working on SLEA initiatives. But now I wonder if it's just what I need to balance out fake-dating with Gabe. Doing SLEA work with Rish will give us time on our own to do one of the things we've always been so passionate about—making sure the lake, land, and trees here are protected from pollution and overdevelopment. If I spend too much time with just Gabe, Rish might think I'm totally over her and there's no chance with us.

But I need her to know there will always be a chance for us.

Feeling proud of my master strategizing, I say, "Oh, great. I'm excited to dig back into SLEA stuff."

"You are?" Mom says. "You seemed a little . . . hesitant about it yesterday."

"Yeah . . . sorry about that. I was just a bit overwhelmed. I needed some time to adjust to things."

"Things" being the introduction of a certain "lightning rod" into my daily operations and a new, sneaky plan to get Rashida to realize her love for me.

"Well, that's great to hear, honey," Dad says, nudging my shoulder with his.

"Are you adjusted enough to come for a hike with us this morning?" Mom asks.

I love a good hike, but I have a fake date to enact. "Actually, I kind of have . . . plans."

"Oh?" Mom says.

"What plans?" Dad asks.

"I'm meeting Gabe and taking her to the farmers market."

I don't miss the glance my parents pass to each other, right across my face. I'm just not sure whether it's a "What great news!" glance or a "What's this about?" glance.

I try to push them toward the first option and say, "It's kind of a date." I add a bashful smile, which is only half fake, because I genuinely do feel a little shy about it.

"A date! Wow."

"Who asked who?"

Hmm . . . which will sound better? I decide to impress them with my fake initiative. “I did. She seems fun, and I guess I just like being around her.” None of that is a total lie, even if the fun parts can be overwhelming and a little intimidating.

“You sure you’re ready—” my dad starts, but my mom quickly cuts him off.

“We’re happy for you, sweetheart.” This time, a clear warning passes from her to my dad.

“Thanks!” I say, mustering up some cheer, even though lying isn’t really my forte. I stand with my smoothie to get out from between them and say, “I’m going to finish this down on the dock. But I’ll see you both later, okay?” My voice is as light as a pool noodle.

“Sounds good. Enjoy the market.”

“Oh, and maybe grab some more kale for our smoothies,” my dad adds.

“Will do,” I say, leaving them to gossip about me so I can just take a beat to myself. I head down to the dock and lie back on one of the lounge chairs. The morning is cool and sunny. I stare out at the lake and take a sip of my smoothie.

I think about what this day is about to bring and find it difficult to quell the nerves that are bustling around in my belly. But I’m determined now. I’m doing this.

TWENTY

Gabe

I'm playing games on my phone when I hear, "Hey, Gabe." I look up to see Maya smiling and wearing a vintage T-shirt, jean shorts, and sneakers. Her hair's in a ponytail, like yesterday.

I wore a pair of red shorts today—the shortest I brought—and kept my hair down. My top is a little less revealing than yesterday, but not by much. You gotta work with what God gave ya, after all.

"Hey," I say, smiling back. I go in for a hug, too, because, like, we're *dating*, right? Maya seems a little surprised but quickly eases into my arms, and I'm not really a hugger, but this is a decent one—fast but firm.

We pull back, and I immediately slip my hand into hers, like we practiced last night—fingers laced, my hand over top of hers. We catch swift looks from a couple of people passing by us and I lean in to whisper in her ear, "Bingo."

She gives me a shy smile, I heft my bag up my shoulder, and we're off to this market.

It takes us about two minutes to get there—the market is behind a row of four small houses that Maya tells me are artist studios. When we walk around the corner of one, a wide array of white canopy tents spreads out in front of us in three rows, each about six to eight tents long, and it seems to me that all of Spruce Lake is here, which I guess is the point if Maya and I want to cause a stir with our little scheme.

Overlapping smells of bread, flowers, and something sweet fill the air, along with the chill strumming from the person by the entrance, playing their guitar.

"Where do you want to start?" Maya asks.

"Let's just walk through the whole thing first," I say, then lean in again to add, "just so everyone can get a good look." Wink.

She swallows and nods. I can tell she's nervous, and I get it. She knows mostly everyone here, I assume, and all of a sudden she's tromping around town with this rando chick from who knows where. At least this random chick is hot.

We meander through the wide lanes between tent rows, and I try to get Maya to loosen up by asking about all the things for sale. Produce, flowers, candles, bread and pastries, jewelry, clay stuff, handmade clothing, etc. It's cute, I guess. I mean, it's not like I've never been to a market before—there's a massive one that Meems used to go to near our place in the city, and she'd bring me along when I was younger—but it's been a while. I get most things online these days.

As we walk, tons of people say hi to Maya and smile at me or glance at our hands, and we stop to chat with a few people. Maya introduces me as "Gabe, who's here for the summer," and most people give me warm greetings, even though I can tell they're surprised by me and Maya together. No one mentions Rashida, and I'm glad for it because Maya's such a sap when it comes to anything Rashida-related.

Near the end of our first walk-through, a voice calls out, "Gabe! Maya!" and we turn to see Canva and Blu in one of the tents. The counter has a bunch of different food on it—healthy stuff, I imagine, and my nose automatically wrinkles.

Maya smiles and waves, tugging me forward. I'm not quite as enthused to run into either of these two—though Blu seems to have kept his promise to stay quiet about my run-in with the chickens. He grins and waves, as well, from where he's playing a card game with some other kid, then hops up to stand beside Canva.

"Hi, you two!" Canva says, her smile wide. She definitely catches our hands, but doesn't say anything about it. Instead, she homes in on me and says, "Gabe, I'm so glad you found the market! It's a great introduction to all the amazing things Spruce Lake has to offer."

Her energy is just bursting out of her, and I find it irritating, personally, but I know I have to pull some positivity out of my ass to sell this situation with Maya. "Yeah, totally! I'm super glad Maya brought me." I grin at Maya and then, because this is what we practiced and agreed on, I lift her hand to my lips and plant a quick kiss on the back of it. Her eyebrows bounce up, but she manages to plaster on a smile.

"Oh my goodness," Canva says now, "you two are so sweet! Gabe, you must be pretty special to nab this one so quickly."

I try to read Canva's face for some kind of suspicion or insincerity, but I find none. Just genuine enthusiasm and pleasure, I think.

This would be a great time for Maya to jump in with just how special I am, but she doesn't, and that's fine—I think this whole thing is already stretching her natural being to the max.

"Here, try this," Canva adds, using tongs to pick up two small pieces of something chocolatey and hold them out to us. "Blu, tell them what it is."

He bends his knees then jumps up, shouting, "Dark chocolate bark with ginger!" Then he barks like a dog, which makes me snicker. Little weirdo.

Maya breaks our handhold and takes the bark, then hands one to me. We pop it into our mouths, and it's sweet and a little bitter with a zing of spice from the ginger.

Okay, Canva, not bad.

"Yum," I say. "Thanks."

"Yeah, that's tasty, Canva. Thank you!" Maya adds.

"My pleasure, you two." Another customer steps up to the booth, so she turns to help them, saying to us, "Have fun!"

I lean over and whisper to Maya, "Should we buy something?"

She shrugs. "Only if you want to."

"But, like, support local or whatever, right?"

She gives me a skeptical look. "I mean . . . yes? That's something we try to do around here anyway."

"Well, watch me do it now, too." Looking back at the table of Canva's wares, I say, "Hey, Blu, can I get some of that chocolate stuff? Maybe a small box? Please?"

He's as excited as ever to add some bark to a cardboard container and take my money before returning to his card game.

After that, Maya and I resume hand-holding and walk through the market again, but this time we stop to actually look at things, and I end up buying the best fucking donut I've ever had in my life, which Maya and I split.

As we're finishing that, I realize that the most important person we're supposed to be all cutesie in front of isn't around.

"Hey—you said Rashida would be here, right? Where is she?"

Maya looks ill at my question, but manages to get out, "Oh. Right. She'll be in one of the artist studios we passed—her dad's."

"Okay, well . . . want to check it out? That's the point of all this, right?" I lift her hand in mine.

"Yeah . . . okay."

She's nervous, but that's what I'm here for. "Cool. Lead the way."

She walks me over to the market entrance, but just before entering one of the small studios, she lets my hand go.

Christ. This chick really needs to up her game.

The studio is tiny, with framed paintings along the walls, and a workspace set up in one corner. Three other people are browsing the art, one of whom is facing the wall, talking to Rashida, who is also facing away from us. Maya comes to a stop just inside the doorway, and I bump into her, but use the bump to keep up our forward momentum. I lean in and whisper, "Maya, you got this."

She doesn't look like she's even close to having this.

I search the walls, trying to find something to distract her for a hot minute while she gets her shit together. "Whoa—what's that?" I point to a small painting of some kind of duck-like bird to our left, near where Rashida is standing. Just as Rashida turns her head to look at us (because my voice is hard to ignore), I slip my hand back into Maya's.

Like clockwork, Rashida's eyes fall directly to our hands, and I have to stifle my smile.

I see Rashida swallow before she manages to get out, "Oh, hey," to us. Then, to the person she was talking to, she says, "Let me know if you have any more questions."

Maya's hand is limp in mine, but I give her a squeeze. "Hey, Rashida," I say. "I was just asking Maya about this painting here." I point to the bird with its red neck and beady red eyes, like some kind of devil duck.

"Oh, uh . . . that's . . ." She looks at the painting for a couple of seconds. "That's a red-throated loon." She turns back to us and gives Maya a half smile. "You know that, Maya."

Maya's chewing the hell out of her bottom lip, and almost startles when Rashida says her name. "Oh? What? The bird—yeah, sorry. I do know that. Duh."

Wow.

Guess I'm running this show on my own. "So this is your dad's art?" I ask Rashida.

"Yeah. Yes." She sweeps a hand out. "His bigger pieces are scattered elsewhere—art galleries and such. "These are mostly prints."

"He's not here?" I ask.

I detect a small glitch in the smile she's likely faking right now, but she clears her throat and says, "He travels a lot for work."

"Right, right. That's cool he trusts you to do this, though. My parents wouldn't trust me to wash their dishes." I grin, even though this is probably true.

Maya finally comes alive beside me. "It'd be cooler if he was around a bit more," she says, a surprising bit of irritation in her voice.

I catch a look between her and Rashida—one that signals some kind of understanding between them. That might be a good thing. Maybe Rashida just needs a reminder of all the stuff they share.

Trying to keep the mood light, though, I say, "Well, I'm gonna buy that one. The loon."

Rashida's eyebrows pop up, and I feel Maya's hand squeeze mine. "Gabe, you don't have to do that," Maya says.

"But I want to. I love art." To be honest, I find nature art kind of boring and dated, but maybe my mom will like it.

"Um . . . did you want to know the cost, or . . ." Rashida says.

"Doesn't matter." This is what Mummy Dearest's credit card is for. She wanted me to make myself at home here, after all, and home is where the wallet is.

As Rashida packages the print for me and rings me up, Maya leans in and whispers, "Gabe, Winston's art is expensive. Are you sure?"

I lean back in, just for the sake of appearances more than anything, and reply, "It's fine, Maya. It's a gift for my mom."

She doesn't look convinced, but shrugs and says, "Okay."

As we're about to go, Maya clearly wants to stick around and talk to Rashida more but needs a nudge. "I'm just gonna run to the bathroom. You stay here, and I'll be right back, okay?"

She looks at me like she's having a little freak-out, but I hand her my stuff and leave before she can back out.

When I return a few minutes later, having chilled around the side of the studio the whole time, Maya and Rashida are leaning over a counter, looking through some kind of art book. Maya's even pointing at something and laughing.

I mentally give myself a fist bump.

"Hey, y'all," I say, coming up behind them. "Wanna split lunch, Maya? Rashida? You want anything?" *Because not only am I dating a wholesome girl, but I am also a very considerate human being, Mom.*

Rashida looks surprised. "Oh, no—I'm okay. But thanks, Gabe. And thanks for buying the painting." She gives me a small smile.

"Yeah, no worries," I say, and return the smile. "Maya? You good to go?" I give her a stick-to-the-damn-plan look, and it seems to register.

"Oh, yeah. Um, bye, Rashida," Maya says with a little wave.

Once we're outside and lost in the crowd, I turn to Maya, grinning, and say, "Not bad, am I right?"

She smiles back. "Yeah—better than I thought it'd be."

"See? You just gotta trust the power of the fake date."

We walk a bit more, and I buy a handmade wooden necklace sold by a lumberjack of a guy whose massive hands somehow carved the most intricate designs into the wood. The necklace I bought has a cool tree design in it. It's not exactly my aesthetic, but it's beautiful, and I plan on snapping a photo of it and the bird painting later to send to my mom—show her some of the good, clean fun I'm having while here.

That gives me an idea. "Hey—can we grab a selfie for my mom?" I say to Maya as we sit on a bench at one end of the market with the plate of homemade bulgogi and rice I just bought. I went for meat when Maya decided she wasn't hungry after all.

"Oh, sure."

"Cool, come here." I place an arm behind her and she shuffles a little closer to me. I let my hand rest on her shoulder, which is warm from the sun. Holding my phone out, I try to form a smile that conveys more "cozy" than "flashy." Maya's smile is something between shy and awkward. I take the photo anyway, because my mom will love that I'm not alongside some shirtless dude with his tongue out.

TWENTY-ONE

Maya

Gabe snaps the photo of us and shows it to me. "Cute, right?" she says.

"Yeah, totally," I say. And it is. I mean, Gabe is a gorgeous girl—wide smile, big green eyes, wavy, lush hair, and she even has a scattering of light brown freckles across both cheeks. She's girl-next-door meets babe-on-magazine-cover.

I'm . . . fine. Cute, generally speaking. I love the light brown of my skin and the eyelashes I inherited from my mom. My dad calls my nose "adorable." Rashida has always said she's jealous of how "perfectly symmetrical" my features are. When she said it before, I always thought it was her way of telling me I was beautiful. Now I realize she was just making an objective observation. A fact. Nothing romantic about it.

"You good?" Gabe asks, after sending the photo to her mom

and putting her phone back in her bag. She says it in that way that sounds like she doesn't really want to know, and I don't blame her.

I know I've been less than sparkling during this first fake date. She's had to carry the load while I wrestle with wishing I was here with Rashida instead. Wishing things could go back to a time when I "knew" she and I would be together. That whole scenario in Winston's art studio made me nauseous, but at least I managed to pull it together when Gabe strategically left us alone.

But I say, "Yeah, why?" now, just to see what Gabe will do.

She just shrugs, though, and pokes around in her bulgogi with wooden chopsticks. "Nothing. Just wondering." She scoops some beef and rice into her mouth and chews. Guess I was right that she didn't want to get into my woes. I get it. I'm kind of sick of my woes, as well.

We sit for a bit, just people watching. Gabe eats her meal, and I munch on the caramel popcorn I bought. Given our agreement, I know I'm not pulling my weight here and decide to try a little harder, whatever feelings are pushing at me about Rashida.

I go for a little of that "close proximity" we talked about last night at the antique shop and scootch my butt over on the bench so our thighs and hips are side by side.

Gabe looks at me, her mouth full and her eyebrows rising.

I lean in and whisper, "I'm practicing."

She smirks, chews, and swallows. She whispers back, "You're a nerd."

"But I'm *your* nerd, honeybunch," I say, kind of enjoying this bit of silliness. I even go so far as to slip my arm under hers and grab hold of her hand again.

She eyes up my "move," one eyebrow still peaked. Then, as though she can't possibly let me win, she sticks her chopsticks in her food, places the container to the side of her on the bench, and crosses one leg over the other so that she's leaning into me and her bare leg is overlapping mine. Our faces are within inches now, and my heart beats a little faster, unused to this kind of closeness with people I don't know well. And Gabe still makes me nervous.

I guess a real couple would kiss, but that's beyond our fake-dating guidelines, so Gabe just sandwiches my hand between both of hers. "What now, Brady-Jayasinghe?"

I lift my eyebrows, surprised to hear her say my name perfectly.

"Impressive, right?" she says, that smirk practically living on her lips.

"Not bad," I say, smiling back.

"What if I kissed your cheek right now? Would that freak you out?"

I can't help the "oh" that escapes my lips, or the way my eyes dart away to see who's around.

"I won't if you don't want me to, obviously, but, like, people are here—they're watching. That's what you wanted, right?"

"Yes . . . yeah." She's right. People have been checking the two of us out all morning, and most with smiles and surprised-but-eager greetings. I wonder if they're just plain relieved to be rid of their secondhand embarrassment for me.

"So?" she asks, her head tilting a little. Her tone isn't pushy, though, which I appreciate.

"Yeah, go ahead."

"I have your full consent to place my lips against your cheek? Because that's what's going to happen." Smirk.

I laugh. "Gabe! Yes, already."

She grins, but then she leans in close, placing her lips against my cheek, only an inch or so from my own lips. She lingers for only a second, but her lips are so soft and her breath against my cheek gives me a shiver.

When she pulls away, her eyes are on my lips, but she quickly looks up and grins again. "Nice, right?" she says, all cocky.

I roll my eyes. "It was fine." But I laugh, because this whole situation is bananas and I can't believe we're doing it.

"Fine, my ass," she says, and goes back to her bulgogi.

"It's all right," I say, the words popping out before I even think to stop them.

She looks back at me and scoff-laughs. "Sassy! I like it."

And I'm not going to lie—I kind of like it, too.

TWENTY-TWO

Gabe

The day after Maya's and my first fake date, I'm officially bored again, so I decide to head back to that crappy beach, because I still need a tan. Yesterday, Maya and I parted ways around noon, because we were both kind of tired from staying up late and being woken by matching annoyances—her parents and my chickens.

As I gather my things together for the beach, including *Fried Green Tomatoes*, I get a text from my mom. Those photos are very sweet, Gabe. Love the painting. Thank you for thinking of me.

That might be the nicest text my mom has ever sent me. I use the moment to see if I can build in the next step of Maya's and my fake-dating plan.

Gabe: np. Farmers market was super cute. Maya wants to meet you. Can we do lunch or something on Wednesday?

She takes a few seconds to message back, and my stomach dips a little. But then the dots start doing their dot thing and a message comes through.

Mother-Figure: Would love that. Let me shuffle some things and confirm later.

Winner winner, chicken dinner.

I head out for the beach from Canva's around one o'clock, except I may have been a bit too cocky about my directional skills before, because I come out of the forest a different way than I went in and the pathway opens up near a boardwalk that has a shop of some kind alongside it. The small building is painted blue and white with fish illustrations all over it.

I do a slow circle, trying to get my bearings. I try my phone. No service, of course.

"Need something?" a gritty voice behind me says.

I recognize that voice.

When I turn, I find my new BFF standing next to the shop wearing the same purple Crocs from before, different pajama pants, and a gray tank top. Both hands carry large white buckets.

"Pardon?"

She nods to the sign on the shop, which says "Need Something?"

Oh, yeah. This again.

"Right. Do you . . . sell maps?" This looks like a place that would actually sell maps.

"What d'ya need a map for? Over here, if the lake is on your right, you're going south. If it's on your left, you're going north."

Helpful. "Great. What if I'm in the middle of the lake. Then what?"

A tiny smirk appears. "Then yer hooped."

I smirk back. "I'm trying to get to this little public beach. You know it?"

"I know everything." She lifts her arm to indicate the way I came and her muscles flex with the weight of the bucket she's holding. I swear she could bench-press me one-handed from the looks of that arm. "That path, turn right at the cluster of carved gnomes, then left at the broken iron gate."

Jesus. "If you could just maybe tell me the non-forest route, I'd appreciate it."

She snorts with disapproval. "The beach is eight minutes up that way." She points with the other arm down the road at the end of the boardwalk.

"Cool. Thanks. See you around."

"But yer gonna help me carry these buckets to the pub first."

I pause. "Am I, Janet?"

"It's Jan," she grumbles, advancing on me.

"Sorry. Jan."

She mutters something—not sure if it's actual words—and hands me a bucket, which is heavier than she made it look.

I peer inside. Strawberries. But, like, teeny-tiny ones.

"What are these for?" I ask as she starts marching off in the first direction she indicated, through the woods.

"Eatin'. What else?"

I stifle a snicker.

"Right. But why are you taking them to the pub?"

"I'm bringin' 'em to Diamond. Why d'ya think his shortcake is so damn good?"

Diamond is . . . Maya's uncle, I remind myself. From the other night.

"I . . . can't say I was thinking about his shortcake, but I will now—promise." I grin at her and get some sweet side-eye and a grunt in return.

A few moments later, she says, "Try one."

"Pardon?"

She stops, faces me, and puts her bucket down. Then commands, "Eat a strawberry!"

Jesus. I wouldn't decline even if I were allergic. I put my bucket down, too, and I pick one out—it's way smaller than the strawberries from the grocery near us and looks a little dirty, so I brush it against my shorts and take a bite. The sweetness bursts in my mouth.

"Holy shit."

"Yeah. Holy shit is right. That's what you get when you grow yer own food."

"That sounds like a lot of work."

She places her hands on her hips. "Work that's worth it."

"Maybe for you. But I prefer someone else doing the work." I grin.

She rolls her eyes, picks up her bucket again, and turns to keep walking. "Yer not as lazy as you act."

I pick up my bucket and follow her. "How would you know?"

"'Cause yer helping me, aren't ya?"

"You didn't give me much of a choice, Jan."

"You always got a choice."

At the broken gate she mentioned earlier, Jan turns right again, and we're out of the forest. Jan marches up to the pub, me hustling behind her, only she goes around back and through another entrance there.

I find myself in the pub's kitchen, and the two men from Friday night—Diamond and Jasper—are tickling each other. I remember that Maya said these two are an item. More lovey-dovey bullshit. No wonder Maya thinks love is for everybody. I'll admit, though, that these two grown-ass men tickling each other is a little cute.

"Quit yer canoodling and come get these buckets, you two!" Jan shouts, but she must think they're cute, too, because she's half smiling. It forms spidery creases around her mouth.

Diamond and Jasper jostle each other to get to Jan first, still giggling like little kids. When Jasper sees me, his eyes light up. "Gabe the babe!" he says, grinning. Then follows with, "You make one helluva Cher, Gabe!"—yet another reference to my incredible karaoke performance the other night. He winks at me as he takes my bucket, and honestly, everything about Jasper makes me warm inside.

Diamond smiles at me and says hello, as well, taking Jan's bucket. Then Jan tells me to follow her through the small kitchen out to the pub.

When we're out past the bar she says, "I'm eatin' here. And you should, too. Then you should stay for our meetin' 'cause it looks like you don't have anything better to do."

Everything comes out like a fact to accept and follow.

"What kind of meeting?"

Instead of answering, she heads to a table in the corner with enough seats for eight or so people. It's almost two in the afternoon on a Sunday, and the place is about a third full. Much less rowdy than karaoke night.

I guess I have to follow Jan to find out anything more, and to be honest, eating with this woman sounds like a dream come true, so I seat myself next to her, our backs facing the wall so we can see most of the bar.

"Ever heard of SLEA?"

She pronounces this as "slay," and I wonder if she means the slang word, dictionary definition, or what. "Um . . . no? I don't think so? What is it?" I ask, hoping it's not some weird small-town cult or whatever.

"Spruce Lake Eco Alliance."

"Ah. Which is . . . ?"

"We keep track of all the crap other people try to pull on us and the land here and give 'em trouble when they do."

Oh God. It *is* a cult. A cult of tree huggers. "Okayyy . . . so, like, you . . . do what, exactly?" I'm already thinking about how to extricate myself from this situation without being maimed by this woman.

"All kinds of stuff. I've got my own stuff going on, so I just help when I can."

Vague. But to be honest, I'm more interested in whatever Diamond is carrying to our table right now.

"Your usual, Jan," Diamond says, placing two dishes down in front of us, "and a complimentary serving of our famous zucchini bites. Wasn't sure if you're into that kind of thing, Gabe."

He smiles warmly at me again, and it looks genuine enough. The snacks are fried to golden perfection, and my stomach growls. "I am *definitely* into that kind of thing," I say, smiling back. Jan's got what appears to be a salmon burger in front of her.

"Would you like anything else?" Diamond asks me.

"Oh, uh . . ."

Diamond jumps in with some specials, which all sound amazing, but I opt for the chicken strips, thinking spitefully of my chicken friends at Canva's.

"Strips it is!" He's about to turn back to the kitchen when he pauses and adds, "Staying for the meeting?" He glances at Jan, who takes a big bite of her burger and chews it slowly, eyes on me.

Can I really say no now?

"Yeah—sure. Why not?" I say, and pop a zucchini bite into my mouth. It's a glorious mouthful of salty, soft, and crunchy. I give Diamond a thumbs-up on the snack.

"The more the merrier. I'm sure Maya will be glad to see you." He smiles again.

"Oh—is she in this group, too?" I ask, my stomach doing a weird little twist, which I chalk up to hunger.

"Yup. And her parents, Rashida, a few others." He adds these "others" like he's testing something out.

Oh. "Cool" is all I say, but I try to sell it.

He smiles at me and turns to go while I grab another bite so I don't have to say anything right away. My brain is abuzz with this exchange.

Is this a good thing? That I'm going to be at this meeting with Maya *and* Rashida? It could be another chance to sell our little act, but this is an unplanned event, and I'm not sure how Maya will handle that. She was nervous enough during our *planned* date yesterday.

My hesitation also stems from the fact that I'm not at all excited about participating in whatever this group is up to. My environmentalism extends as far as driving Meems's hybrid when she was still around and turning off the lights when I leave the room . . . mostly.

But . . . joining a group like this might also add points in my favor with my mom. I'm dating a nice girl. I'm buying local. I'm volunteering with some kind of do-gooder organization. I'm my parents' dream come true.

TWENTY-THREE

Maya

When I walk into Jasper's, my energy is not *quite* reaching Diamond's or my parents' levels, but it's definitely better than it was when I arrived to Spruce Lake. I'd left Gabe feeling pretty good about how our "date" worked out yesterday, and even better after I had a chance to sleep in a little this morning.

I'm also kind of looking forward to seeing Rashida at this SLEA meeting. Still nervous. Still heartbreaky. Still uncertain about everything. But after hanging out with Gabe—even though it was fun being silly and doing something old with someone new—I guess I'm excited to do something familiar with a familiar group, and to see if I can reconnect with Rashida over something we love.

My parents are with me now as we enter the pub, and they are *ecstatic* that I'm accompanying them to the SLEA meeting. When we enter, Prince is lying on his side next to the bar, as usual, and thumps his tail when he sees me, which gives my mood another little boost. I stop to give him pats, and he gives me lazy licks in return.

I rise and follow my parents toward the back of the pub, where we always sit for SLEA meetings. Various hellos greet us, but then I hear my dad say, "Oh! It's you—the superstar from karaoke night!"

And my mom turns to me and says, "Maya, your friend is here!"

My . . . ?

When my parents split to sit down at the table, there's Gabe, sitting next to Jan, with a half-eaten plate of chicken strips and fries in front of her. She gives me a sideways peace sign and a smile.

I'm momentarily off-balance. I didn't expect to see Gabe until Wednesday, for our next fake date with her mom. And I definitely didn't think I'd be navigating her and Rashida here at the pub again. At a SLEA meeting. This kind of flies in the face of the fancy little strategy I'd envisioned. Hard to spend some quality time with Rashida when Gabe—my supposed crush or whatever—is *right there.*

My face must communicate some of my bewilderment and uncertainty, because her eyes grow wide and she tilts her head a little—and even though I've only known her for a couple of days, I already know that she's trying to prod me back into the role I'm supposed to be playing.

I try to rally—"Oh, hey!" I say. "Gabe!"

My voice is too high, but she matches my tone with a cheerful "Hey, Maya!"

I take a breath and vow to chill out already.

The next few minutes are a shuffle of people arriving and saying hi and ordering food. My parents ask Gabe about the market (they already gave me the third degree about this) and she provides all the right answers to help convince everyone we had a great time. "It was really fun." "Maya's an excellent tour guide." "We split the donut of my dreams."

At the table already are some longtime SLEA members—a core bunch. We'll spend half the meeting just getting caught up and chatting, the rest on actual planning.

The seats next to Gabe are already taken by Jan and Buddy, and thank God my parents don't make a big stink about me sitting next to her. I'm kind of relieved to not have to pretend any kind of physical dynamic with Gabe right now. I'm still not super smooth at that part, and I'm sure I'd be even worse with Rashida here.

On one side of me is my mom, who's seated next to Buddy. Davie, one of my next-door neighbors who Rashida and I grew up with, is next to Jan, and my dad is next to him. Jocelyn and Casey are next to my dad, and there are two empty seats squished in between me and Casey—for Diamond and Rashida, I assume. I'm not sure where Rashida is—she's usually early for everything.

As if in response, Diamond arrives with a veggie pot pie and side salad—Rashida's favorite meal here—and places it on the table at the empty seat beside me. When he sees me glance at it, he says, "Rashida's just in the bathroom. Want one of these, too? With fries?" He winks because he knows I love his pot pies, as well.

"Sure—yeah. Thanks." I smile at him, but I can feel myself getting flustered. I take another breath.

A French fry lands on the table in front of me. When I look up, Gabe is grinning at me. "Thought I'd share."

I catch a few others at the table noticing this little exchange, including my parents, which is a good thing.

Okay. Okay. This will be fine. I can reconnect with Rashida and also play along with Gabe to suggest we've got something going on.

I pick up the fry and shove the whole thing in my mouth. "Thanks," I say, grinning back at her. Then I steal one of Rashida's cherry tomatoes and throw it to her. "For your kindness."

She fumbles the tomato but manages to grab hold. "Sharing is caring," she says, and pops it into her mouth.

"So how'd you get roped into this?" I ask, keeping my voice teasing and light, but genuinely interested in the answer.

She points a thumb at Jan, who's telling one of her marathon stories to Davie. "No choice. Ran into this one by accident, and next thing I know, I'm here." She shrugs.

That makes sense. Jan can be very persuasive. And by persuasive, I mean bossy. I'm about to ask if Gabe knows what she's getting into when I see Rashida enter the pub from the little hallway that leads to the bathrooms.

When she sees me, her eyes flit to Gabe, and then she's worrying her bottom lip with her teeth like she always does when she's stressed about something. I wonder if the something is me, Gabe, me and Gabe as a pair, or something else entirely.

Okay. Showtime. I catch Gabe's eye, and she gives me a little nod and a wink. We're on the same page, I think.

Rish pulls out her chair and sits. She turns to me. "Hi," she says, and gives me a small smile.

"Hey."

Diamond serves me my pot pie and takes his seat next to Rashida.

She just stares at me like she's expecting me to say something and I'm a little stuck for words. Gabe must see this, because she pokes in with "Hey, Rashida, my mom loved the print you sold me."

Rashida turns toward Gabe. "Oh—I'm glad. Is she a fan of nature art?"

Gabe's grin is so big I know she's faking when she says, "Sure is! Loves her loons."

My mouth quirks at this. Somehow, she's managed to put me at ease again.

I try to keep the momentum going by turning to Rashida and saying, "Hope you don't mind, but I stole one of your tomatoes. Sorry." I shrug and scrunch my lips to one side in fake apology.

She narrows her eyes at me with a small lift in her lips. Without breaking her gaze, she reaches over and grabs a handful of my fries just as Diamond says, "Rashida, those are hot!"

Rashida's eyes grow wide and she drops the fries back onto my plate, letting out a very un-Rashida-like squeal. I grab her hand immediately with my left hand and ice from my water glass with my right, and then start to smooth the ice over her open palm.

"Quick-thinking, honey," my mom says next to me.

"I'll get the cold pack from the freezer," Diamond adds, and heads to the kitchen.

"It's not that bad," Rashida says, looking at me. "Worth it to get my germs all over your fries, anyway."

I roll my eyes. "Gross."

"*You're* gross."

"Mature."

"I'll show you mature." She closes her hand around the piece of ice I'm still applying to her palm, yanks at my collar, and drops the cube down my shirt before I can even react. The ice slips right into my cleavage (what little I have) and nestles in there, sending a shiver through me.

"You little—" I say as I dig it out.

"Now, now, kids," my dad says, amused.

Most people at the table have stopped what they're doing to watch this little scene between me and Rish—one that's a repeat of so many silly moments between us. It feels good—natural. Like old times. Like we skipped over the weirdness of the last couple of days and straight back into Rish and Maya.

Maybe I don't even need a secret plan to prove to Rashida we're meant to be. Maybe she actually gets it now? After a year away from me? Or maybe we're just back to best friends and nothing more. How am I supposed to know which it is?

For now, I'll work under the assumption that we're just friends until I have proof we're not—the proof, of course, being the kiss I've pictured thousands of times in my head.

Diamond comes back with the cold pack and people continue eating while Jan finishes her story. I dig into my pot pie as Buddy asks Gabe how she's liking Spruce Lake.

She glances at me, a gleam appearing in her eyes as she says, "Honestly, the best part of being here is hanging out with Maya."

I try to smile back at her—convince everyone at this table that I like her and she likes me and I'm over Rashida and getting a life, like we planned.

But then Rashida says, "That makes sense. Maya's awesome." She's looking at me when she says it, though, not at Gabe. And I may be wrong, but her eyes dip to my lips?

Wait. What's happening?

As I'm recovering from the whiplash this whole situation is giving me, Diamond inserts, "Okay! Let's get this meeting rolling, shall we?"

Thank God.

TWENTY-FOUR

Gabe

"Okay, so notices have gone out to everyone on our email list, and posted to the sustainability forums across the island and mainland," Rashida says. "I think we're going to get a huge crowd."

I glance around the table. Most people have finished their food and are listening intently to Rashida, like she's some kind of CEO of Spruce Lake and not just a teenage girl. After Diamond brought the group's attention to SLEA business, Rashida took control of the meeting, and I can't get over how seriously everyone seems to take her, even though as far as I can tell, she's just an overly intense kid with no real life beyond all this protest stuff.

But so far, I've focused enough to discover that SLEA is bigger and more organized than I assumed. It includes a ton of people in Spruce Lake and more in Miller's Bay—the town my mom is currently working out of and where a company called Lux has its closest headquarters.

SLEA already managed to block a permit Lux applied for last year to change zoning laws for a section of Tipper Park, which is the forest surrounding Spruce Lake. But their most recent application passed, and now SLEA is trying to disrupt Lux Corp's progress before Lux can break ground on a swath of land at one end of the lake to build a massive resort—one that will mean cutting down ten acres of trees. SLEA is also suspicious of the resort's impact on the lake, which is a water source for the town.

SLEA's next action is a protest meant to put pressure on Lux and draw media attention to SLEA's cause—which I guess is to protect all things nature-y.

Rashida and Diamond have organized a huge number of people to show up at the Lux build site in Tipper Park on the day they're supposed to break ground dressed in the bare minimum of lake clothing for a massive sunbathing demonstration.

"Think body parts painted with protest slogans, signs with facts about Lux Corp's impact on the environment, and maybe even some bare boobs," Jocelyn happily explained to me.

The code name is Project Babes in Wonderland—dorky, but I kind of love it. I'm definitely down with the public nakedness aspect.

"I contacted my friends at CHEK and KWSN and they're going to send reporters," Casey says.

Diamond squeezes Casey's shoulder. "You're a champ."

"You all have news contacts?" I ask, impressed and also trying to get a sense of the scope of this protest and how much I want to be involved, if at all.

"Casey has tons of contacts in news and TV because they have a journalism degree," Maya explains.

"Yeah," Casey adds. "I ended up working in sustainability, but stayed in touch with some of my classmates who are journalists now."

"Wow," I say, fairly sure I'm the least accomplished person at this table. Nothing new there.

Before Rashida can launch into a bunch of boring logistics and stuff, I ask, "So, like, this is supposed to stop Lux from . . . what?" SLEA seems organized, but Lux also seems like a gigantic company.

Rashida tilts her head at me, trying to figure me out, I suppose. I keep my face completely pleasant and friendly, which is not easy, because I not only have a resting bitch face, but also a very active bitch face.

"We're hoping to gain enough media attention that more politicians get involved. It's happened before," she says.

The guy next to Jan, Davie, who's been sneaking glances at me like I won't notice, pipes up. "Yeah, two summers ago we staged a huge protest on the lake—everyone on floaties—and got so much coverage that the mayor from Miller's Bay used our cause as a campaign platform. She won her district again and has been a total ally ever since," he says, and everyone who was there nods and smiles at some shared memory I'm not seeing.

"Floaties?" I ask.

Maya explains, "Yeah, hundreds of floaties of every shape and color parading across the lake. It was incredible."

She smiles at Rashida, who smiles back and adds, "We got some flak for using plastic floaties to make a statement about sustainability, which was totally valid"—everyone around the table nods at this—"and so we adjusted this time around to bathing suits and towels instead."

I nod slowly. "Cool," I say. But what I'm really thinking is, why bother? Like, this town could use some shaking up, right? Wouldn't a fancy resort create jobs and more tourism, put Spruce Lake on the map? Sounds all right to me. Trees come down sometimes, right? But there're a shit ton of them around here. What's a few less? Especially if it means Spruce Lake might have more money for other stuff?

I'm not about to say any of this now, though—mostly because I don't want to get crushed to death by some tree huggers.

Rashida turns back to logistics and then the meeting wraps up a very long forty minutes later. Most people leave, but I sit tight as Jan finishes her thick-as-mud coffee next to me and watch Rashida and Maya to see what happens—if Maya will need me to play wing-woman again. She's been holding her own for the most part—after their cutesie French fry and ice episode—and I can't help feel a little proud of her for it. Like my little baby chick is finally cracking out of her shell.

I watch the two now, as Rashida packs up the rest of her meal in a container that she seems to have brought herself—*Who does that?*—and Maya hovers next to her, fidgeting with her bracelet. Now that the meeting has broken up, she seems a little lost again.

Time for mama bird to step in. "Hey, Rashida," I call out across the table, "any suggestions about where Maya should take me next?"

Our next official "date" is already set for Wednesday—my mom messaged me during lunch and confirmed she could meet us for a quick meal. But it can't hurt to remind Rashida she should be a little jealous right now, too.

Both Rashida and Maya turn to look at me. I give them my friendliest smile.

"Oh, well . . . there's a nice hike a little ways from here?" She glances at Maya, who glances back but keeps fiddling with her bracelet.

"Ooh, yeah—not a big hiker," I say. "That sounds like more of a 'you' thing." I point at the two of them, hoping Maya will play along.

She seems to get the message, because she finally stops fidgeting and says, "Right. Yeah. Maybe you and I could climb Baldy this week, and I can take Gabe somewhere that doesn't involve . . . dirt." She smiles at me, and I grin back, even though a tiny prick of something unpleasant pokes at my chest. I can handle a *little* dirt. Maybe.

"So you're not . . . big on the outdoors, Gabe?" Rashida asks.

I try to read her face, but can't tell if she's being bitchy or not. "I'm not a big fan, no." I add quickly, "But that doesn't mean I don't care about nature." I need this SLEA group and my mom to believe I'm all ethical and stuff, after all.

"Right. No, of course not. It's cool that you came to the meeting today. We can use all the help we can get," Rashida says. She looks at Maya. "I've gotta run some errands tonight, but let's definitely do that hike later? Or even row out to Sun Island? Maybe?"

I watch closely as Maya blinks several times, rubs her nose, then finally gets out the words, "Yes. Yeah. I'll text you."

At least she finally got there. Good job, little bird.

Maya says she's just going to run to the washroom, and I wonder if I should follow her to check in, but then Jan, who's been plugging away on her phone since the meeting ended, probably trying to ignore the teenage drama unfolding around her, says, "Well?"

"Well, what?" I say.

"You in or what?"

"In . . . to . . . ?"

She rolls her eyes in a way that makes me just love her more. "SLEA, girl. SLEA!"

I crack up, because damn if this woman is telling me I slay without realizing it.

"What's so funny?" she grumbles.

"Nothing, nothing. Just—never mind. But yeah, I'm in." I say it before I really think about it—mainly because I can't say no to this woman. But even after I say it, I don't regret it. If my mom thinks it's so great that I'm dating this nice girl and doing nice things, then what'll she think of me *volunteering* with some local, do-gooder group who's trying to save the planet? Talk about good-kid points.

"Great," Jan says. Then she stands abruptly, adding, "You need something useful to do," with finality. "Come on, Rashida. Let's make a run to Miller's Bay and get you those supplies you needed."

"Oh, thanks, Jan. But you don't have to—"

"Shut yer trap already. You know I'm gonna. That e-bike of yours is great and all, but you can't carry all that stuff on it."

Rashida half smiles at this, and I can see these two actually *are* BFFs, and I'm a little jealous.

When Maya returns from the bathroom, I'm leaning against the bar, gay-flirting with Jasper, who's better at flirting back than Maya is.

"Hey," I say as Jasper disappears into the kitchen, leaving the two of us alone.

"Hey," she replies.

I watch her for a beat to see if there's anything weird going on with her but can't really tell.

I take her wrist gently and pull her toward the exit. In a lower voice, I explain, "Just FYI, I had no idea you were going to be here."

She shakes her head. "It's fine. It's just . . . I'm clearly not great at dividing my attention between two girls I like—fake or not." She smiles at me.

Placing my hands on her shoulders, I say, "But you pulled through, bro! I think the plan is working. And I can see what you mean, about you and Rashida clicking together."

Her eyes turn bright at this. "Right?" she says. "I don't know how *she* can't see it."

"She will. Especially if she feels the pressure of potentially losing you to another girl. A very *hot* girl, might I add." Smirk.

She laughs and shakes her head. Once we're outside of the pub, she says, "Okay, so what's the plan for Wednesday? Did you get ahold of your mom?"

"Yes! And she's down for lunch. Is there a good place somewhere between here and Miller's Bay?"

She thinks for a moment, playing with the hem of her tank top. This girl is such a fidgeter. Finally, she says, "Yeah . . . there's a cute spot not too far from here, actually. How would your mom feel about vegetarian Vietnamese?"

Ugh. But I just say, "Sounds good. I don't have a car or anything—"

"We can bike!" she says, like this is good news.

"Pardon?"

"Yeah—you can borrow my mom's bike! It's a beautiful ride through the forest—and don't worry, it's only about twenty minutes and mostly a very even pathway."

"Mostly?"

"You'll be fine, Gabe. Consider it an additional fake date."

"But if two girls ride through the forest and no one sees them, is it even a date?"

She laughs again, and I realize I like making her laugh. "Lots of people take that path. We'll be seen, don't worry."

"Fine. But just so you know, I haven't ridden a bike in over two years."

"Gabe. Seriously?"

"Why bike when you can Uber/taxi/drive?"

"Um . . . so many reasons?"

I roll my eyes, but I also kind of like the idea of cruising up to lunch with my mom on a bike. That sounds wholesome as fuck.

"Okay. See you Wednesday?" she says.

I shrug. "Sure. But if you get bored before then, hit me up. It's not like I have much else to do."

Her eyebrows rise a little, and maybe she's surprised I'd want to hang out outside of our fake-dating deal, but it's not like we have a terrible time together. And besides, I *know* I'm gonna be bored.

"Okay, sure."

We stand there for a moment. I glance around. Plenty of people are walking by, so I lean in and whisper, "'Kay, I'mma hug you now, all right?"

She nods. We hug, and I add a small peck on the cheek for good measure. "Bye, boo," I say, and walk in what I hope is the direction of the beach.

TWENTY-FIVE

Maya

By the time I get home from the SLEA meeting, my parents are already down at the dock and it looks like they're getting ready to go for a canoe ride. Evening paddles around the lake are one of our favorite things—whether it's paddleboards, kayaks, or canoes, there's nothing quite like meandering along the water as the sinking sun sets it alight with golds and yellows and oranges.

As I wander out to the dock, my dad calls, "Hey, honey!" from where he's holding the canoe steady in the water.

"Wanna come?" Mom asks as she places the paddles across the canoe one by one.

Do I? The alternative would be to hang out here by myself. I could read, I guess. Or go for a swim. Neither seems very appealing—too much room for overthinking this afternoon's events and whether or not Gabe is right—if Rashida is starting to see what she's missing.

"Yeah, sure," I say now, hoping they don't ask me *too* many questions about Gabe, but knowing I should prepare for some.

"Hooray!" my dad shouts like a nerd. "Get in."

We all climb into the red canoe—which my mom has had for ages and which is named Rose for her color—and my mom and dad push us off from the dock. I'm sitting between them, my dad at the bow and Mom at the stern. We set off at a leisurely pace and I decide I made a great decision to join them—what's better than being paddled around the lake like a queen? I think about Gabe and how much she'd probably love this, too, even if it involves a canoe, since she regards herself as a "queen built for luxury."

As we pass by the Morris cabin and then the Allegrettos' dock, my dad, predictably, says, "You know you have to tell us everything about Gabe now, right?"

Oh jeez.

"What qualifies as 'everything'?" I ask, stalling the inevitable. "I'm still getting to know her."

"Tell us what you know," Dad says.

"Or anything you *want* to share," Mom adds.

I think about this for a moment. I want to share at least a few things—to show them that Gabe and I have been getting to know each other, and like each other. Which is all true. I mean, she's still someone I'd probably never regularly hang out with, and her aversion to nature is disturbing, but we've had some nice moments, and she does make me laugh.

"She's hilarious, for one. Sarcastic and cheeky, which is fun."

"She does seem fun," Mom says. "Definitely not shy, judging from karaoke."

That's true, I think, but I also think about some of the moments that seem to sneak through—where she also seems a little unsure, or even . . . contemplative? But I decide to keep things a bit simpler right now with my parents.

"Where'd you two meet, again?" Dad asks.

"Kind of by accident. She got lost and found my spot in the woods."

"Oh! Wow. Lucky," Dad says. "I should try getting lost and see if I can find your little sanctuary, finally."

"No, you really shouldn't," I say. He's been trying forever to get me to reveal the spot I discovered after he abandoned me in the woods all those years ago.

"So are you two . . . ?" my mom says, trying for nonchalance in her tone, but not achieving it.

I shrug to myself, watching the water whoosh by, because this is a tricky question. We've only known each other for a couple of days, so "dating" feels a little much. But I'm also not about to tell my parents we're "hooking up," because gross. And "seeing each other" sounds like something old people would say.

"We're just hanging out," I decide, but add, for the sake of Gabe's and my plan, "But I like her a lot. I think it's going to be a fun summer."

My dad shouts, "*Aha!*" and I startle.

"'Aha' what?"

He twists around and gives me a sly smile. "Your mom was right, then."

"About?"

"About you coming here, even if you didn't want to."

"Jack . . ." my mom starts.

I roll my eyes. "Yes, Dad. Parents are so smart, and children should always listen to them."

He and my mom giggle like little kids. "I'm just glad things are looking brighter for you, sweetheart," Mom says.

She's not wrong. My heart is still a Ping-Pong ball in my chest every time I'm with Rashida, and I still have no idea how she feels about me or if she'll ever see what I see.

But at least now I'm trying to do something about it, rather than just avoid her and my feelings.

"Remember that time we got married in this canoe, Hessy?" my dad says now, and I roll my eyes again. He literally can't be in this boat without telling that story.

"No, Jack, I think I've forgotten. I'm sure Maya has, too. Why don't you tell us again?" This is Mom's standard response, because we're going to get the whole spiel whether we like it or not. He begins his typical, animated version as we paddle along, letting the setting sunlight wash over us and waving at the neighbors who've come out to their docks to eat their dinners or enjoy an after-dinner swim.

I've heard this story a thousand times. And even though I roll my eyes each time, I've always loved it. What could be more romantic than meeting on this beautiful lake, falling in love here, getting engaged in your favorite fishing spot, and then exchanging vows in a bright red canoe named Rose?

A bit of sadness pokes into my chest, because of course it does. My parents' love story always gave me hope and something to look forward to. Now it just leaves me with questions about if I'll ever have what they do. But as the water flows past us, I try to breathe through the pricks in my chest and focus on what still might be possible.

TWENTY-SIX

Gabe

"I thought you said this would be easy!" I yell ahead to Maya, my ass bumping against this bike seat that was made for much smaller asses.

"I said 'mostly even'!" she yells back.

After another fifteen minutes and a close call with a dog running beside its owner, Maya and I arrive to a trio of buildings set back from a larger road. A couple of cars are parked outside.

"Oh, so we could have driven?" I say, indicating the cars and road as we park our bikes.

"And miss out on all your complaining?" she says, grinning at me.

Cheeky.

I pull off the helmet she insisted I wear and try to bring some body back to my hair, but that twenty minutes added a sheen to my skin, and now my hair is damp, too. *Gross.*

"You look great, Gabe," Maya says, watching my struggle with a gleeful look in her eyes.

"Yeah? You like the sweaty look on your girls, do you?"

She shrugs. "I don't hate it."

"Well, I hate it, so be a goddamn gentleman and gimme your hair tie."

"*My* hair tie?"

"Yes. I forgot mine, and I need to get my mane off my neck."

She scoffs but relents. As I'm tying my hair back, she says, "Your hair really is a wild thing, huh?"

She says it with awe in her voice, and I like it. "Damn right. She's got a mind of her own."

"Fitting."

We make eye contact, and the smile she gives me pushes a little bump of confidence through my chest. Just what I need for this lunch date with my mom.

"Come on. My mom is almost always late, so let's grab a table," I say.

This vegetarian Vietnamese place is quaint, like everything else around here. A small fountain sends trickling sounds through the space, and the decor is all light greens and yellows. Peaceful. Which is good, since I'm a little nervous about this whole thing. It's not like I usually bring my "dates" home to my mom, after all.

After the server brings us some water, which I gulp down because that's the most exercise I've done in a while, Maya asks, "So is there anything I should know about your mom?"

God. Where to begin. But we're keeping shit simple here, so all I offer is, "She's kind of corporate. Wound a little tight. And she wants me to be a bit more . . . grounded." *Or just someone else entirely.*

"Okay, so I'm the nice, small-town girl who grounds you? Is that my role here?" She's half smiling, so I assume she's okay with this.

"Yeah. Exactly."

"Got it."

My phone buzzes, and it's a message from my mom saying she'll be a few minutes late. *Shocking.*

Instead of letting myself get irritated, I turn my attention to Maya and ask, "So do your parents think I'm the shit, or what?" I grin.

She pushes at my shoulder. "I think their words were 'fun' and 'not shy,'" she says.

I'll take what I can get.

"Do they seem happy that we're hanging out?"

"I think so," she says, fiddling with her napkin. "They're mostly just happy for me to get over my heartache so I'm not 'moping around' anymore."

"Ouch."

"Yeah. They don't get it. My mom and dad, like I said, met here, fell in love here, got married here, and now they get to live happily ever after. I bet they think I'm just ruining an already good thing by trying to change my relationship to Rish."

"Do you—"

"But to me, it's not a change, you know?" she continues. She's revving up, I can tell. I shut my trap and let her do her thing.

"For me, it's just this story that started the moment we met and then it was like this path was all set out for us. Like, we've always gotten along so well, are passionate about so many of the same things, love spending all our time together—why *wouldn't* we end up girlfriends, eventually? And I guess I pictured things playing out like they did for my parents. They got married right on the lake—like, *right* on the lake. In my mom's canoe. With the justice of the peace in there and everything."

She looks at me like she expects a response to this, so I offer, "Wow. Cool." In reality, it sounds like a fucking nightmare to me. Three people in a tippy canoe, trying to maneuver around marriage vows with no escape except jumping into cold water? No thanks.

"And eventually, Rashida would inherit her cabin, I'd inherit mine, and we'd combine properties and live in Spruce Lake year-round, and that would be that."

Whoa. I can't help but step in now. "So, like, you had your whole life pictured with her?" I can't imagine seeing that far into the future. Or trusting any relationship enough to see it past next week.

"Yeah—I guess I did," Maya says. "It seemed—seems—obvious to me."

After a few minutes and more water, my mom finally appears at the entrance. She removes her sunglasses and surveys the restaurant. I give her a wave, and she heads over. She's got her hair back in a low chignon, as usual, because her hair let loose is as full and wild as mine. She's wearing heels, a fitted black dress suit, and a high-collared white shirt. Standard corporate wear.

My hands automatically move to my hair, smoothing out any bumps and tightening my ponytail.

When she gets to our table, apologizing for being late, Maya gives me a funny look and I realize normal families probably hug in situations like this. I haven't hugged my mom in literal years, but this "date" is supposed to change things up, so even though it feels completely unnatural, I stand and move to hug her. There's an awkward moment where my mom is confused, but she reciprocates. The hug is loose and clunky, and when it ends, she says, "Oh, Gabe—you're a little damp?"

"Sorry, yeah. We rode bikes here."

As she takes her seat, her eyebrows rise. "Bikes?" She looks at Maya. "You got Gabe on a bike?" Her tone is surprised, but she's also smiling, and this feels like a win.

Maya glances at me and smiles back at my mom. "Ha—yes. But she didn't put up too much of a fight." She glances at me again, and I realize I haven't introduced them.

"Maya, this is my mom, Karen. Mom, Maya."

"Pleasure to meet you, Maya." Mom reaches over and shakes Maya's hand like we're in a business meeting or something. I try not to roll my eyes.

The server takes our orders, and I try for another win. "So, Mom, Maya's family's been in Spruce Lake forever."

"Oh?" my mom says, laying a napkin on her lap.

"Well, not forever, exactly, but for a couple of generations, at least. My grandparents built our cabin and now we mostly use it in the summers."

"That sounds lovely. Are you right on the lake?"

"Yeah—we're really lucky."

My mom turns to me. "And, Gabe—how is your place working out? Better now?" she asks, referring to my earlier, panicked call after the chicken "coup" (because "coop," get it?).

Since I'm trying to be Good Gabe—or at least A Little Bit Better Gabe—I nod and respond, "Yes. I'm getting used to it. The owner is super generous." Not *not* true.

"That's good to hear." To Maya, she adds, "As you might know, Maya, Gabe isn't used to roughing it. She's been very lucky, too."

There's no malice in her voice, I don't think, but her words set a small fire alight in my chest, nonetheless. *Lucky, my ass.*

When I don't say anything, because I'm trying to swallow the pissy words burning to get out, Maya pipes up with, "Well, you'd be impressed, then, because she's even been hanging out in the *forest.*"

My mom's eyebrows jump again in surprise. "*This* Gabe?"

Maya's hand is suddenly on my arm, her thumb rubbing against my skin, which is still warm and sticky. "This Gabe," she says, smiling at me. I'm both impressed by her commitment to this role and genuinely comforted by the gesture and words. The burn in my chest subsides a little.

After Maya tells my mom a bit about her spot in the woods, our food comes—an assortment of vegetarian dishes like spring rolls, lemongrass tofu, and some kind of noodle bowl. We let Maya order, since my mom and I are definitely not vegetarian connoisseurs.

The food would be better with meat in it, but my mom and I both admit it's tasty. As we eat, my mom peppers Maya with questions—about her cabin, the town, her parents. Maya plays her role perfectly. But really, I think she's just being herself. She *is* a nice girl, from what I can tell—even if she's a bit sulky over Rashida.

My eyes dart to my mom in between bites of food. For the past couple of years, the only expressions I've known were either all business or irritation or exasperation. Now, though, there's something softer there, and I'm not sure if it's just because she's looking at Maya and not me or what. Maybe she's playing a role, too—caring mom who's happy for her kid.

When there's a pause in their conversation, I say, "Oh, I almost forgot to mention—I'm volunteering with this group Maya's a part of. I think I'm going to help them fundraise and such."

My mom's phone pings from where it's been on the table beside her the entire time because of all her important business things. Instead of responding to me, she picks it up and frowns. I already know what's coming before she says it.

"Shoot. I'm sorry, you two, but I need to head back to the office."

She's been here for thirty minutes and her plate is half full, but whatever. Maybe I should be thankful she came at all.

"Hectic days," she adds. "I'm sorry, Maya. But you two stay and enjoy the rest of your lunch. Order whatever else you want. Gabe, just use the credit card, okay?"

"Right. Yup." I'm trying not to be irritated, but this is a redo of so many interrupted meals and moments for the sake of my mom's work that it's hard to stay calm.

Thankfully, Maya is *genuinely* a good person and says, "That's totally okay. It's so nice you were able to come at all—Gabe said you're really busy. Thanks so much for lunch."

My mom smiles at her as she stands and collects her things. I can't seem to get my own legs to stand for another awkward hug, so I just wave goodbye and say, "Yeah, thanks for lunch, Mom."

"My pleasure. I'm so happy I got to meet you, Maya. Maybe we can do this again sometime. August should be a little less busy."

"Great. Sure," Maya says.

She's smiling at my mom, but I can tell she's probably thinking, *August?* because Lord knows neither of us signed up for this fake-dating thing for that long.

"And, Gabe, this," my mom says, making a little circle with her fingers in my direction, "is a good look on you. I'm proud of you, honey." She gives me a small smile and waves goodbye to the both of us before hustling out of the restaurant.

After she's out of sight, Maya turns to me and says. "Well? Not bad, right?"

I give her a half smile and nod. "Yeah. You nailed it."

She studies me for a moment longer than I'm comfortable with, and I look back at my food.

"You okay?" she asks.

I scoff. "One hundred percent," I say, and take a massive bite of spring roll.

This is what I wanted, of course—for my mom to see I can be committed and grounded like she wants me to be. For her to be proud of me for once. But I also can't help but wonder what will happen if—when—the real Gabe pokes through again.

TWENTY-SEVEN

Maya

Gabe and I agreed we'd meet up on Friday for a third date and try tackling karaoke again—except this time I'd actually get my butt onstage and sing with her. Before then, though, my plan was to see if I could spend a bit more time with Rashida. We keep trying for a hike, but she's been so busy with SLEA stuff, we haven't had a chance yet.

It ended up that I didn't have a ton of time, either, though, because my parents have become obsessed with cleaning out the cabin and collecting items for a garage sale that SLEA is organizing to fundraise for Project Babes in Wonderland.

This means that I, too, have to clean out the cabin, which I am not at all excited about.

"It'll be fun!" my mom says.

"Think about the treasures we'll find!" my dad adds.

They're standing at the doorway to my room, and when I groan and flop sideways into my bottom bunk, my mom offers, "Why don't you just start in here and we'll see how it goes? I'm sure there's some stuff you can find to donate. Your dad and I will start going through the rooms upstairs."

I glare at them with the one eye that isn't smushed into my pillow. "Yes. Fine," I mumble.

"Great! Love you!" Mom says, and sends me air kisses as she quickly pushes Dad out and away like she's afraid I'll change my mind or have some kind of hissy fit.

I sit up slowly and take in my room. It's small, and I'm only here during the summer. How much stuff could there be?

Turns out, there's a lot of stuff. Apparently, I have used every square inch of available space to hoard things I don't want anyone else messing with. There's stuff under my bed, in my closet, crammed into my desk drawers, behind and on top of my dresser, and lined up against the floor next to the window.

Diamond would say, "One thing at a time." So for the next hour, I plug away at the stuff in my closet and in my desk. Everything from sports equipment to stuffed animals to junk jewelry to an *amazing* sticker collection I forgot about appears out of dark corners and dusty drawers.

I try to be methodical about my sorting—starting out with Keep, Donate, and Recycle/Trash piles on my bunk beds like you see in those home makeover shows. But that lasts about twenty minutes before I realize that my Keep pile is overflowing, that only one item—a chunky, fake jade necklace—occupies the Donate pile, and that the Trash pile sits completely empty.

I stare at the items in my Keep pile. I don't want to get rid of any of them. And why should I have to? I don't, do I? They've been perfectly happy filling up my space all this time.

I'm about to replace everything in its rightful spot when I hear our cabin door thunk open, the tinny sound of the doorbell clanging shortly after like it does whenever the door closes.

"Hello?" I call out, unfazed by someone just walking in. That's just how it is here.

I hear an "Eeee-*yu*!"—Rashida's and my special call—from the living room and then Rashida appears at the entrance to the bunker. My heart skips, seeing her here. I'm instantly both excited and nervous. This is what I wanted, though—to spend some time with her—so I try to get myself together.

She takes one look at the tornado of my room and me standing in the eye of the storm with an armful of stuffies and says, "Girl."

"I know" is all I say.

"Is this for the garage sale?"

I nod, feeling exposed.

"Want help?"

"Desperately."

She grins. "Come on—it'll be fun. Think of the treasures!"

I try to ignore the echo of my dad's comment in hers and grin back. "That's the problem—too many treasures. I don't want to get rid of any of them!"

She walks over, takes the stuffies from me, and places them on the bed. "But they could be treasures for someone else, too, right? And you just keep the memories?"

"I *guess*," I say, unable to keep the whine from my voice.

She laughs. "Oh, wow. You're in a state. Go drink some water. I'll start by going through your stuffed animals and narrowing them down to three. Then you get to choose *one*, got it?"

"Ugh. *Fine.*" I stomp past her to the bedroom door, turn, and add, "*Bossy.*" But I'm smiling, and we both crack up.

I do feel better after a glass of water—Rashida always seems to know when I'm dehydrated—and so I don't even mind that Mr. Huff the stuffed dragon or Bella Swan (the stuffed swan, duh) are in Rish's to-go pile when I return.

Rashida's on the floor sitting cross-legged with the three finalists in front of her, lined up like contestants on a game show: Toasty the stuffed marshmallow, Pucker-Up the trout, and Ribbit the Pacific tree frog, who has Velcro on her toes and can wrap around things.

I sit cross-legged in front of her, too, with the stuffies between us. "Interesting. Didn't *you* give me all of these?"

"Listen, these are merit-based choices *only*." She grins.

I roll my eyes. But as I scan the three items, I'm horrified to feel my eyes get wet.

"Hey. What's up?" Rish leans over and puts her hand on my knee, which just makes things worse.

What would happen right now if I brought up last summer? My feelings for her? Will I ruin everything if I do? She's seemed kind of tentative around me so far—but also maybe a little bothered by Gabe and me? But then she hasn't even brought up Gabe, which I for sure thought she would by now. Maybe she's not jealous at all? Is it too soon? I haven't really given Gabe's plan much time to work. Should I wait?

Gabe's voice shoves through these thoughts, telling me to "calm my ass down" and "let this shit work." I can't believe she's already in my brain like this, but I decide I should wait. I should definitely wait.

"It's nothing. I'm just sad I have to give away any of these. It's silly," I say, squishing Toasty between both hands.

We're silent for a few moments, then Rashida says, "Remember those incredible onesies we found at Forevermore when we were, what, eight or nine?"

Forevermore was a thrift shop in Miller's Bay. It's no longer there (ironically) because a mall went up six years ago, and Forevermore just couldn't compete with all the new and shiny stuff.

"Yeah—eight," I say. "Yours was gold. Mine was silver."

"With lightning rods and little stars!" she adds.

We were beside ourselves when we found those onesies. We even performed in them at karaoke night that summer, singing "Nothing's Gonna Stop Us Now" by Starship. We got a lot of wear out of them—my mom sewing up holes and tears repeatedly before we eventually had to give them up because they were falling apart.

"What about them?" I ask now.

"Can you imagine if whoever donated those hadn't? Where would we be now?"

I roll my eyes at her. "Okay, After-School Special." This is what we'd call each other when one of us got cheesy or preachy because of some TV show from the last century that my mom told us about.

She laughs and pushes at my knee. I realize her hand's been there the whole time. "It's true, though! All those memories—poof. Gone." She spreads her fingers and hands in front of her like she's revealing magic.

"Yes, okay, I get it. I'm contributing to someone else's memories if I donate these. God."

"God ain't gonna help you here. Let's just do this, okay? Choose." She indicates the three stuffies.

I stare at Toasty in my hands. At Ribbit and Pucker-Up. I think of the times Rish gifted me with each. Two birthdays and a congratulations for coming in third at the annual Spruce Lake fishing derby.

"I can't. You choose for me." It's a cop-out, but I don't care.

She sighs and blinks at me, exasperated. "Maya . . ." She's always been more decisive and disciplined than me. When she looks down at the stuffies, though, she scrunches up her nose and takes a few seconds before finally saying, "Fine. Just keep all three. You're still getting rid of, like, a butt-load of stuffed animals, at least."

I'm a little surprised at this move—it's unlike her to give in like this, and even though I'm trying not to make it mean too much, I wonder if she's having a hard time letting go, too. I *hope* it means she sees how much we have together and that it's worth holding on to.

TWENTY-EIGHT

Gabe

I'm sitting at Canva's kitchen counter, half listening to her and trying not to hurl as she shows me something called a SCOBY that she uses to make kombucha. I can't decide if it looks more like a giant scallop gone bad or a melting breast implant.

I rub my eyes. For some reason, I woke up before the chickens had a chance to wake me—early enough to partake in a hot breakfast with Canva. I was relieved to see that there were eggs involved, but didn't realize that breakfast would also include both Blu and Canva nattering on about their natural food experiments. I wonder if Canva knows Blu also eats processed candy like Cookie Monster eats cookies.

Blu is seated on the stool next to me, eating his breakfast, too. I've learned over the past few days from both Maya and Canva that Blu lives here during the summer. He's not Canva's biological nephew, but Blu still calls her auntie. I gather that he's a bit of a handful and his parents send him here to keep him busy with a very active Canva. I can relate to some of that—the getting rid of your annoying kid bit, anyway. I think Blu's a little enamored with me—always grinning and making egg references. He's all right, I guess.

When Canva turns back to the fridge, I check my phone while Blu spins around and around on his stool singing some made-up song about kombucha. I messaged Maya yesterday to figure out our next date details and if she wanted to grab dinner before karaoke tonight to bump up our visibility in town—but she said she'd have to get back to me because her parents have her doing a bunch of stuff around the cabin. Haven't heard from her yet.

Not a big deal. We've still got karaoke, and I'm hoping to put on another show this town won't forget, especially after the past couple of days of hanging out by myself and reading *Fried Green Tomatoes*, which is cute and all, but, like, this girl needs more stimulation than a book's gonna give me.

"Hey, any ideas for things I should do today?" I say now to both Blu and Canva.

Blu just shrugs, grins, and says, "Feed the chickens?" then keeps spinning. He's a little stinker, but this makes me smirk.

Canva leans over the counter and thinks for a moment. "Well, there are plenty of nice hikes around here."

WTF with everyone's obsession with hiking around here. "Cool. What else?" I say.

"How about . . . kayaking?"

I scrunch up my nose and give my head a little shake. Not planning on drowning today.

"Renting a bike? There's a beautiful forest ride near here."

My cooch still hurts from that bike ride with Maya. "Anything that's a little less . . . outdoorsy? I'm still easing into all that." In other words, I don't want to do any of that.

"Um . . . oh! I don't know if you'd be into this, but it *is* indoors."

Now we're talking. "Okay . . ."

"Blu and I are helping sort through donations at the local high school for an upcoming fundraiser. We could use all the help we can get."

Two problems with this: One, it sounds like work. And two, donations sound dirty. But options seem limited, and it does sound like a good way to keep myself busy. Plus . . .

"Is this fundraiser for SLEA, by any chance?" I ask. Someone mentioned something about a garage sale at the meeting on Sunday.

"Yes! You know about SLEA?" Canva asks. Her whole face blows up with excitement. I mean, she seems like a generally excited person, but this really sets her alight. These people sure do love their activism.

"Yeah—I went to a meeting. At the pub? Jan kind of forced me into it—but I didn't mind."

That last part is partially true. I like Jan. I like Maya. And even though I didn't get the reaction I wanted from my mom at lunch for joining SLEA, I'm hoping I can still work that angle—especially if the fake-dating works and Maya ends up back with

Rashida. At least I'll still have something wholesome I can use to impress my mom.

"Oh, super!" Canva replies, smile as big as ever. "Jan's a hoot, isn't she?"

That's one word for her. "She sure is," I say.

"Well, then you must know that we're having a garage sale the Saturday after next to raise money for the upcoming protest. All the donations have been piling up in the school gymnasium, so a few of us have been going down there to sort, organize, and tag. What d'you think? Could you spare a bit of time? We'd really appreciate it."

Usually, I'd have no trouble saying "forget it" and finding a less sweaty-sounding activity to do, but Canva's so earnest and Blu's grinning beside me and I'm trying to be Good Gabe, so I say instead, "Yeah, I can help for a bit."

Canva literally claps her hands together and squeals like I've just said I'm buying her a new car. Or . . . a new bicycle or rowboat or whatever. Even Blu flings himself around on the stool and lets out a "Wooo!"

Okay, calm down, people. But I can't help but smirk at their zeal.

The Spruce Lake High School gym is hilarious. I swear it's the size of my basement. I assume sports isn't a thing here, but then I notice several banners on the wall boasting swimming and rowing championships, so I dial back my judgment.

This tiny gym is chockablock full of all kinds of shit, though. It's like that antique place Maya took me to, except less curated and more overwhelming.

A few people are already here, organizing. Three I recognize—Jocelyn, Casey, and Davie from the SLEA meeting—and the others recognize *me* from karaoke. Everyone seemed happy to see me, which is unexpected, but kind of nice.

Canva wastes no time in handing me a price tag thing and directing me to label a bunch of stuff on a table. Once I've done that, I'm instructed to organize clothing along some racks by type of garment.

These tasks I can handle. I hope she doesn't ask me to do anything that'll mess up my nails, though. I already feel kind of grubby, thanks to Canva's instructions for what I should wear today.

I've got on an oversize T-shirt (because this didn't sound like a job I wanted my boobs on display for) and a pair of sweatpants I brought for chilling in private, because Canva told me to wear long pants and something I didn't mind getting dirty. I'm also wearing the trashiest shoes I brought—scuffed and weathered kicks I've had for over two years that I just can't seem to part with because they're comfy as hell.

Not my hottest outfit, but that doesn't stop Davie from coming up to me with random stuff and telling me why I should buy it. I get the sense that he's into me from all his glances the other day at the meeting, plus his goofy attempts to tease me today. He's kind of funny and hot, but I'm not feeling it. And besides, I'm fake-taken.

Anyway, I'm glad I'm wearing this outfit now as Canva points me toward a bunch of dusty books to sort through. I crouch down to poke around in the boxes. So many books. Everything from cookbooks to novels to dictionaries and *lots* of outdoor guides—*100 Hikes on the West Coast, Lake Living, Plant Medicine 101.*

The guides remind me of Meems. After she took off, Mom didn't bother doing any of this—sorting through Meems's stuff to get rid of it. Whatever Meems left is still all there, in our house—her clothes are in the closet, her super-gay rainbow apron is hanging on the same damn hook in the kitchen, her travel guides and do-it-yourself books still take up a whole shelf in the study. Even her favorite fucking relish is on the same shelf in the fridge.

I definitely wanted to shove all that shit out the door after we realized Meems wasn't just gone for a short stint. Why would I want reminders of her?

But when I tried to bring it up with my mom, she was pissed—I wasn't sure if it was because she thought Meems was coming back or if she resented me even asking, since I was the reason Meems left in the first place.

About three weeks after Meems left, I'd been looking for a notebook or something I could use for the course I was taking. While rooting around in the study, I looked up and saw that damn row of travel books and outdoor guides, and I kind of lost it, I guess. Why didn't she take her shitty adventure books if she wanted to screw off around the world? Didn't she need them to figure out where to go to get the hell away from us?

I'd started pulling the books off the shelf and throwing them haphazardly into whatever bags I could find. I left them by the front door to drive to the thrift store the next day.

But when my mom came home that night, she'd found me in

the home theater, where I was watching bullshit TV instead of doing my coursework. She'd been fuming.

"Why are all those books by the front door, Gabe?"

I didn't even sit up from where I was lying on the sectional—didn't even take my eyes off the screen. "Why not?" I said, like a little jerk.

"Those aren't going anywhere, so put them back." Her voice was even but seething, and it pissed me off.

I finally sat up. "What? Why? *You're* not going to read them. *I'm* sure as hell not going to read them. Meems isn't coming back for them, and even if she does, sucks for her. We can't just keep all her crap around. It's not going to change anything."

"Gabe!" My mom's voice rose. "They will stay where they are. *You* don't get to make the decisions around here, got it? You haven't exactly proven yourself to be a good decision-maker, have you?"

She didn't say it out loud, but I'd heard the next sentence anyway. *If you'd made better decisions, maybe she'd still be here.*

I put the books back that night, slamming them into place and wishing I'd kept my damn mouth shut.

I stare at the boxes in front of me. I get why people clear out their spaces. Why remind yourself of shitty things—especially if you caused those shitty things?

For the next hour, I work like a fiend, pretending that all this stuff is my own, my mom's, and Meems's—and that I can organize it, label it, and get it the hell out of here.

TWENTY-NINE

Maya

Dad hands me a box from the trunk of our Subaru while Mom grabs some garbage bags from the back seat. The car is full of stuff from our cabin. In the time it took for me to go through my bedroom, Mom and Dad finished cleaning out the loft, their own bedroom, and the sunroom.

Oops.

But I don't feel bad about it. Rashida and I took our time, going through everything and playing little games to see who remembered what about each item we found.

And though Rashida turned into a bit of a hard-ass after that initial bout of leniency with my stuffies, I could tell it was hard for her, too, packing up some of these bits of us to give away.

She finally asked about Gabe when we found a collection of rocks we'd gathered together at Sun Island hiding in a tin box beneath my bed. Something about the way she asked—"You haven't taken Gabe to Sun Island yet, have you?"—made me wonder if she really was jealous and gave me a little bump of hope.

I told Rashida I hadn't taken Gabe there, and wouldn't. She looked like she wanted to ask more, but then Mom and Dad came in to check on us.

I pass Jocelyn now on my way into the high school gym as she comes out to help us unload.

"Hey! Your friend Gabe is hilarious. And she's been working like a machine."

I stop walking, hitching the box up into my arms a bit more. "Gabe's here?"

"Yeah—been here for, like, three hours or something. Hasn't even taken a break."

"Wait. You're thinking of the right person?"

"Um, yes, Maya. Hard to confuse her with anyone else. It's not like you bring a lot of cool new girls around. Love to see it, by the way." Jocelyn winks at me and continues on.

My cheeks warm at her words. Even if it was Gabe's and my plan to make people—especially Rashida—think I've moved on, I'm finding it kind of weird how *quickly* people seem to embrace this idea, even if it gets them off my back. It's almost like people *want* me to give up on what Rish and I have. But why would they?

"Ha ha—right," I call after Jocelyn, trying to sound casual. "She's hard to miss, I know."

I slow-walk into the gym, trying to gather my thoughts. Gabe keeps popping up in unexpected places, but there's no way she'd know I'd be here now. Maybe this is some part of Gabe's plan I don't know about? I can't imagine Gabe *choosing* to help with this, except for some ulterior motive. But three hours of hard labor is a lot to fake.

When I enter the gym, I pause to scan the space, even though this box is getting heavy. My eyes land on Gabe off to my left. Her back is to me, but I'd recognize that mane of hair anywhere. Right now it's tied back in a high ponytail and she's on her knees, hunched over a pile of utensils and sorting through them. She's very focused, placing forks with forks and knives with knives like she's playing a game of solitaire or something. It's actually so cute.

I frown. Not cute. Just . . . nice. That she's helping.

I finally put the box down and am about to walk over when Blu pops up in front of me.

"Hi, Maya!" he practically sings, then gives me a big hug around the waist and runs off to who knows where. When I look back over at Gabe, she's looking at me, then blinks and gives me a little wave. I wave back and walk over.

As I get close, she stands and glances around. No one is near us, but it's obvious a few people are watching.

I take in her outfit—it's definitely the most modest clothing I've seen her in. Baggy black sweatpants, a gray T-shirt that's at least three sizes too big for her, and well-loved kicks. Not even any makeup—just the bright red nails. It's hot in this gym, and she must be sweltering. But I don't miss how attractive she is, even in these clothes. She almost looks sporty. Or just—comfy.

She tucks some hair behind her ears and says, "I'm a bit sweaty, but we should probably hug or something? You know, for appearances?"

"Well, as you said, I like my girls sweaty," I reply, and immediately feel embarrassed, because I never say things like that, even as a joke.

She busts out laughing, though, which makes some of the embarrassment fade, and then she pulls me in for a hug, which makes the rest of the embarrassment disappear.

"You're definitely sweaty," I say as we come out of the hug.

She laughs again. "Hey! Some of us are working hard here."

This appears to be true. "Yeah—I can see that. And I'm a little surprised? Is someone coercing you somehow?"

She shrugs and grins. "Bish, you don't know me," she retorts, all sass.

I laugh again but also find myself wanting to know her more.

She's about to say something else when I hear my mom behind me.

"Maya! There are more boxes!" she calls out, but when she sees Gabe, she smiles and shouts, way too enthusiastically, "Oh, *hi*, Gabe! Never mind, Maya. I'll get the rest. You stay right where you are!"

Oh my God. I look pleadingly at Gabe. "Are your parents as embarrassing as my parents?"

Her face shifts for the briefest moment, and I remember that she said her moms weren't together anymore.

"Oh, Gabe, sorry—I forgot—"

She's back to grinning in the next second. "No, no—don't worry about it. All parents are embarrassing. But yours are still better than mine, trust me."

I watch her for a beat, but she seems all right, so I say, "I should go help them anyway. And you look like you're doing some very intense utensil organization here, so heaven forbid I interrupt."

She smirks and looks down at her masterpiece. "I'm actually almost done here. Are you staying, or . . . ?"

Do I want to stay in this hot gym organizing even more things after spending several hours already on my own room? Then I realize that Gabe's spent just as much time working away. And then I just really want to get out of here and do something that has nothing to do with organizing old things at all.

"No," I say.

An eyebrow cocks. "Okayyyy . . . ?"

"And neither are you."

Both eyebrows pop up. "Oh?"

"Finish your utensils while I grab these boxes. Then we're getting out of here. I have an idea for date two-point-five."

THIRTY

Gabe

"Um, absolutely not."

Inflatable tubes are bobbing around in the water in front of me and Maya, waiting to be ridden down a bumpy river. We're at a spot unofficially called Salmon Run about a ten-minute drive outside of Spruce Lake. According to Maya, it's called that because people throw themselves along it on these tubes and crash around the rapids like salmon on their way to spawn or whatever. Several people are doing so, right now, and Maya thinks I'm going to, as well.

Her parents let her borrow the car once they unloaded it, and after quick pit stops to change into our bathing suits, she drove me here with these inner tubes shoved into the back of the car. She seemed to think I'd welcome a refreshing water activity after that hot gym, and she's not wrong, but this is not what I imagined.

"I kind of pictured us just floating in a calm, boring lake with beers in our hands," I say.

"Gabe, I promise it's not scary at all. Literally no one ever falls in, and I'll be right there with you. And we're wearing life jackets. And I've got first aid training."

"That last part was unhelpful."

She grins. "I didn't think you were someone to back down from a challenge," she says, like a real jerk.

I narrow my eyes at her, then turn to watch some people bumping through frothy water about a hundred feet down, their feet and arms flopping around, screams of delight emanating like that shit is fun.

"How about we give it ten minutes, and if you hate it, we can get out," Maya says when I remain quiet and unconvinced.

"A lot can happen in ten minutes," I say, placing my hands on my hips and staring at her for a few moments. She keeps smiling. I narrow my eyes again and shake my head, but I'm really *not* someone to back down from a challenge. Goddamn her for knowing it.

"Five minutes?" she negotiates.

"Ugh. Fine."

Of course, it takes us about twice that time to get me balanced in the tube and out on the water, because this body is made for luxury cars and leather couches, not rubber tubes. But we finally set off with the tiniest paddles—because apparently I also have to push my own damn self through the water—and float away from shore, a short rope connecting our tubes so I'm not lost to the wilderness.

After a minute of getting my bearings, I ask, "Do you and Rashida come here a lot?"

"Rashida doesn't love it because she thinks it's too touristy, but I don't mind it."

"You don't care that she won't see us?"

She shrugs. "I'm sure she'll hear about it. I figured enough people would be around to see us. Lots of locals come here, too."

"Cool, cool," I say, concentrating on not falling into the water so all these locals and tourists don't get to see me drown.

We float a bit more, our tubes bumping up against each other now and again.

"I'm not hating that book, *Fried Green Tomatoes* or whatever." I'm not sure why I bring this up now. Maybe I want Maya to know I'm reading it? Or maybe I'm still not great at extended silences.

Her eyebrows rise as she paddles. "You're reading *Fried Green Tomatoes*?"

"Yeah. Hope you don't mind I borrowed it from your box thing in the woods?"

"You went back to my spot?"

Oh. Should I not have? "Sorry, yeah—the other morning—but I won't go again if you don't want me to."

"No, it's fine. I'm just surprised. But I like that you like it."

"Really?"

"Yeah. I mean, sometimes I like to be there alone, for the quiet and solitude. But if you enjoy it, too, use it."

She smiles at me, and despite the cool water at my feet, a warmth moves through me.

"Thanks," I say. *Back to the point, Gabe.* "Anyway, the book is pretty good. But the back-and-forth between past and present is kind of annoying? Like, who cares about Evelyn? I just want more Idgie and Ruth. Why can't they start making out already?" I wink at her.

She blushes, but manages to get out, "Yeah, I always want more Idgie and Ruth, too. But I like how the story goes back and forth. I mean, I prefer the parts set in the thirties, but Evelyn's story is important, too."

"Yeah, yeah—she learns from the past, blah blah blah, gets to be all impacted by Idgie and Ruth's story or whatever."

"Well, yeah—"

"Okay, but it's a little boring to follow this middle-aged woman discovering herself, is what I'm saying."

She fake gasps. "Evelyn's not boring! She's totally reinventing herself. It's cool. Wait and see . . . I think you'll like what she gets up to."

I shrug. "If you say so." We're quiet for a few seconds, but then I add, because apparently I've turned into a book club nerd, "I do kind of like how cozy the story is. I can see why you'd be into it, I guess—Spruce Lake is very Whistle Stop, but more West Coast and less the American South, right?" I cock an eyebrow at her, and she smiles back.

"Yeah, that's definitely part of it. I love the small-town feel for sure. But I'm kind of surprised *you* like that part."

I frown. "Why?"

She gives me a skeptical look. "Um . . . because you still don't seem super keen to be here."

I shift in the tube, getting a bit too wobbly for a moment before I settle and continue. “Do I love being pulled away from my friends and my giant house and all my stuff for an entire summer to stay in the tiniest town with a very strict vegetarian and be woken up by rabid chickens and eaten alive by mosquitoes? No. But it’s not *all* that bad. Just not what I’m used to. These ‘dates’ are helping.”

“Yeah?”

“Yeah.”

We share a look before she says, “Even this one?” and nods toward the frothy part of the water that’s coming up fast. My stomach twists at the sight.

“Umm . . . we’re not actually going through that, are we?”

“We are.”

“But, I mean, we could just float around here, take in the sights. Watch everybody else?”

Maya rolls her eyes. “Can you just trust me, please?”

“Trust is for chumps.” I frown, looking from Maya to the foaming water. But the thing is, I kind of do trust her. At least I trust her enough to not get me killed. Pretty sure, anyway. “Ugh. Fine.”

Maya grins and uses her paddle to push us toward the rapids. “Don’t worry, they’re not actually that fast, and it’ll only take thirty seconds to get through them. Just lie back, relax, and hold on.”

I bring my paddle in and grab the tube handles, saying, “If I had a buck for every time . . .”

I make dirty jokes when I'm nervous, okay?

Maya laughs awkwardly, and it makes me wonder what her experience with sex is. If she's been in love with Rashida all this time, does that mean she's never made out with anyone else?

I don't have time to further contemplate Maya's sex life, though, because shit's about to get real.

Maya shouts, "Hold on!" and I do, for dear fucking life.

THIRTY-ONE

Maya

Our tubes slide into the first slope, and the moment we hit a bump, Gabe's eyes go wide and her grip on the holds tightens, her arms going rigid.

"UM" is all she says at first.

"Easy, Gabe. I got you."

She trains her eyes on me. "You better."

I guide us through the various dips and angles of this part of the river. It's really not that fast, but I have to remind myself that I've been doing this for ages, and that everything's a little nerve-racking the first time around.

I watch Gabe as we go and can tell she's trying hard not to freak out. She's breathing through her mouth, staring ahead of her, periodically closing her eyes, and releasing brief, very un-Gabe-like screechy sounds. Her efforts tug at my heart.

"You're doing great," I say. "We're almost through."

"Cool. Great. Love this."

I can't help but chuckle and am happy when she half smiles, as well.

After one last dip, we land in placid water again, and Gabe collapses against her tube like we just plunged down a waterfall.

A few people who went through the rapids before us and are floating nearby cheer and whoop for us. They're teenagers I know vaguely, and I imagine they can tell that this was Gabe's first time.

Gabe perks up at their applause and gives them a queen's wave, saying, "Thank you, thank you." Her voice is a little wobbly, but then she looks at me and adds, "Now what?"

"Now we float some more. Your favorite."

"That's it?"

"What do you mean, that's it? That seemed like enough for you."

"It wasn't that bad."

"Really?"

"I mean, it *felt* bad for a bit, but it was fine."

"Really?"

She shrugs. "Show me something else."

I eye her up. Her face is both a challenge and a hint of something else—eagerness? Excitement?

"Okay, fine. Come on."

We paddle farther down the river where there's a bit of beach area. After we drag our tubes onto the beach and take off our life jackets, I lead Gabe up onto some rocks. There aren't a lot of people here, so this might not serve our secret plan very well, but I figure she won't want an audience for this part anyway, given her nerves about our previous activity.

"Ever cliff jump before?" I ask.

"Um, *no*?"

Her expression is so incredulous, I laugh. "Good, 'cause we're not doing that." I grin.

She gives me her middle finger.

"But I dare you to jump off this small rock." I point at the one we're standing on. It's only about five feet from the top of the rock to the water, but I remember my first time jumping into the lake off the diving board attached to Rashida's dock. It took me ages to finally try.

Rashida's always been the one to urge me into things, like when I was too scared to try water skiing until she went first and then she had to spend half the summer we were nine teaching me how to do it. Every time I bailed, Rish implemented the encouragement sandwich—a base layer of energetic praise, topped with some tough, constructive feedback, finished off with one more reassuring compliment, and—if I needed it—a little hug for good measure. I knew what she was doing the whole time but didn't care. The sandwich helped, and I knew she just wanted me to feel confident.

I want Gabe to feel confident now, but her bravado has fallen, and she actually looks worried sick. I don't say "It's not that high" or "Anyone can do it" because I don't think either will make her feel good about trying. And she seems like someone who'd just throw an encouragement sandwich out the window.

Instead, on an instinct I don't know the origins of, I take her hand and say, "I'll do it with you. Ready?"

She looks at my hand in hers, and though her face doesn't appear any less worried, she swallows and her grip tightens around mine. A small nod makes me smile, and we step to the edge of the rock.

"It's deep enough, right?"

"Totally."

"And we're going feetfirst?"

"Yup."

"You won't let go?"

"Not until you let go of me."

She's staring at the water and still seems unsure. I'm not jumping until she's one hundred percent ready. But something tells me she *wants* to be one hundred percent ready.

Whatever made me take her hand urges me now to lean over and plant a little kiss on her shoulder, even though no one's here to see it. "You got this."

She's more than surprised, I can tell. She's looking at my lips. She bites her lower lip, and a corner of her mouth lifts.

"What are we waiting for?" she asks, raising an eyebrow.

I grin and squeeze her hand.

"One . . ." I start.

"Two . . ."

"Three!" we shout, and jump in together.

THIRTY-TWO

Gabe

Maya and I unload the inner tubes from her car and lean them up against her cabin. She was going to drop me at Canva's first so I could shower and get ready for karaoke, but I told her I'd just walk from her place. I might get lost again, but I guess I wasn't quite ready for our fake date to be over yet. Plus, no one that important even saw us tubing, so I figure this way, at least her parents will see us together and then we can really make a splash (because *lakes*, get it?) at karaoke tonight.

We'd spent another hour at those rocks, jumping and swimming and floating, and then sunbathing on our inner tubes. I'd even jumped off the rock on my own, then watched as Maya jumped off a much higher one, admiring how easy she made it look and then laughing as she took my directions for different diving poses. "Queen waving to subjects." "Woman drinking tea." "Whip, then Nae Nae."

I'll admit—the whole afternoon was fun, even if I have sand in places sand should never be.

As she closes the car's rear door, she says, "Can I ask you something?"

"Ask whatever you want," I say.

We're still wearing our wet bathing suits with clothes over top, so we're also sporting very sexy wet spots on our boob and crotch areas. "You said your parents aren't together anymore, right?"

Oh. Not too keen on this topic. "Yeah, that's right." I flap out the towel Maya lent me and start to refold it. Before she can ask a follow-up question, I ask, "Are you hungry?"

"Oh—are you? I could make us a sandwich or something?"

"You sure? We could also just grab something in the village if you want—my treat. Part two of our 'date.' More people will see us that way, right?"

She wrinkles her nose, which I'm already starting to realize is her tell when she feels uncomfortable, and I wonder what's up.

"Actually, I wouldn't mind a little break from fake-dating until karaoke, if that's okay? But we have all kinds of stuff in the fridge—no meat, but cheese and eggs and stuff."

"Oh. Yeah. That sounds good." Honestly, I wouldn't mind a break from the dating show, either.

We head inside, and her parents—Jack and Hesara, I found out at the SLEA meeting—are already in the kitchen crafting something that makes my stomach growl immediately.

"Hey, you two!" Hesara says. "Just in time for dinner—homemade pizza. Join us?" Jack gives us a big smile, and they both have flour on their faces and on the matching aprons they're wearing, like this is some kind of rom-com and they're about to kiss for the first time or some shit.

Christ.

Maya looks at me now like this is all completely normal, which I suppose it is for her. "You in? They even make the dough. Karaoke's not for another two hours."

"It smells amazing. I'd love some." To her parents I say, "Thanks for letting me crash your pizza party." I've been crap to my own parents, but I can turn on the charm for other adults, no problem.

"Our pleasure! We haven't been able to properly get to know each other, have we?" Jack says, grinning. He wipes his floury hands on his shorts, and Hesara points at his apron, her face a mix of scowl and amusement. Maya grabs a dishcloth and hands it to her mom, who swipes Jack's ass with it, and they all laugh. I watch the whole happy family scene with a bit of amusement, too, but something else simmers in my stomach, as well. I don't like it, whatever it is.

"No, we haven't," I say, but I'm not sure I really want them to get to know me now, either. Something about their closeness is making me just want to get out of here. "Actually—sorry. I think I got too much sun today or something. I think I just need to—" I point to the door and make a move to go.

"Oh, honey," Hesara starts, "do you want to lie down for a bit?"

"No, no—I'll be okay. I'll just head back to Canva's and rest there. But thanks." I catch Maya's face, and it's got confusion all over it. That's fine—she'll be fine in this happy little cabin with its flour-filled kitchen and totally in-love parents. "Enjoy your pizza!" I add, to convince them everything's just *fine*, and head out the door.

I barely make it up the four steps to the road and Maya's caught up to me. "Hey—Gabe. Are you okay?"

"Yeah, yeah. Like I said. Just feeling a little woozy, is all."

"Well, I'll walk you."

I object, but she insists.

We walk silently for a while, down the road and then onto the forest path to Canva's. I can tell Maya's sneaking glances at me, but trying not to say anything.

Damn. Way to ruin a perfectly good day, Gabe.

"Sorry," I say, finally breaking the silence. "For being weird."

"That's okay. Is it actually the sun, or . . . ?"

I swallow. The path through the forest is cool and quiet. I think I'm slowly figuring out which path leads to Canva's and which one leads to the café, but the rest is a crapshoot.

I'm not great at sharing my feelings or whatever. For some reason, whenever I get big emotions, all I want to do is take my mind off of them—it's just easier, I guess. Maybe I got that from my moms. When you're angry or sad or depressed or whatever . . . leave. Or work a lot.

My emotions feel big now, and honestly, if Maya was someone I was actually dating, I'd probably just pull her to me and start making out (with her consent, obviously). But we're not really dating, and Maya doesn't seem like a spontaneous make-out kind of girl, anyway. Even just for fake fun.

But she is, apparently, the kind of girl who will take your hand when you've been quiet for a while, because that's what she does now, and—kind of like that kiss on my shoulder before—something about it makes me feel . . . comforted, or safe. Or something.

"You asked about my parents before," I say.

"Yeah. But you don't have to talk about it if you don't want to."

My throat feels thick, so I swallow again before saying, "They're not together. My one mom split a few months ago, and I haven't heard from her. And my other mom—who you met—may as well be on another planet most of the time. I think I mostly just disappoint her. That's why I wanted her to meet you and see that I could do something right."

"Oh. I'm sorry, Gabe." Her hand squeezes around mine.

I shrug. "Is what it is."

"It sounds like a lot to me," she says.

"Yeah, well with parents like yours, I'm sure mine sound hideous. Your family's like something out of a Disney movie."

She laughs lightly. "Yeah, and I always thought that was a good thing."

"It's not?"

"It is—don't get me wrong. I'm thankful. I just always thought what they have is the norm, even though my rational brain knows it's not. Like, Rashida's parents aren't great. Her mom took off, too. And her dad's kind of MIA, as well. Like your mom."

"Oh. That sucks."

She nods. "And I know other parents and families aren't like mine. But growing up with my mom and dad, it just made me want what they have so badly."

"Why can't you have that?"

She shrugs. "I guess I can. But I thought I was going to have it with Rashida, and I'm not sure that's true anymore."

"Maya. You're eighteen. I think you have some time to find your epic romance or whatever." I almost roll my eyes, but that feels a little shitty right now, so I don't.

"Yeah. I know you're right. I'm just having trouble seeing past what I thought was going to happen, I guess." She's quiet for a moment, then asks, "Were you ever close to your parents?"

I think I was happier talking about her stuff, but respond, "Not really. Or, at least, it doesn't feel like I ever was. Maybe as a little kid?"

"Are you just different people, or . . . ?"

"Um . . . yeah? I'm . . . a pain in the ass, like I said." I try a laugh, but it comes out a little pathetic.

Maya stops walking and her hand in mine tugs me to a stop, as well. We're in the middle of the path, and the heat of the day kind of hovers around us. She's looking at me, and I frown. "What?"

"I feel like I'm not the only one here stuck to some story I created in my head."

My eyebrows lift. "Pardon?"

"Don't take this the wrong way, but I kind of think you're full of shit."

I scoff. My hand automatically loosens, but hers doesn't.

"What's the *right* way to take that?" I say, somewhere between offended and amused.

"I mean—you're not *just* Gabe who's a pain in the ass. Or Gabe who's 'trouble.'"

I *do* roll my eyes now, because this is starting to feel a little too much like that one therapy session Meems made the three of us go to where the therapist talked all about "possibilities" and "self-stories." Barf.

"Okay. Sure. Fine. I contain multitudes. Can we move on now? This wet bathing suit is starting to chafe, you know what I'm saying?" I try a grin, but she just tilts her head and contemplates me for a moment. Something in my chest hitches at the way she's looking at me. I shift my gaze before any other weird shit can start moving around in there.

"I'm going to hug you now, okay?" she says, out of the blue, and my head turns sharply back to her.

"What?"

"We've practiced hand-holding and cheek-kissing, but I feel like our hugs could use some work."

"Are you serious?"

"Yup. Can I?"

What the fuck is this? "Sure. Let's practice hugging," I say with another eye roll, but my chest is doing more annoying shit.

She lets go of my hand and wraps her arms around my waist. I encircle her shoulders, but keep my arms loose and give her a little pat on the back.

"Don't you dare pat my back, Gabe," she says, her chin pushing into my neck as her mouth moves. Her arms squeeze a little tighter. "Act like people are watching and you need to sell it."

Fine. I give in a little so we can get this done with, and I tighten my arms. We're both damp and sweaty, but she smells like coconut sunscreen and fresh water. My chin automatically lowers until it's found the little pocket between Maya's neck and shoulder, and my heart rate finally begins to settle. My eyes land on a small bundle of mushrooms growing from a tree stump behind her.

We stay like that for a few beats, and when Maya eventually pulls back, our faces are close and our eyes meet. A small wrinkle settles onto her brow, and her eyes fall to my mouth. I instinctively wet my lips with my tongue.

But then a rustle and flash of movement behind her startles me, and I immediately envision myself being mauled by a bear.

I grab on to Maya's arm and tuck myself into her like the weakling in a horror movie. I don't care how pitiful I seem right now, though. I'm not gonna die by bear. "What the hell is that?"

Maya turns casually, like we're not about to get attacked by one of the most terrifying creatures in nature, and when she sees whatever it is, she turns back to me, smiling. Her face is full of amusement, and I know I'm about to be very, very embarrassed.

"It's a deer, Gabe."

Jesus.

She pries my death grip off of her arm and slowly brings me forward to watch as Bambi himself nuzzles through the bush and stares at us, his big eyes gleaming and his jaw working away at a leaf or something.

"Oh" is all I say, feeling like the biggest jackass.

"What did you think it was?" she asks, her voice laced with laughter.

I side-eye her. "Murderer? Rabid chicken? Human-hating bear?"

She grins. "I mean, yeah, those are all probably right around the corner, too."

"Shut up," I say, and give her arm a little push.

She laughs and says, "Look. He can't take his eyes off you."

I look back at the deer, and he is, truly, staring at me. He's pretty damn cute, I guess. But he sure has shitty timing.

THIRTY-THREE

Maya

Gabe and I both decide we're not up for karaoke tonight. We reschedule date number three for tomorrow, and I tell her I'll message with an idea as soon as I think of one. When I get back to my cabin, my brain and body are buzzing. Another warm, firm hug outside of Canva's created two competing urges in me. One is to see Gabe again as soon as possible, even if something feels dangerous about it. Or maybe not dangerous, but just . . . complicated.

The complication has to do with the second urge, which is to find out what's going on with Rashida. Things felt so good with her as we sifted through my room and all those memories. But also—different? And I'm trying to figure out if that shift has to do with Gabe.

Because those hugs were . . . not fake.

But these confusing feelings can't be real, right? I've only known Gabe for a week. Letting myself believe that there might be something happening with her when I've been in love with Rashida forever seems absurd. Maybe it's just everyone else's crap getting to me—urging me away from Rashida.

In other words, while I eat spicy spinach and mushroom pizza with my parents, my brain is hectic, and my parents just add to that commotion by asking a thousand more questions about Gabe.

"Was she okay?"

"Is she not used to this much sun?"

"Her parents are where again?"

"Is she going to keep helping with SLEA?"

"Would she want to come to dinner another night?"

I try to answer as many questions as I can, given that I *want* my parents to see that I'm into Gabe and completely fine about Rashida, but the fact that I don't feel completely fine about either Gabe *or* Rashida makes me flustered.

"Maya, is everything okay?"

Oh jeez. Not this again. "I'm good. I just got a lot of sun today, too, I guess. Haven't quite got my summer legs yet."

"Yeah, it was hot today. You spent all day at Salmon Run?" Dad asks.

"Yep."

"Did Gabe like it?"

"I think so—she was nervous at first, but then got the hang of things."

"That's good," Mom says. "She's a bit of a city girl, I take it?"

"Yeah." Then, feeling a little defensive, I add, "But she's definitely starting to enjoy it here." This isn't a lie, I don't think.

"She's a little different than your usual . . . pals," my dad says, tactful as ever.

"Pals?" I say, giving him a "Really?" look.

"You're not . . . pals?" he says, glancing at my mom.

"We're . . ." *What are the right words here?* "More than pals."

"Oh! Spicy, like this pizza!" he says, grinning.

"Ew, Dad."

He and my mom giggle. "She seems lovely, Maya," mom offers. "I'm glad you're having a good time."

I nod and take a bite of my pizza, letting them think Gabe is a casual summer fling and not someone with girlfriend potential—which of course she isn't, I have to remind myself. I can't picture us becoming anything more than friends, even if I'm starting to have confusing thoughts about her. We clearly want different things when it comes to romance . . . in that I want it, and she doesn't.

But my perplexing thoughts and feelings about Gabe continue after dinner. Despite my goals with Rashida, I find myself texting Gabe to see if she wants to go on a short hike the following day—it's a Saturday and plenty of people will be out and about to see us. I add that maybe we can take a couple of "action shots" of her in the woods to send to her mom to sweeten the deal.

But I know, even as I type these words, I'm not just thinking about action shots or public exposure. I know that I just want to spend more time with Gabe, to see what it's like after our time together today.

My confusion just grows, though, when she doesn't text me back by the time I'm getting ready for bed two hours later. As I crawl under the covers, I'm left wondering if we didn't have as good a time at Salmon Run as I thought. If I'm misreading that hug in the woods and the moment just after it, before the terrifying "bear" interrupted us.

THIRTY-FOUR

Gabe

When I get back to Canva's that night, I'm more exhausted than I've been in a long time, but in a good way. I feel sleepy and my arms are a little sore from organizing and paddling and swimming. I sit by my pool at home a lot in the summer, but rarely do I actually swim. Something about all that water time seeps into my bones, and I just feel content.

Well, mostly content. After Maya walked me back, I'd wanted to ask her to hang out a bit more—even if we decided against karaoke—but thought that might seem a little desperate. I didn't really want to hear her say no, either. But it was hard not to think about that soft kiss on my shoulder and why she did it. Or those hugs. Or how both made me feel like she cared if I felt safe or not.

But she dropped me off without asking if I wanted to hang

out more, so I guess she was eager to get back to pizza with her parents. Or maybe she was just tired, too. Which is fine. It has to be fine. Because she's in love with Rashida, and my job is to make sure they live happily ever after.

Anyway.

After saying hello and catching up on garage sale updates with Canva and Blu, who are playing cards in the kitchen, I have a hot but time-allotted shower, and collapse on my bed. It's only seven thirty, but I could fall asleep right here and now.

I start to, but then my phone buzzes. I left it at Canva's all day, which kind of sucks, because I would've loved to snap a couple of photos of me and Maya on the tubes, but I suppose phones and tubes on rivers don't mix anyway.

I check my phone and it's my mom.

Mother-Figure: Hi Gabe, wondering if you have time to chat today or tomorrow?

Huh. We barely chat when we're in the same room, let alone in different towns. Maybe my whole "dating a wholesome girl" schtick is working and she just wants to, you know, catch up? Or maybe I'm in some kind of trouble, as usual. Either way, I'm not going into a call with my mother uninformed, so I text back: What about?

Mother-Figure: Yes or no?

Jeez. Definitely sounds more like an "I'm in trouble" conversation than a "Let's catch up" one. This puts me on the defensive, and I gear up for whatever's about to be thrown at me.

Gabe: sure. Now?

My phone rings two seconds later.

"Good evening, Karen," I say, constructing a little barrier around me.

"Gabe. Don't start."

"Start what? You're the one who called."

I hear her sigh. I'm being a brat. I can't seem to help it with her. But I try. I walk to the window and look out at the trees just beyond the backyard. "Sorry. What did you want to talk about?" I ask.

"How are you?"

"Me?"

"Yes, you. What are you and Maya getting up to?"

Is she actually asking about my life?

"Any more biking adventures?"

She is *asking about my life!*

"No, but she took me tubing today. I jumped off a fucking cliff, and—"

"Language, Gabe."

"Sorry—but it was pretty cool. We went through some rapids, too," I say, bending down to peer into the small mason jars on the windowsill with their swirling, reaching roots.

"That sounds wonderful. I'm glad you're staying out of trouble."

I bristle at this, even though that's exactly what I want her to think. But does she have to *say* it?

I turn one of the jars in a circle, then realize I might be disturbing the little ecosystem or whatever, so I stop and straighten up, my eyes landing across the backyard on the line of trees there. "Yeah, not only that, but I've been volunteering with this local organization, too—helping them organize this huge garage sale." *How's that for staying out of trouble?*

"Wow. Sounds like you're really trying something new."

Exactly.

"And Maya seems lovely."

She is.

She pauses, and I'm about to offer more about my time with Maya when she says, "Listen, Gabe, I just wanted to let you know that your mother messaged me yesterday. Apparently she'll be traveling in South America for several months. She might be out of cell service for a while."

There are so many trees lining the backyard, but my sight line gets stuck between two that seem thicker than the rest. One has a birdhouse attached to the trunk. One is bare. The space between them looks slim and dark. I wonder if I could slide in there.

My free hand finds the window frame.

"Gabe? You still there?"

I have to swallow once, twice.

"Gabe? Honey?"

It's the second word, not my name, that brings me back from the trees and the gap between them.

"Sorry. Yeah?"

"Did you hear what I said?"

"Yes. Real shocker, huh?"

"You're upset."

"I'm not. I'm not surprised or upset. Why should I be? She's been gone for weeks. Without a word. Why should I care now?"

"I care."

My fingers find the glass jar again, and I stare into the green leafy things sprouting from the opening. "About what?"

"That she's leaving for so long." There's a pause. "That she's gone."

Do roots just absorb water though the tips? Or the whole, long tendril, or what?

"Gabe? You're really fine?"

I shrug, even though she can't see it.

I hear her sigh. I'm probably exasperating her. I should probably care.

"Well, I just thought you should know, in case you were expecting her to reach out at all."

I wasn't. "Cool. Thanks for the update." My voice is hard again, I know. I turn to collapse onto the bed and stare up at the ceiling.

We're quiet for a few seconds, and I almost say bye and hang up, but she adds, "I'm sorry about this, Gabe. Do you—need to talk about it at all?"

I almost laugh at the apprehension in her tone. Part of me wants to see what she'd do if I said yes, but instead, I say, "Nope."

"Okay." I can hear relief in her voice. But then she adds, "I *am* happy to see you making something good out of this summer, though. I hope we can find another time to meet up?"

My surprise at her words constricts my throat for a few seconds, but finally, I get out, "Sure, yeah."

"Okay. Well. Good night, Gabe."

We hang up, and I continue to stare at the wood beams above, the feelings in my chest twisting and tight. Part of me can't believe this fake-dating thing is actually working out for me and Maya. I should be happy about that, despite the fact that Meems is so *un*happy with me that she can take off for months at a time.

But Maya is getting what she wants with Rashida, and my mom actually seems to think I'm doing something good here. That I'm *being* something good. That's one less mom disappointed in me than I had before.

The happiness I should feel refuses to take root, though, because I realize that what I felt in the forest today with Maya is what I really want—not this pretending for others. And that freaks me the hell out, because there's no way she wants that with me.

So when a text comes through and it's from her, asking me if I want to go on a hike tomorrow, and when she makes sure to add that a ton of people will be around to see us and that it could impress my mom if we send her a photo of me in the forest, I don't answer it.

Because her invitation confirms for me that this is all still very fake for her and that I need to fight off whatever feelings I'm having that are real.

THIRTY-FIVE

Maya

It's been two days since I've seen or heard from Gabe. From what I hear via Davie, she's been working her butt off at the high school, sorting for the garage sale. I thought about going over there and talking to her, to see if she's just suddenly and rapturously committed to fundraising for SLEA, or if I did something wrong, or what.

But my own insecurities stop me. Once again, I feel like I've read someone completely wrong. I let this whole fake-dating thing muddle my brain and make me think that Gabe and I were possibly, maybe heading into some other territory.

Ridiculous.

And then this morning, Rashida messaged me, asking if I'd take the dogs up Old Baldy Mountain with her, and I said yes, because going on a hike with Rashida is precisely what I want to be doing. I love hiking, just like Rashida does. We love nature. We love fitness. We love our silly, slobbery dogs and how they bound around us as we hike.

These are all things I could never see Gabe loving. And from her unresponsiveness after I invited her on a hike with me, I have to assume I'm right.

But then, I never guessed she'd be so into organizing used stuff, either.

I try to set Gabe aside, as she seems to have done with me, and refocus on Rashida, because that's who I should have been focusing on all along. As I head out to meet her, I also wonder if this might be an opportunity to see if anything has changed in her feelings for me.

I walk down the road toward Old Baldy now with Prince in tow. It's the biggest mountain around here, but really not that big. A thirty-minute mostly gradual hike up, shaded by arbutus and cedar trees.

Prince snuffles around the entrance while we wait, and then I hear an "Eeee-*yu*!" from down the road and turn to see Rashida and Poppy walking toward us.

Prince bounds over, and his whole body wriggles as Rish bends to squish his smooshy face, then he abandons her so he and Poppy can sniff and lick at each other.

"Hey," she says, straightening up. I can tell she's sizing me up a little, trying to figure out where we're at, too. After our bedroom sorting session the other day, we haven't seen much of each other, either. She's been busy with SLEA stuff, and I've been—or was—busy with Gabe.

"Hey!" I smile, trying to channel some of the confidence and calm assurance I'd been able to generate with Gabe at Salmon Run and apply it here. *I can do this. I can figure this out and not fall apart.*

"Ready?" she asks.

Maybe? "Yup. Haven't been up yet, and I miss the view."

"Let's do it." She grins and sets off.

The trail starts out steep, and both of us are breathing a little harder within minutes. Prince runs ahead and back, getting all his energy out, and I wish I could do the same with all the nervous energy I'm carrying without looking like a "complete weirdo," as Gabe would probably say.

Once we hit the more gradual part of the trail, talking becomes easier—at least physically. But I'm still trying to figure out how to play this. Keep it casual? Chat about Gabe and see how she reacts? Ask her outright about last summer?

Before I can decide on anything, she asks, "What'd you get up to the past couple of days? More organizing and donations?"

I take this opportunity to tell her about Gabe helping with all the donations, and then about tubing at Salmon Run—how fun it was to show her something new and help her go outside her comfort zone.

Based on her response to Gabe's presence so far, I expect some discomfort or tension. Maybe some awkwardness. But she doesn't respond with any of that.

"That's cool" is all she says—not even with any underlying resentment.

I'm both surprised and hurt by this.

But then she follows with, "You're better at things than you think, Maya. Sometimes you just get freaked out about new stuff."

"Salmon Run and tubing isn't new to me, though," I argue.

"But taking someone *new* to Salmon Run and being the one who had to do the encouraging is. Right?"

"What're you talking about?"

She sighs like I'm exasperating her but says, "Who's usually the hesitant one here?" She points between herself and me.

"Me, I guess."

"You *guess*? Maya. Be real."

"Fine. Bossy."

We grin at each other, but then she frowns.

"What?" I ask, hopping over a muddy patch in the trail.

"You really like hanging out with Gabe?"

Ah, there it is. This question is more in line with what I thought—maybe hoped—Rish would ask.

"She's super entertaining." A small pang darts through my chest at this, because I know that's not *all* Gabe is. But I'm trying to sort things out with Rashida, and I don't want her thinking I have anything special with Gabe. That wasn't the point of fake-dating, anyway. Gabe would agree with me, I'm sure. It was her idea, after all.

Rashida is quiet for a few moments, picking up a stick from the ground and holding it out for a yapping Poppy to jump at. "Yeah. Entertaining is right. But she also seems a little . . . superficial, maybe?"

A flare of defensiveness rises in my chest, despite what I said before, and she must sense it, because she adds, "But I get it—she definitely seems fun."

She's more than that, too, I want to say, but don't. Instead, as we near the top of the mountain, I stop in the shade just before the trees open up and say, "She's been at the high school a ton, sorting through stuff. She seems to want to help, at least."

Rashida keeps walking with a "Hmm."

"Hmm, what?" I say, continuing after her.

"She just doesn't seem all that . . . aware? Don't you think? I mean, she's very . . . *animated* . . . but does she actually know anything about environmentalism? Or is she just bored?"

That bit of defensiveness flashes hotter now. Is she saying this because she actually means it or because she's jealous, like I wanted her to be? Either way, I'm not sure I actually care. "She's *learning*," I say. "There's nothing wrong with that."

"Oh, totally," Rashida says, but like she doesn't really mean it. She steps into the sunshine. "She just isn't the kind of person you'd usually hang out with, I guess."

I see her glancing over, and *this* feels something like jealousy. "I can hang out with different types of people, Rashida."

She looks back at me. "Okayyyy . . . Are you trying to tell me something?"

Am I?

We're at the lookout now, and we both take a moment to appreciate the view.

Baldy isn't that high, but from the top, you can still see for miles: trees in all directions, mountains in the distance, Spruce Lake nestled between forests. The lake is beaming with reflected sunshine right now, and I must be squinting, because Rish holds her hand above my eyes, shielding them from the brightness.

"Nerd. Stop squinting," she says.

Something about the gesture and her calling me a nerd and her tender bossiness breaks the tension from before. My heart pinches. She's right beside me, and I can see her skin is glowing a little from our exertion. My urge is to turn to her and give her a hug, but I resist, and I'm not entirely sure why.

Instead, I act as though I'm about to bite her hand, and she squeals with fake indignation. We tussle, and I pull my signature move (also my *only* move)—grabbing her, twisting my leg behind hers, and dropping her to the ground with a light bump.

Prince and Poppy join in the fun and start jumping around us and yapping.

Once her ass is on the ground, I rise and lift my hands like Rocky, prancing around and shouting to the universe, "And it's Maya for the win! Queen of Baldy Mountain!"

I grin at Rish, who's leaning on her elbows and shaking her head. "I let you win that one, obviously."

I drop my arms and roll my eyes. "Sure you did. You've never been able to withstand my trip-and-drop."

I reach out my hand to pull her up, but I should have known better. She yanks me down, and I fall half on top of her. Prince and Poppy are in our faces in no time. We're an entanglement of arms and legs and paws and tails and slobbery dog tongues.

"Ugh! Okay, okay!" Rish cries out, pushing Prince off of her while I lift Poppy off of me and plop her to the side.

When I twist back to face Rish, she's turned to me, and we're right in each other's faces. My breath catches.

I always thought my first real kiss would be with her. She and I had both kissed other people before—when you go through all of high school mostly just seeing each other in the summer, it's likely that there will be a game or two of spin the bottle or some brief, haphazard kisses in the corner of a party at some point. But those weren't real—at least I didn't count them as such. Those were forgotten in no time, didn't send explosions through my chest like I thought kissing Rashida would.

I've always loved the scene in the movie adaptation of *Fried Green Tomatoes* where Idgie and Ruth are in the kitchen and they start throwing flour at each other. I remember wishing they would just kiss already, but they never do. Their whole relationship is hinted at, but there's never a kiss. There's no doubting how much they love each other, though.

The potential between me and Rashida had felt so real to me, too—like it was clear Rashida and I were both on the same page, in the same moment, wanting the same thing. And it was just a matter of time. But like Idgie and Ruth, we spent our summers wading through hints and possibilities.

And then when I finally did take the plunge last summer—that potential burst into oblivion. We'd never been on the same page or wanted the same thing, apparently. I'd made everything up in my ridiculous brain like some cheesy summer romance novel—only someone tore out the final pages where the lovers finally got together. The hints and possibilities were red herrings, meant to throw me off and then shock the hell out of me when—plot twist—Rashida just wanted to be friends. No miraculous kiss, no triumphant declaration to the rest of Spruce Lake who would surely be ecstatic to see us finally get together. No enduring romance like my parents.

But. The way she's looking at me now, so intently. There can be no doubt she feels the same way I do, can there?

"Rish . . ." I start to say, but then we hear a loud hacking noise, and both of us turn our heads to see Prince doing that gross thing dogs do when they've eaten something they shouldn't have and are trying to cough it up, his jaw wide open and aimed at the ground.

We both scramble onto our feet and run over. Rashida gets right to the ground again, on her knees, and grabs Prince's snout then jams her fingers in to swipe around in his throat. Prince is struggling against Rish's hands, so I stabilize his hindquarters between my knees and hold his shoulders as steady as I can.

Finally, after several seconds that feel like forever, Rashida's fingers pull out a plastic wrapper that some jackass left behind out here.

Her hand is covered in dog slobber. Prince sniffs at the wrapper, sneezes violently, then gives a full body shake.

Rashida holds the disgusting wrapper between her thumb and pointer, her face twisted into anger. "What the actual fuck! How hard is it to throw your trash in a trash bin! What the hell is wrong with people?"

I'm pissed, too, because Prince is my favorite dog in the whole world and Diamond would be devastated if anything happened to him.

But my heart also sits heavy in my chest because that moment from before between me and Rashida was headed right where I wanted it to go, and I can tell from the energy emanating from her now, the moment is gone. At least until I can get it back.

But I also realize that if I want another moment like that with her, I need to end my fake-dating scheme with Gabe, and even though that's technically a good thing, the task feels like added weight in each footstep back down the mountain.

THIRTY-SIX

Gabe

My goal over the past couple of days has been to be as useful to SLEA as possible. Keep myself busy and out of trouble. Avoid any dangerous situations with nice girls who are in love with other people.

I've been back to the high school, continuing to sort and label. Jan came by with a bunch of plants she said she got from "her associates." She put me in charge of creating a garden section, saying, "Yer in charge of making all these green things look nice and stay alive. If any one of 'em is dead before Saturday, my associates are comin' for ya."

So that was terrifying, and I had my work cut out for me with trying to figure out how to keep "green things" alive, but I didn't mind. I kind of liked having this one thing to look after. And the crew sorting for the sale actually seemed to appreciate my help.

I didn't even mind that I saw Maya and Rashida walking into some park this morning, looking all outdoorsy and like they were headed on the hike that Maya had invited me on. Easily replaceable, I guess.

It's fine. Our next agreed-upon "date" isn't until Tuesday, anyway. Contributing to SLEA is my life now, I've decided. Besides, I don't want to have those feelings I had with Maya if she's still pining after Rashida. Or if they're actually getting together or whatever. That was the whole plan, right? The goal? And it seems to be working.

Could be a rare success for you, Gabe, I tell myself.

So when I make my way over to Maya's cabin on Sunday for a SLEA meeting, trailing after Jan, who's making sure I don't get lost but also marches at a speed that makes me trot to keep up with her, I prepare myself mentally to focus on SLEA, keep a careful layer of "casual" between me and Maya, and be as pleasant to Rashida as I can. I am an environmental machine now, I tell myself. At least when things with Maya and me end, I'll still have that to prove to my mom that she can be proud of me.

Jan walks me down around Maya's cabin and out onto her dock where a few SLEA members are lounging and enjoying a charcuterie board under a large canopy. It's five o'clock, so the sun is directly across from us and lighting up this side of the lake in a wash of gold. I have to admit, the fact that food and socializing seems to be an integral part of SLEA meetings makes it a lot easier to like SLEA meetings.

Jack and Hesara, Rashida, Canva, Jocelyn and Casey, Davie,

and that girl Shannon who talked about her cats nonstop at karaoke are here, plus Jan and me, of course.

And Maya.

I momentarily lose focus on any goals I had when I see her. She's not wearing anything special—just a loose gray tank top and red running shorts, her hair in a ponytail. But my stupid heart picks up its pace nonetheless.

Focus.

She gives me a little wave and a smile, but doesn't get up for a hug or anything, and I wave hello to everyone, then take a seat very intentionally between Jan and Davie, even though Davie continues to try out his goofy brand of flirting with me. He seems harmless, though—hasn't let his eyes roam lower than my chin, even though I'm wearing my red bikini top underneath a sheer white tank.

The meeting gets started, and I mostly listen, ask a couple of clarifying questions when I need to, and offer to take notes on my phone so I have something to do.

Like the last meeting, Rashida presides over this one. I smile and nod at everything she says and keep my smartass comments to myself. I notice she gives me a couple of confused glances, but that's fine. I'll just win her over with my dedication to SLEA. Because I'm here to be useful.

"What time did you want us there next Saturday?" Casey asks, directing her question to Rashida, of course.

"We'll open to the public at nine, so if everyone could get there by eight o'clock, that'd be great."

Eesh. Eight o'clock on a Saturday. Fun. But I plan on being there the whole damn day and ask, "And what about at the end? Do you need help with any leftover stuff? Where's it going?"

Rashida stares at me for a second, her eyebrows lifted, but then says, "Oh, we're just going to leave any remaining items in the gym and take it to thrift stores over the next few days." After a moment, she adds, "But thanks for asking, Gabe."

"No problem!" I say, injecting supreme cheer into my voice. "Happy to help wherever I can."

"You've already been such a big help, Gabe," Canva says, smiling at me, and I'll admit, the words and the smile infuse me with genuine appreciation.

The meeting moves on to things like who's doing what jobs at the garage sale, last-minute advertising blasts, and such. I sign up to wander the sale, chatting people up and encouraging them to buy stuff, because I know I'll kick ass at this.

The conversation then moves on to the protest in a couple of weeks at the Lux worksite. The idea is to cause some publicity that will delay Lux's resort project. I lean over to add more cheese and crackers to my plate, listening carefully.

"What are our numbers, you think?" Hesara asks. She and Jack have literally been holding hands the entire time—even when one of them leans forward to grab food. It's ridiculous. I can see why Maya's become so convinced love is grand and all that, even if her parents are an exception, as far as I'm concerned.

I glance at Maya now, though I've mostly been trying to keep my eyes trained anywhere but at her. She's sitting next to Rashida and listening intently to everything coming out of Rashida's mouth. I swallow back the lump that rises in my throat at this.

"I think our numbers are great," Rashida says. "Like, in the hundreds. That's the word I'm getting from my contacts, anyway," she adds, like a boss. I can't blame Maya for hanging on her every word, I guess.

"Awesome," Canva says. "What's our plan if Lux calls the cops?"

"They'd do that?" I can't help but ask.

Jan scoffs, but not unkindly. "They sure as hell would, Gabe. Won't even think twice about it. Cops are the answer to everything with some of these companies."

"Who here's been arrested?" Jack asks, half smiling. He raises his hand (not the one holding Hesara's, heaven forbid).

Hesara raises her hand. So do Jan and Casey.

"And Diamond, too, right?" Rashida asks.

"Yep," Jan says. "Kinda comes with the territory when ya put yer body on the line." She pops a grape into her mouth like this is just everyday talk.

I sit back. "Holy" is all I say.

"What do we do this time? If the cops come?" Shannon asks.

"I think it's going to be very difficult for them to arrest a bunch of people in bathing suits," Jack says with a smile, "which is part of the point of the bathing suits, but we'll stick with our usual methods: always have a buddy, mask up if you don't want to be in any photos or anything, and we'll hand out our regular info in case anyone does get arrested."

"What kind of info?" I ask.

"We've got some great lawyers on standby—so their phone numbers are on there—plus some legal info people should be aware of in case of arrest."

Holy shit. These people aren't messing around.

"Jan, are you and your defenders around for this one?" Rashida asks.

Defenders? Is this a Marvel movie?

"We're thinking about it," she says, all sketchy, and now I'm legitimately wondering if she's in a gang or something. I tuck that bit of info away to ask her about later.

Eventually, the conversation veers into non-SLEA topics. Canva, Shannon, Jocelyn, and Casey leave, and Jack asks if anyone wants anything. When he and Hesara go up to the cabin to get more drinks, it leaves me, Maya, Rashida, Davie, and Jan on the dock.

The tone definitely shifts to something between confusing and tense, or maybe that's just how I feel.

Jan eyes up the four of us and then stands, leaning back to stretch and swinging her arms around a few times. "Well? Who's up for a swim? You all look like you could use some cold water."

"I'm in!" Davie says, and Rashida follows with, "Me too."

The three of them and the dogs are in the water in no time, racing to God knows where, which leaves me and Maya standing on the dock, watching them.

I can feel her looking at me, but for some reason, I can't look back.

"So . . ." she begins.

"Yeah?" I say, still staring out at the lake.

"I think our plan worked."

Fuck this goddamn pinch in my chest.

"Oh yeah?" I say, as clearly and cheerily as possible. I finally look at her, and she's chewing at her bottom lip.

"Yeah. I mean, it feels that way—with Rashida."

Don't be weird about this, Gabe. "That's great, Maya. My mom's pretty stoked about me helping with SLEA, too. I don't think it'll even matter if we're not dating anymore."

"Oh—well, that's perfect, then."

"Yeah."

"Um . . . what should we tell everyone?"

I shrug. "What do you want to tell them? This is mostly your thing, right?"

She nods and her eyes fall to my lips for a moment. Contemplating my words, I guess.

"Maybe we can just say we decided to be friends? I mean—I'd like that anyway. To still hang out. If you want to, I mean."

I shrug again, because I'm all about nonchalance right now. "Yeah. Sure. Sounds good. I might let you break it to the group, though, okay? I'm actually gonna head out. All this volunteering's got me wiped, you know?"

"Oh, okay. But I'll see you sometime this week maybe?"

"Yeah . . . or maybe just at the garage sale next weekend. You should probably focus on Rashida, don't you think?"

She nods again, but this time looks out to where Rashida is cutting through the water like a goddamn Olympic swimmer. "Yeah. Right."

I turn to go. "Okay, see ya then."

"Hey, Gabe?"

I keep moving, but turn my head to say, "Mmm?"

"This has been . . . fun. Thank you."

I give her a sideways peace sign because I don't know if I can trust my voice anymore.

That's me. Super fucking fun. And maybe that's exactly who I'm meant to be.

THIRTY-SEVEN

Maya

"Your change, ma'am," I say to Jan, giving her a small smile.

"Don't you frickin' 'ma'am' me, buster," she grumbles, and takes the lidless Tupperware containers she just bought away with her. Lord knows what she's going to do with them, but she's the resourceful type. They'll probably turn into homemade birdbaths for her front yard or something.

The garage sale is in full swing. Out in the school's parking lot, Buddy and Dennis are barbecuing hot dogs and selling cookies, muffins, and lemonade. People are moving in and out of the gym, between the tables holding kitchenware, clothing, books, sports stuff, and more.

I'm in charge of one of the money tins, Rish is in charge of the other at the opposite end of the gym. She and I have hung out a lot this week, mostly preparing for this garage sale, but it's still been nice—like old times. No almost kisses like on Baldy Mountain yet, but I'm trying to be patient. I don't want to be seen jumping into something with Rish right after "breaking up" with Gabe, anyway.

Once Gabe and I ended our arrangement on the dock last week, I started telling people—including Rashida—that Gabe and I decided to be friends and that I'm completely okay about that. Which I mostly am, I think, although I've definitely felt her absence this week. Most people seem to believe me—maybe because I'm not pining over Rashida like I was at the beginning of the summer. I guess I feel less desperate than I did two weeks ago.

Rashida's response when I told her was . . . a little confusing. It was almost like she expected it. Maybe because she didn't really see Gabe and me fitting together anyway. But the hug she gave me after felt like both relief and something else—something more like comfort or coming home. It made me think I did the right thing by ending things with Gabe.

Anyway, today Gabe's floating around, randomly pointing things out to people as though she's just another customer. *Oh! Look at that cute top. Man, these books are in great condition.* It was her own sneaky plan, apparently, and it's working. And from here, she seems like the same gregarious Gabe. She must be fine with our arrangement ending, too.

"How's sales?" my dad asks now, popping up beside me. He and my mom are in charge of reorganizing merchandise when it gets too messy. The people who come to these garage sales don't play. It's been chaos since we opened, and the need to tidy up after rampaging customers is continuous.

"Great," I say, indicating the coins and bills filling up my money box.

"Most excellent, my daughter," he says, kissing me on top of my head.

He's such a dork. But to their credit, neither he nor my mom have asked about Gabe or Rashida, thankfully.

Diamond *did* mention this morning—not so casually, might I add—that Gabe sat at a table by herself last night at the pub, eating dinner and reading a book. I assume the book was *Fried Green Tomatoes*, although maybe she found something else to read by now.

The thought of Gabe sitting alone at the pub reading is both sweet and sad. Maybe she wanted to sit there by herself, but it's hard to believe that. She hasn't reached out to spend time together either, though.

A burst of laughter comes from the clothing racks, and I see Gabe throwing a scarf around Blu, who's already wearing an enormous sun hat. Blu starts strutting around, and Gabe turns up the music. She herself is wearing a long hippie skirt that I swear was my mom's and a headband with cat ears.

"What's happening down there?" Dad asks.

"Looks like some big city energy taking over," I say, and can't help smiling at the sight.

I ask Dad to look after the money box for me for a minute, and I head over to the makeshift fashion show that seems to have sprung up.

As soon as she sees me, Gabe's lightheartedness seems to falter, and I think I've made a mistake in coming over. But her face shifts into a grin and she focuses her attention back on Blu, whose hand she takes in hers. They start to catwalk together, much to the delight of the people milling around.

Gabe starts going up to people, full of flirtation and persuasion.

Placing a hand on Judith Garner's shoulder, she asks, "You want vintage at fair prices? Have I got a deal for you!" She swings her hips this way and that and says to a bewildered and amused tourist, "This gorgeous hippie skirt? Five dollars regular, but for you . . . two bucks!"

After a few minutes of Gabe and Blu's antics, Rashida's got a line in front of her seven or eight people deep. She's having a hard time keeping up, so I make my way over.

"Need help?"

She looks up, blinks at me once, and nods. "Yes. Please."

Within about twenty minutes of Gabe and Blu strutting the "runway" and accosting strangers and locals alike, we've sold over a hundred dollars' worth of clothing.

"Nice work, Gabe!" Rish says.

Gabe glances at us, shrugs, and takes the headband off. "Just doing what I can to help," she replies, her energy from the past several minutes suddenly muted. I don't have time to figure out what's up, though, because my dad calls me back to take over the other collection table, and the rest of the sale is as busy and chaotic as ever.

By the end of the day, we've made over twenty-three hundred

dollars, which will help pay the food costs for the protest, plus some transportation expenses to get people to and from the construction site. It's not a ton of money, given how much work it was to organize this sale and how much the costs associated with these protests can be, but the SLEA crew seems pleased.

Immediately after we've wrapped up the garage sale, my parents zip home, grab their camping stuff, and then head off for a night to their favorite romantic spot about an hour away. They do this—just take off spontaneously for adventures. Sometimes I'm invited, sometimes not.

Tonight, I'm not, which is fine with me, because hanging out with my mushy parents isn't my top priority right now. My priority is spending more time with Rashida.

Davie invites a bunch of us (the younger SLEA members) over to his and his brother Sean's place for a party that night. Their parents have been away all month, and they have people over all the time, but I'm not sure I feel like going to a party after such a long day.

As a few of us are organizing some things before we leave—the last hour of the sale we cut prices in half and it was a total zoo—Davie pleads, "Come on, team. We deserve to celebrate, don't we?"

"Yeah, we've got beer and snacks," Sean adds. "All you have to do is bring yourselves." He sidles up to Rashida where she's collecting displaced shoes into one area and flings an arm over her shoulder. "Rashida, babe, I'll even make you one of my five-star s'mores." He wiggles his eyebrows at her. We've known him and Davie our whole lives, so this is less creepy and just the usual annoying.

She rolls her eyes, but to my surprise (because she's not the biggest party person), she says, "Fine. But I can make my own s'mores, and they're better than yours, anyway."

"Ouch," Sean says, but he's grinning.

"Gabe?" Davie says. "You've gotta come. You haven't experienced Spruce Lake until you've been to one of our parties." He's grinning, too, and it's clear he has a thing for Gabe—and, I mean, who can blame him? But a pang of jealousy flashes in my chest, which just mixes in with the other feelings I can't quite get ahold of.

Gabe's untangling a snarl of extension cords and smirks back at him. I wait for her to say something sassy or sharp in return, but she just replies, "For sure. I could use a beer."

Davie lights up, and my stomach dips.

"Two for two! Maya? Casey? Joss?" Sean turns to us. Then everyone turns to us, where we're shoving leftover clothes into garbage bags.

Jocelyn and Casey are both enthusiastic yeses, and now I feel the pressure to say yes, too, even though I'm still not sure I'm up for a party. But because I know I'll have FOMO if both Rish and Gabe are at Davie and Sean's without me, I say, "Sure."

THIRTY-EIGHT

Gabe

"Well, hello, hello, Big City," Davie calls out as I roll into his place, liquid provisions in my arms. Once I knew both Rashida and Maya were going to be at this party, there was no way I was doing the night sober. Sorry, not sorry. I just want to chill and have a good time tonight. I deserve it after the week I've had. I don't think I've ever worked so hard in my life. And for free, for shit's sake. Not to mention the other stuff this week—the back-and-forth between hollowness and heaviness in my chest, refusing to get the hell out.

"Hey, Small Town," I say. "I brought stuff to share." I indicate the paper bag I'm holding. The selection at the gas station / bookstore / café / sushi joint was better than I thought it would be, and in the bag, I have gin, tonic, limes, peach cider, and a bottle of rosé, 'cause I'm a classy bitch.

"Sweet, thanks," he says. "You can put it over there with the beer."

I grab the bottle of wine—who needs a glass?—and set the rest down next to a cooler full of canned beer and ice.

"Where're your pals?" he asks.

I guess he means Rashida and Maya. Because as far as everyone else knows, Maya and I are pals now, and everything's just dandy.

"Who knows?" is all I say, not wanting to get into it. I had to focus on my feet as I walked past Maya's cabin to get to Davie and Sean's tonight—to avoid peering into her windows like a creep.

After the garage sale, once I'd returned to Canva's for a shower and nap, my brain started racing. I'd successfully distracted myself all day with fashion shows and cheesy sales pitches and screwing around with Blu, but the quiet of my room at Canva's settled around me like oppressive heat, and my thoughts filled the space. Napping didn't work, so I dressed (looking mighty fine in a burgundy *Flashdance*-style T-shirt and black jean shorts, my hair down and wild like she wants to be), walked to the store, and then made my way over here.

"I hear there's a pool table," I say now. I heard this from Davie himself, when he was trying literally all day to convince me to come to this party.

Davie's eyes light up. I've been giving off "friend zone" signals to kibosh any funny ideas he has now that Maya and I have "broken up," and he seems to have gotten the hint, but he's still a bit puppy doggish around me. He's actually a sweet guy—and maybe in another time and place I'd give it a go, but just the thought feels impossible to me right now, and I don't want to think too hard on why that is.

"There *is* a pool table, in fact," Davie replies. "Want me to teach you how to play?" He grins.

I roll my eyes. "LOL. Let's go. I'll be nice." Davie laughs and heads out of the kitchen, and I follow him. As we make our way through the party, I recognize quite a few people—Casey, Jocelyn, and a bunch of others from SLEA and around town who smile and wave at me. A few people even lean in for hugs, 'cause they're drunk or maybe just small-town friendly.

Davie leads me down some stairs. "So which are your favorite hot spots in Spruce Lake so far?"

"Hot spots?"

"Yeah, Maya was showing you around, right?"

Oh. That. I play it chill, saying the first thing that comes to mind, rather than thinking too hard about my favorite parts. "Tubing was cool," I say, my voice coming out more monotone than enthused. But despite my efforts, the voice in my head still needles me. *Holding hands. Jumping together. Forest hugs. Comfort.*

We enter the basement, which has a pool table, air hockey, and a small bar. Glass doors lead to a deck that holds a hot tub. Pretty sweet setup. I should've just been hanging out with Davie and his bro all summer. Would've been a lot simpler.

"I guess Maya didn't take you to Sun Island, did she?"

"What's that?" I ask after he tells the guys playing pool to hurry up and finish.

"It's the teeny-tiny island across from us. Maya and Rashida are way too protective of it. Like, they used to throw rocks at me and Sean when we were younger if we tried to join them. It was their special place or whatever."

Cool. Love that for them. "They're pretty tight, huh?" I ask, even though I already know the answer. Maybe I want confirmation or something.

We're standing by the pool table, chosen pool cues propped up in front of us in our hands. He shrugs. "Yeah. 'Thick as thieves,' as old people might say. I'm glad Maya's been chilling with you, though."

This surprises me—not just because Davie has had a clear crush on me, but also because everyone seems to love the shit out of Rashida here. "Why's that?"

He shrugs again and leans his chin against the pool cue tip, which is definitely going to leave a green powdery spot on his skin. "Maya was pretty gutted last summer. I heard she did this whole thing where she borrowed Jan's ice cream paddleboat from the shop, decorated it with lights and stuff, and then showed up at Rashida's to finally tell her how she felt. You probably know this already, though. It didn't go well."

I didn't know the details, but that tracks. Maya seems like the grand-romantic-gesture type. "Huh. That's rough" is all I say.

"Yeah. But, like, in some ways, I'm glad it finally happened, you know?"

"Glad what happened?"

"They finally cleared up whatever's actually going on between them so they can move on. There's been way too much buildup."

I don't know how "cleared up" things are between them, judging from Maya's whole plan to get Rashida back this summer and the fact that she thinks things are going her way now, but I'm not about to stick a wrench in Davie's theories. In fact, I'm done with this conversation.

I call to the guys still playing pool, "Hey, my dudes—what's taking so long?" I give them a friendly smirk, though.

They eye me up—predictably, from top to bottom—and one guy responds, "Check this out." He grins and then tries to sink the four, but misses.

Everyone laughs. "Wow, impressive," I say, but I keep it light. I'm not out to destroy any egos tonight.

Finally, the game ends and Davie and I rack up. I try to lose myself in sharp hits and the thunk of the balls in their pockets, rather than thoughts of private islands for two where I'd never be invited.

THIRTY-NINE

Maya

When I walk into the cabin next door, Sean's in the kitchen. "Hey, a-hole. Why're you playing such trash music?" I say, summoning up as much lightheartedness as I can, even though a big part of me would rather be at home watching Netflix on the covered patio.

Sean nestles into my side like a cat—his "signature move" he calls it, which explains why he's single. "Hey, kid," he says, even though we're the same age. "Glad you finally made it over." He's grinning and already tipsy, but his expression is genuine and warms me a little.

"Beer and some other stuff are over there," he adds. "Want anything?"

"I'm okay for now, thanks." I might have a drink at some point—to help loosen me up, but I'd prefer to have my wits about me. It's a fine balance between liquid courage and liquid chaos, after all.

"Cool," Sean says. "Wanna head to the basement? I think Gabe is thrashing my brother at pool." He grins, because Gabe and I are just friends now and everything's totally chill and normal and great. And maybe that's the truth. It's hard to tell since we've barely seen each other this week.

In any case, I need a minute before diving into whatever's going on downstairs. "I think I'll just hang out here for a bit, as much as I'd love to see her annihilate Davie." I smile.

"Sounds good. I'm gonna get down there—don't wanna miss this."

"Sure."

When he's gone, I grab a glass and some water from the tap, just to have something in my hands. I stare at the refrigerator door and read through the magnet tile poetry either Davie or Sean has created. It's bad, but amusing. I start creating my own poem.

I get lost in my literary musings when I hear, "'Terror is a nightingale feasting on my toes?' Wow, Maya. Do you need to talk?"

I guess I was so engrossed in my poem, I didn't notice Rashida walk in and stand beside me. She's wearing one of my favorite T-shirts of hers—the one that says "I'm with her" and has a picture of the planet on it—and baggy black pants. Her braids are up in a bun, her hands in her pockets.

"Oh hey," I say, trying to read her face. Lifted eyebrows, steady eyes.

"What's with the angsty poetry?" she asks.

I look at the poem. I try for some humor. "This isn't angsty. This is genius."

"Sure it is." She rolls her eyes.

For the next several seconds, we stare at the fridge, but I can feel the same uncertainty I felt on our hike—that need to figure things out with her, one way or the other. I take the plunge, because this tension between me and her is excruciating. "I—need to talk to you," I say, still staring at the fridge.

"Okay . . ."

I glance sideways at her, and she's staring at the fridge, too, frowning. Four guys invade the kitchen, all deep voices and rowdy laughter. My resolve weakens. *This is not the time or the place, Maya.* "Maybe not this minute, but—"

I hear her sigh with what sounds like relief. "Yeah. Let's just try and have a good time tonight."

"Right. Yeah," I say, mad at myself for wimping out, but determined to talk to her by the end of the night.

"Okay, so what're we drinking?" she asks.

"You want to drink tonight?" Rashida drinks even less than I do.

"Why not? Just a little?"

One drink won't hurt. "Okay. Sean said that stuff is for the taking." I point to the cooler full of ice on the floor.

She rummages through the beer, decides none of it is to her liking, and then peeks in a couple of the paper bags. "This one has peach cider."

She looks at me, and we both make an "uh-oh" face and start

to laugh. Peach cider has not been our friend in the past. The first time we got drunk together was on a two-liter bottle that Sean bought off a friend for us. We were thirteen and that stuff tastes like candy, so we just kept drinking the whole thing. It was bad. Like, double-vomit bad.

Neither of us will be touching the stuff tonight, but the memory makes me nostalgic for those ridiculous times with her.

"Gin?" she says.

"Is there anything to mix it with?"

"Yeah—tonic and limes?"

"Yum—that's the one."

As she makes two gin and tonics on the lighter side, she asks, "Is Gabe here yet?"

I try to read her tone, which I've always been good at, but I can't tell now if she's just curious or if there's any uncertainty or jealousy in her voice or what.

I try to keep my own tone light as I say, "I think she's kicking Davie's ass in pool."

Rashida's eyes narrow. "Oh, this I want to see."

"Really?"

"Yeah. Don't you? I'll always watch Davie get his ass kicked." She grins and heads for the stairs. I take a sip of my drink and just focus on following her.

When we get to the basement, it looks like most of the party is down here. My eyes find the pool table, and I notice three things: One, Gabe looks gorgeous as ever and is gulping from a bottle of rosé. Two, she's the only girl at the table and is getting a lot of attention from the four other guys besides Davie and Sean who are standing around. And three, when she sees me and Rashida, she immediately looks away, hands her wine bottle to one of the guys, and nails a shot, which causes a jeering "OHHH!" from the guys toward Davie, who, I gather, is indeed getting his ass kicked.

Gabe places a hand on Davie's shoulder and gives him a little shake. "Sorry, pal—looks like you're about to go down hard," Gabe says, grinning and eliciting another boisterous reaction from her audience.

Even with my nerves and uncertainty, it's hard not to love Gabe's energy right now. Maybe it's just the alcohol, but she seems to be in her element.

Davie rolls his eyes. He's a good sport, though, I'll give him that.

Gabe leans over the table and nails the eight ball into a corner pocket. She's quick and precise and barely looks like she's trying. It's actually very impressive. And hot, if I'm being honest.

Gabe drops the pool cue on the table like a mic drop and raises her arms in victory. "And that's how it's done, bitches." She grabs her wine away from the guy and takes a gulp, then holds it out to me and Rashida. "Cheers, queers."

It's the same bravado from before—before rock jumping and scary "bears" in the woods—and part of me is glad to see her cheekiness back, but I also find myself missing the quieter moments with her, too. My hand in hers. The way she looked at me before we jumped into the water together . . .

Get ahold of yourself, Maya. I take a breath as Rish just shrugs.

"Cheers to that," she says, and clicks her reusable mug against Gabe's bottle. I follow suit, and we all take a swig of our drinks, none of us making eye contact.

"Please tell me one of you is better at pool than this guy," Gabe says, indicating Davie, who folds his arms in mock indignation, but then grins and bows like he's done something impressive and wanders away.

"I'm terrible at pool," I say quickly, which is true. But I also need a moment to gather myself and sort these unwanted tangles in my chest. Playing pool against Gabe right now wouldn't help with that at all.

I'm both surprised and a little relieved when Rashida says, "I'll play. But it's been a hot minute, just FYI."

FORTY

Gabe

"I feel like you're the kind of person who's good at everything," I say to Rashida, because, honestly, I'm tired of all my overthinking and overfeeling, and all I wanted to do coming to this party is drink, play pool, and have a good time. So I add a wink now and hope it works some charm on her, because we're gonna keep this game of pool light and breezy. Everyone's gonna see that I am just fine about all of this. Maya and Rashida are closer than I've ever been with anyone, including my own moms. It was stupid of me to think I could get anywhere in the middle of that, so I'm just staying the hell out of it.

My charm must work on Rashida, because she smiles and grabs a cue. To my surprise, she downs the rest of her cup and asks Maya if she can get her a soda. Maya looks relieved to have something else to do. Maybe she wishes it was just her and Rashida hanging out. Maybe she's just kind of done hanging out with me.

I refocus on racking up the balls, and Rashida and I settle into a pretty even game. Most of the guys have wandered off, probably realizing that I'm not interested in them and that Rashida and Maya probably aren't either, since it sounds like they've both been gay and out for a while.

I'm really good at pool—better than Rashida is, for sure. But I go a little easy on her, hoping it will continue to keep things chill and show both her and Maya everything is great.

After a couple of minutes, Rashida asks, "So, like, your mom just sent you here for the whole summer alone?"

I line up my shot. "Yeah, we have some trust issues. Meaning . . . she doesn't trust me at all."

She watches me take the shot. I sink the six.

"You two aren't close, then?" she asks.

I scoff before I can stop myself and then hit the next ball way too hard.

Rashida says, "Sorry, you don't have to answer that."

Get over yourself, Gabe. "Nah, it's fine. We're not super close," I say. *But I'm working on that.*

"Me neither," Rashida says, missing the three.

"You're not?" I ask her as I plan out my next shot. I realize I haven't actually seen Rashida's parents while I've been here, unlike Maya's parents, who seem to be everywhere with all their smooshy business. Then I remember Maya mentioning something about Rashida's dad.

She shrugs. "No. My mom moves around overseas, and my dad is kind of a famous artist, so he's super busy with that."

"That sucks, dude. Sorry." I know this sucks, because it's super familiar. "One of my moms is probably climbing some mountain in Peru right now—haven't seen or heard from her in a couple of months—and my other mother is super busy with her job, too."

"Oh. So we basically have the same parents," she says, "except yours are lesbians?" There's a small smile on her face, and both the comment and smile make me laugh.

"Ha. Yeah. Guess even lesbians can be shitty parents." I scan the table. If I keep hitting balls like this, I'm going to end the game in no time, but I kind of want to continue this conversation. Maybe it's the booze working its way into my system and making me sentimental or something. Or maybe it's because winning can look a lot of different ways, and not being the only one with shitty parents feels like a win right now.

I miss the next shot on purpose.

"Your dad's super famous, you said?" I ask as Rashida checks out her shot options.

"Yeah. His work is basically the poster child for green campaigns around here."

"Oh. But you're into nature and stuff, too, right? You have that in common at least?"

Her face turns steely, and I think I've made a mistake, but then she hits her ball hard, sinks it, straightens up, and says, "Yeah. Except he thinks my form of activism is too brash and dangerous—'unnecessarily reckless,' in his words."

"Huh." My brain's a little fuzzy from the wine I've had. I'm trying to get my head around what she's saying. "So he thinks bathing suit protests are too harsh? I don't get it."

She sighs. "It's not the bathing suit part so much as the getting in the way of bulldozers and the risk of being arrested and the news stories. He just doesn't get why I need to be so 'political.' It's total bullshit, but it's fine. I do my thing, he does his."

"It really doesn't bug you?" Something in her expression feels familiar. Forced indifference.

"I mean, would I prefer a dad who totally got me? Yeah. But whose parents really get them?"

I think of Maya's parents, who seem pretty damn great. But then, she also said they didn't get her heartbreak over Rashida. This just reminds me of Maya's feelings for Rashida, which makes me take another gulp of wine.

Instead of replying to her question, I miss another shot, and we just trade a few more missed shots back and forth.

Finally, my curiosity gets the better of me, despite my goal of keeping things light and breezy. "Do you keep in touch with your mom at all?" I'm thinking about Meems, of course, and if I'll ever hear from her or if I screwed that piece up forever. Unfortunately, Rashida's answer doesn't exactly inspire confidence.

"Nope" is all she offers. Then, maybe realizing what I was thinking about, she adds, "But that's kind of a special case. Like, she and my dad fought for as long as I could remember anything. She just wasn't happy with him. I guess her need to get away from him overpowered her need to be my mom." She gives me a tight smile.

I feel for her. But I also remember a time when my moms didn't fight all that much—before I became a total pain in their ass. It sounds like Rashida's mom wasn't trying to get away from her the way mine is trying to get away from me. At least she can't blame herself.

I feel a sting in my eyes and will it away with the help of some more wine.

"That still sucks, though," I manage to say, because it does. AWOL moms are AWOL moms.

She just shrugs and hits a ball that misses its mark.

I assess the pool table. I see at least three shots I can make, easy. I aim for a much harder shot and miss.

"Well, maybe we should trade parents. My mother would love your commitment and drive," I say. "And my other mom could take you camping or whatever."

"Great. And you would . . . help my dad . . . paint?"

We both look at each other for a moment and then crack up.

"Right. That wouldn't work. Guess there's no easy solution for disappointing your parents," I say.

We half smile at each other in that way that acknowledges the funny, sad truth.

Maya arrives with refilled cups and eyes us up, uncertain. "Who's winning?" she asks, and this could be a question about so many things.

"So far, things are pretty even," I offer.

"Except I'm pretty sure she's letting me keep up," Rashida says, narrowing her eyes at me.

Maya still looks unsure of this combination of Rashida, me, and camaraderie, but smiles anyway. She looks hella cute in her overalls and crop top, a small section of her torso visible at the sides. When I catch myself checking her out, I tuck some of my chaotic hair behind my ear and direct my eyes to the pool table instead.

Sean appears with a bag of marshmallows in one hand and says, "Still playing? Hurry up—it's s'mores time!"

Rashida looks at me. "You heard the boy. Quit missing shots and finish this already." She cocks an eyebrow.

I smirk. I sink four balls and finish with a cheesy behind-the-back shot to end the game. Rashida rolls her eyes, but a smile hints on her lips. "Whatever. Next competition is swimming. Let's see what happens."

"Not a goddamn chance," I say, grinning and determined to bring back Good Time Gabe.

FORTY-ONE

Maya

After the pool game, the three of us spend some time out by the bonfire while Sean acts a fool, trying to entertain any girl who might be interested, Davie plays songs on his guitar as various drunk people try to sing the words, and people make s'mores with varying degrees of success.

Rashida and I end up sitting on a log bench, our legs pressed up against each other's, her arms bumping into mine as she lays out everything she has to do between now and the protest next week. She doesn't drink that often and her expressions and gestures are extra animated. This is what I want, of course. Me and Rashida around a bonfire, the lake close by as we share our plans to keep the trees in Tipper Park standing, to make sure this water we love so much stays clean and full of all its living, swimming things.

But my eyes keep flicking to Gabe, who's been alternating

between singing along with Davie and doing silly dares with some of the other guys. She's pure chaos for a while, but then she starts singing some country song I'm not familiar with, but that's leisurely and low, and her body seems to settle a little.

I'm nodding at what Rashida is saying, but I can't take my eyes off Gabe. She's got about half a bottle of wine in her, but her voice comes out clear and easy—not like her unruly karaoke performance at all, but somehow just as magnetic.

She's leaning over her lap, sitting on a lawn chair, singing straight into the fire. But maybe she senses me staring—and now I'm definitely staring—because her eyes shift to me and instead of looking away like she seems to have been doing all day, her eyes stay on mine. And somehow I manage to keep mine on hers, as well, even though my brain is telling me I'm just confusing everything.

Whatever this moment is, it's broken in the next instant when I hear "Aren't you two cute?" from behind me and Rish, and we turn to find Sean's face *right there*, and we can't even be mad at him because he giggles like a little kid, which makes us laugh and the tension release is a relief.

"Last one in is a burnt-ass marshmallow!" we hear next, and Sean is suddenly whipping off his shirt and running down to his and Davie's dock. Davie stops strumming on his guitar immediately, lays it down, and runs after his brother, not to be outdone—and also to keep an eye on his tipsy sibling.

Rashida and I look at each other. Rashida shrugs. I shrug back. We both stand and start picking our way through the crowd to the dock, but something doesn't feel quite right, and I turn back to see Gabe still staring into the fire, her song ended prematurely.

"Give me a sec?" I say to Rashida, who throws me a thumbs-up and tries to catch up to Davie and Sean.

I approach Gabe tentatively. Her body language is so different from earlier—the swagger and sass turned to quiet and maybe even a little calm. I don't want to interrupt her, but I also can't imagine getting into the water right now without her, which just stirs more confusion in my chest.

"Hey?" I say, coming up beside her chair.

She looks up, her eyes shiny from the firelight. A split second of something like relief flashes across her face before it's replaced with a cocked eyebrow. "'Sup?" she says, complete with a little nod.

We don't know each other as well as Rashida and I know each other, but I know this energy from her, and it's pure bullshit. "Come swimming?" I say, pushing past my insecurities and her dismissiveness.

She glances behind her at the lake and frowns. "You want me to jump into frigid water at night?"

The sass in her voice is familiar and somehow comforting. I send some back her way. "Frigid? Really? Is it winter? Are we at the North Pole?"

She narrows her eyes at me. "I'd rather sit here by the warm fire with my bottle of wine, thanks."

I narrow my eyes back. "No you wouldn't. Come on, Gabe."

"I'm not even wearing a bathing suit, Maya."

"No one is."

She glances behind her again, then back at me. Something besides defiance or nonchalance crosses her face.

"I really want you to," I say, meaning it and realizing just how much I've missed her.

After another beat of that something else, she rolls her eyes and says, "Oh, Christ. Fine. But if the water's cold, I'm coming after you."

I grin, even though she's back to her bravado.

We make our way down to the dock, where a few people are already swimming and where Davie and Sean have just plunged in. Rashida's half undressed, as well.

Gabe is somehow in her bra and boy shorts before I've even removed my shirt, and I'm once again enamored by every curve on her body, even in the dim light given off by the cabin lights and moon.

I catch Rish watching me watching Gabe, and I busy myself with removing the rest of my clothes. Soon, Rish and I are both in the water, unbothered by the cooler night temperatures. Gabe, though, is still standing on the dock in her underwear, staring into the water.

"Gabe! Come on!" I say.

Rish joins in. "Yeah! The water's nice, we promise!"

"It even *looks* fucking cold!" she says, her face an unfamiliar mix of nervous and embarrassed.

This look on her—it reminds me of Salmon Run, and something both nervous and warm flutters in my belly. Gabe's boldness and brashness drew me in from the start, but seeing her a little vulnerable—even if it's just over a short jump or some cold water—just nudges that part of me that makes me want to know her more.

But that part of me is also scary as hell. Because I don't really know her or what she wants. And who I thought *I* wanted is already in this water with me.

So why do I want Gabe in here with me so badly, too?

"Gabe! You jumped at Salmon Run! You can do this!" I shout.

She hesitates a few seconds more, then scrunches her eyes shut, plugs her nose, and jumps in, a haphazard mix of feetfirst and cannonball style. She comes up sputtering, and this is the first time I've seen her in a completely unsexy way besides her fall from Ruth. My heart does a twist at the sight.

"It *is* cold, you assholes!" she shouts at us, but she's laughing. Soon we're all chasing each other and splashing and laughing and yelling and then singing "I Got You Babe" from karaoke at the top of our lungs. Gabe is actually able to keep up with the words this time.

And then all the other people in the water seem to have drifted away, and the three of us are floating on our backs, staring up at the stars. This is one of Rashida's favorite things to do, I know. We're all quiet for a while, except for the odd splash from Gabe, who isn't quite as adept at swimming or floating as we are.

I feel a hand take mine in the water, and turn my head. It's Rish's hand. She's not looking at me, and maybe this is just muscle memory. We've held hands in the water too many nights to count. Maybe she's just enjoying the night and not thinking at all. Maybe it's just our friendship playing out as it always has.

Only—it doesn't feel quite the same. Comfortable and easy, yes, but my chest doesn't pinch the way it always has, over and over. My lips don't tingle with want for her.

I hear a splash from beside me and turn to see Gabe watching. She immediately looks away, up at the sky, but I can see her swallow from here. I reach out and take her hand, too, because I really want to, and when my fingers lace through hers, she still doesn't look at me, but she doesn't let go, either. Her hand is firm around mine, and I love how that feels, even as the knowing it brings fills me with a kind of panic.

Because I realize that ending my fake-dating deal with Gabe was the right thing to do, but not because I needed to be with Rashida. But because I want to be with Gabe for real. I still don't want to "end" anything with Rashida, but I need to change it. And I need to explain to her exactly why and how before I can move on.

FORTY-TWO

Gabe

Fuck. Maya's hand feels way too good in mine, and though every part of my brain is telling me to let go—*She's holding Rashida's hand, too. She's trying to get back with Rashida, Gabe*—my entire body seems tethered to her in this water. We stay like this for a while, and I try to figure out my next move, but all I can think is, *Why does her hand feel so good in mine?*

When we finally get out of the water, I feel the emptiness of my hand immediately and even though my body is vibrating with nerves and my natural impulse is to get the hell out of here, I realize I don't want to leave without at least talking to Maya, even if it means I'm about to embarrass the hell out of myself.

I like her. I know I like her. I don't *want* to like her. But I do. And suddenly every part of me wants her to know it. I guess I just need to hear her say to my face if she doesn't feel the same way.

Instead of struggling back into our clothes while dripping wet, Maya suggests we go back to her cabin to get towels, and honestly, even though Rashida is included in this little scenario, I'm not mad about getting my cooling body inside a warm cabin and drying off.

We slip on our flip-flops in the dim glow of the bonfire and patio lights and make our way through the still-plentiful partygoers to Maya's property. Her parents don't seem to be around, which is kind of a relief—some distance from their perfect little romance is probably a good thing if I want Maya to see me as any kind of viable option. Which is exactly what I want, I'm realizing.

Maya gets us some towels, and we wipe down on the patio, then head inside. My skin is covered in goose bumps, but the cabin is actually hot inside, and I love it.

"Do either of you want some warmer clothes?" Maya asks. Her eyes are on me, and I force myself to hold her gaze, even though my stomach lurches with nerves. When I don't say anything at first because my mouth suddenly feels dry, she touches my wrist, and even that small skin-to-skin contact renews my resolve. "Gabe? Clothes?"

"Yes. I'd love some." *Because I plan on staying for a while—long enough to have this goddamn conversation, at least.*

"I can just grab some from next door," Rashida says. "I think I might actually take the boat out for a little night ride—get some cool air in my hair, you know?"

Perfect. I didn't hate the time I spent with Rashida tonight—in fact, I kind of enjoyed it—but whatever I'm gearing up to say to

Maya will work a lot better if the girl she's loved forever isn't in the room. Just that thought "loved forever" makes me ill, but I try to stay focused on what I really want right now—which is Maya, alone, so I can just tell her how I feel already.

"You two wanna come?" Rashida adds now, and I try not to groan.

"Oh—um . . ." Maya glances at me, then back at Rashida.

Her hesitation makes my resolve waver. Something sharp pokes at my chest.

"Only if you want to, obviously," Rashida says, eyeing us up.

Maya suddenly looks . . . panicked?

Which makes me panic.

"I—that sounds nice. Did you want to go . . . ?" She looks at me now, but the tone of her voice makes me think she's not really asking me if I want to go.

Spikes form at my throat. "You two should go. I'd rather warm up here." I don't want to say these words, but I also don't know how else to manage the shit in my throat. I become hyperaware of my bare skin, the thin towel around me.

"Are you sure?" Rashida says, a wrinkle in her brow.

"Yup."

"Maybe just a quick loop around Sun Island?" Maya says, glancing at Rashida, then back at me. "Gabe, you can stay here—we can hang out after?"

You mean after you and Rashida enjoy a moonlit boat ride to your special little love island and you finally get your magnificent kiss or whatever? No, thanks.

But I say, "Sure, yeah," just to end this conversation.

Rashida's frowning, but when we all just stand there for a moment, she says to Maya, "Okay, I'll get on some clothes, grab the boat keys, and meet you down at my dock in a minute?"

"Yeah—me too. I mean . . . I'll get changed and meet you."

"Cool . . ."

Rashida leaves, and a shiver moves through me, even though the cabin is hot. My legs feel like mush.

Maya and I just stand there for a second. She's staring at the door, and I'm watching her. Her face is all frown and lip-biting.

She finally turns to me and comes close. Her proximity makes me bristle.

"Listen—I just need to—" She shakes her head and looks at the floor.

"You need to go, so go," I say, making sure my voice stays even.

Her eyes meet mine, and all I can see is that panic—like she needs to hang on to what just walked out the door.

"Yeah—I just. Um." She starts pulling on the overalls she was wearing, not even bothering to change out of her wet bathing suit first. Her eagerness to leave sends a wave of nausea through me. "Just give me a minute, okay, Gabe?" She's already moving toward the door. "I'll be back—I promise. Make yourself at home, okay?"

I want to just accept what she's saying. But watching her hustle out the door before I've even said, "Okay, sure," causes an ache so big in my chest that I have to clutch the towel wrapped around my body, my hands fisting into the fabric at my chest.

What follows the ache is a resurgence of that familiar spike—of something much harder and sharper.

After Maya leaves, I change and gather my stuff—because hell if I'm sticking around, waiting for Maya to get back with Rashida. That sharpness in my chest has settled in, it seems, and I keep picturing Maya and Rashida speeding across the lake in Rashida's boat like they're in some action movie or something, then swooping onto their secret little beach for two and kissing there, under the stars.

I pull out the copy of *Fried Green Tomatoes* where it's been living in my bag and toss it onto Maya's couch. *Sorry, Idgie. Sorry, Ruth. Romance is for schmucks.*

On my way out, I notice the photo wall that spreads above the couch, no rhyme or reason to the display—a mishmash of frames, sizes, and distances from each other. Some photos even have cardboard frames with rocks and crumbling bark stuck to them, thick glops of dried glue spreading out in every direction.

I'd smile if I wasn't so pissed. This has gotta be Maya's work. Maya as a nerdy little kid slapping together these ugly-as-hell frames and her parents using them anyway. That's what some parents do, I guess—love their kids' messy shit no matter what. I swallow against my self-pity, but then I see that at least half of the maybe twelve or so photos on the wall include Rashida.

Maya and Rashida as toddlers, stuffing their faces with birthday cake.

Maya and Rashida as tweens, taking a selfie on their bikes.

Maya and Rashida more recently, it seems, sitting on a rock on some little beach—probably *their* little beach. Maya's arm around Rashida's waist, Rashida's arm hooked casually around Maya's neck. Their lips in closed-mouth smiles. Maya's head resting on Rashida's shoulder.

They look so comfortable with each other. So content.

Gee, Gabe, maybe that's because they're best friends. Maybe it's because they've known each other their whole lives and will probably always come back to each other because that's how it probably is for people who have their people and can trust them and love them wholeheartedly?

The sharp pinch in my chest turns into a full-blown clench, and my face crumples for a moment.

What the hell is this?

I shove the heels of my hands into my eyes. *Get it together, Gabe. No one here cares about your feelings. And you don't care about theirs, either.*

But I know, as I stare at this picture wall and my heart hurts, that I *do* care, whether I like it or not. And I want Maya to care about me, too. I want whatever this is that I'm seeing in front of me—not just a kiss in the woods or even a firm hand to hold—but someone to lean on and care about and just be content with. I want all of that.

Which is super fucking annoying.

So I do what makes the most sense to me, and I leave.

FORTY-THREE

Maya

"Ready?" Rashida says, once we're both in the boat.

I glance up at my cabin, hoping Gabe is still there and will wait for me. My stomach is flush with nerves, worrying I made the wrong decision to come with Rashida. But I knew if I stayed with Gabe, I'd only be half present, wondering if Rashida understands just how confusing this has all been for me and wanting to find some kind of clarity between us. I guess I need to know we'll still be all right before I can move on to anything with Gabe.

"Yeah. You okay to drive?" I ask. She had a drink a while ago, but maybe I'm really asking if *she'll* be completely present for this talk.

"I'm completely sober, don't worry," she says, steering us into the dark lake toward the island, the boat's lights glowing across the water.

The lake is quiet at this time of night, and Rashida cruises at a relaxed speed. The night air is refreshing, even if I'm a little cold from the wet bathing suit I'm still wearing under my clothes.

"Are *you* okay?" Rashida asks, glancing at me from the driver's seat.

"I'm . . . a little all over the place, to be honest."

I see her nod in the partial darkness. "Yeah."

"Yeah."

The ride to Sun Island takes about three minutes, and we're already almost there. And I haven't even broached the things I want to say. As she approaches the small chunk of land, I ask, "Can we pull up and kill the engine for a bit?"

"Oh, okay." She eyes me up but obliges.

Once she settles the boat alongside the small floating dock Diamond helped us build a few years ago and then hitches us to the cleat, she swivels on her chair toward me, and I do the same. Our knees touch.

Now that we're here, facing each other, quiet all around us except for the small slaps of water against the side of the boat, I suddenly feel shy. But I need to get this out.

"Rish . . ." I'm staring at my knees but force myself to look at her. She's eyeing me up, and she almost looks . . . scared?

Before I can get my next words out, she stands, kicks off her flip-flops, steps onto the edge of the boat, and dives into the lake. The boat heaves to one side with her weight and tips back and forth.

I stare after her, openmouthed. *What the . . . ?*

Moving to the edge of the boat, I call out, "Rish?"

She pops up several feet away and turns to face me. The boat lights reach around her as she treads water.

"What the heck are you doing?" I shout, confusion and irritation circling each other in my chest.

She wipes a hand down her face. "I just . . . I needed to be in the water for this."

"For . . . ?"

"For when you tell me you can't be friends with me anymore." She looks away from me, and I can see her chewing at her bottom lip.

"*Rashida.* What in the world are you talking about?"

"I totally get it," she finally says. "You need to move on."

Wait. What?

My chest burns. I don't know if I'm just shocked or annoyed or angry or what. I'm not even sure if my feelings are more about what she's saying or the fact that she botched my whole plan—again.

Whatever I'm feeling, it makes me jump feetfirst into the lake, clothes and all, just like her. My head bobs up a few feet away from her, and I immediately take a swipe at the water, sending a nice, big splash her way.

She flinches and yells, "Hey!"

"Hey, yourself! What the hell are you even talking about right now?" I splash her again.

"Stop. Splashing. Me." Each word is punctuated with a splash of her own. I turn away, but as soon as the splashing pauses, I turn back and plunge through the space between us. She pinches her nose, knowing exactly what's coming. In seconds, my hands are on her shoulders and her head is under water, but not for long. Like clockwork, her arms are around my waist and she uses her incredible leg strength to thrust herself and me up from the water and launch me sideways. I sputter for a few seconds and can hear her laughing.

I splash her again, still mad, but also connected to so many past moments by these antics—play fighting in the lake like we've always done. Except I'm not playing right now.

"Stop laughing, you ass!" I shout. "I was *trying* to say something important!"

We're treading water a few feet away from each other now. Her tank top is billowing around her chest.

"So *say* it already!" she shouts back.

I open my mouth to tell her everything I've been feeling—how hard it's been, letting go of what I thought we were, trying to sort out these feelings I have for her *and* for Gabe. How scary it is to think something is so obvious and real and then find out that it isn't. At all.

But what comes out of my mouth is, "We'll always be friends, dumbass! No matter what."

She gazes at me for a few moments, and any traces of laughter disappear. "Even if . . ."

"What?"

"Even if *all* I want is friendship?"

I know I'm starting to veer toward something different with

her, and I know I like Gabe, but her words still jab at my chest. I swallow back the hurt and stare at Sun Island, just to our left. That small beach where we've spent so much time together. I turn back to her, eyes wet.

"Yeah. I think I can finally accept that. But I guess it still freaks me out—how wrong I was about us." My eyes flick to the sky, the tiny pinpricks of light dotting it. "It's just hard to trust my feelings now, I guess."

I hear her sigh—maybe with relief, maybe with exasperation—and then she says, "Maya, I love you more than I love anyone in the world. You weren't wrong about that part. What you thought we were is changing. But we care about each other, right? You can trust that."

My eyes shift back to her, and her head tilts to the side, her face soft. Her words help to ease the frantic heartbeat reverberating through every part of my body, but not completely.

"*Sucks* to change," I say, but with a soft laugh.

She laughs, too. After we both had to read *Lord of the Flies* in tenth grade, we said "sucks" to everything . . . in particular "Sucks to pipelines" and "Sucks to clear-cutting."

"You don't mean that," she says. "It looks like your taste in girls is changing, right? I'm sorry it didn't work out with Gabe."

I watch my hands move through the water in front of me. I should tell her about Gabe's and my fake deal, but what does it matter now, when my feelings for Gabe have turned into something more real?

When I don't say anything, she adds, to my surprise, "You

know, Gabe is . . . definitely a change. But I think I actually like her? Do you think she's okay? Back there on her own?"

"You don't?" A panicky sensation climbs up my chest.

"Well, from our conversation tonight, it sounds like our parents share some of the same crappy parenting styles," Rashida says.

Oh. I forgot about how Rish and Gabe have that in common. A mom who left and another parent who doesn't pay enough attention.

She looks away and adds, "It's probably just hard, being left behind. Even if it's for a good reason."

I watch her face in the boat's lights. I love her profile—she's got this perfect round nose and long eyelashes, a killer jawline. Right now, though, she's biting at her bottom lip again.

I think about the way Gabe talks about her parents, about that barrier that goes up sometimes when she's unsure or maybe feels threatened. Or just . . . scared?

"But," I say, reading between her words, "it's like Gabe pushes away, while you don't do that at all. I mean, you never seem *angry* or put up walls. I've never even heard you say anything bad about your mom."

She shrugs in the water. "I *am* angry at my mom, all the time, but maybe I just deal with things in a different way—and have more people to depend on. But I get the fear. The feeling like you did something wrong and that's why people leave."

Hurt pierces my chest, hearing her say this. "Rish." I bring her in for a hug, our legs kicking beneath the surface, holding us up. My heart thumps away in my chest, and it's going to take some time to let go of the visions I did have of me and Rish together, but at least this feels like some kind of opening to do that, finally. "I love you, no matter what. And I meant it—we'll always be friends."

"I know. And I'm lucky," she says, then leans her head back to look at me. "I've had you, and your parents, Jan and Diamond to fill in the blanks. I'm not sure Gabe has anyone else. Does she?"

Her question lands like an anchor in my stomach. "I'm not sure, either."

"Maybe you should find out?" She gives me a small smile, and I nod.

We release each other in the water and swim back to the boat, then haul ourselves aboard. Now all I can think about is getting back up to my cabin and asking Gabe about these things—and letting her know she has *me* if she needs someone.

After Rish drives us back and we say good night with one more soul-filling hug in our sopping-wet clothes, I enter my cabin hoping to find Gabe relaxing in the living room or on the porch. But instead, all I find are empty rooms and *Fried Green Tomatoes* lying on the couch, some of its loose pages scattered beside it.

FORTY-FOUR

Gabe

The next morning, I wake up to simultaneous sounds of birds chirping like I'm in a goddamn Disney movie, the chickens of course, and Canva and Blu having breakfast. I shove a pillow over my head and try to stay in bed as long as I can before I finally have to pee.

I wait until I don't hear any more voices and head to the bathroom.

When I see myself in the mirror, my outsides definitely match my insides. My hair was still wet when I went to bed, so it's a savage mess. I never removed my makeup properly, so raccoon eyes stare back at me, dreadful and dark. And I have three angry, red mosquito bites just below my right collarbone that make me want to tear off my skin.

So yeah. Fitting.

I don't want to be here anymore.

I gave this a fair shot. I tried to fit in, helped out some hippies, and even—almost—let some girl get close. Too damn close. Now I need to get far away.

I clean myself up as best I can, pulling my hair into a ponytail and scrubbing my face. My eyes still look bloodshot, and the ointments I brought do fuck-all to stop the itch of these bites, but at least the raccoon eyes are gone.

Maya texted me last night—just Where'd you go? and Can we talk?—but the hell if I want to sit down with her and have a heart-to-heart about how "this was all a lot of fun" and "sorry I gave you mixed signals," but "I've sorted out this better, real thing with Rashida now, so good luck to you."

No thanks.

I pick up my phone to call my mom, to explain to her that I really did try, but I hear her response already in my head.

It's been two weeks, Gabe. You lost the girl and you're giving up on volunteering already?

I can hear the disappointment already, too.

My options are shitty any way I look at them. And to be honest, I don't actually want to stop helping SLEA, even if being around Maya feels like torture. Maybe I can figure out a way to get my mom to let me stay with her, but still help with SLEA? Miller's Bay and Spruce Lake aren't that far from each other. Or—Rashida and the others said that Lux is based in Miller's Bay. Maybe I can do reconnaissance or something.

Before I can even think up a proper plan, though, my phone buzzes in my hand and I see my mom's face light up the screen.

That's some creepy shit.

"Mom?"

"Gabe? Where are you right now?"

Her voice is all pissy, and it immediately puts me on the defensive again. "What? Where do you think?"

"I mean—where *exactly*? I'm coming to you now."

If her tone didn't sound angry, I'd be surprised and excited by this—her coming to see *me* out of the blue. But instead, I'm surprised and freaked out. "What? Why?"

"Just—tell me where you are. Are you at the B and B?"

"Yeah. Yes. But—"

"I'll be there in twenty minutes. Don't go anywhere."

She hangs up.

What the hell?

I spend the next five minutes running through all the things I might have messed up, all the ways I could be in trouble. I mean, I got my drink on last night, but I didn't even do anything dumb like I usually do, except for maybe letting myself believe Maya was into me for a hot minute. I haven't crashed any cars, broken anything at the B and B, done anything embarrassing.

If anything, I've been wholesome as hell.

But this is fine, I tell myself. When she gets here, I'll have my bags ready to go, and I'll tell her SLEA needs me to do some work in Miller's Bay. That it's super important and it just makes more sense for me to stay there. That I won't cause her any trouble at all or distract her with my bullshit because I'll be too busy doing very crucial, very unselfish work for SLEA. She'll be so damn impressed by my commitment and drive and virtue, she'll let me stay with her.

I pack my shit up and roll my suitcase through Canva's front door, then wait in the driveway.

When my mom drives up a few minutes later, she's in a massive black SUV, unsurprisingly. I frown when I see the words detailed on the side, though.

Lux Corp by Omni Industries. Revitalizing and energizing communities across the west.

My empty stomach suddenly feels nauseous.

My mom gets out of the back seat—because obviously she has a driver . . . gross. She's in her usual chignon, dress pants, black blazer, and a blue dress shirt. In this weather. On a Sunday.

When she takes off her sunglasses, I'm a little surprised by how tired she looks. I guess corporate bullshit takes a lot out of you.

My body vibrates with nerves and irritation and a sick feeling that I've messed up again somehow.

"Gabe," she says as she approaches, trying not to twist an ankle in her heels on the gravel driveway. She's tapping at her phone, frowning.

"Hey," I say from where I can't seem to move my feet. "What's going on?"

She stops a couple of feet away—no hug, awkward or not, this time, I guess. She glances at my suitcase beside me, ignores it, and holds her phone out to me. "Gabe, what is this about? What are you trying to pull now?"

I peer into her phone, confused as ever.

What I see is a photo from some local news site of the garage sale yesterday. In the photo, I'm dressed in a long skirt and headband. Blu is beside me in his ridiculous outfit from our impromptu fashion show.

"Oh—that's just from this fundraiser we did yesterday," I say. "It was for—"

"I know exactly what it was for," she interrupts. She scrolls up on her phone and shows me the screen again. "It says you were raising money for the Spruce Lake Eco Alliance? Are you kidding?"

My brow furrows. I'm so fucking confused. "Why would I be kidding?" But then I remember the SUV behind her. "Wait—"

"You realize, Gabe, that this little group you've been helping is trying to disrupt *everything* I'm working toward right now, right?"

"But—"

"Omni has been keeping an eye on them. It sounds like they're a bunch of career protesters—troublemakers, really—who've been causing havoc for the company for years. And this is the group you've been helping? Are you just trying to get back at me or something? For making you stay here this summer?" She scoffs and shakes her head. "I should have known all this was too good to be true." She rubs an eye with the heel of her hand. "Jesus. I'm so tired of this, Gabe."

The disappointment of this last statement is so much worse than her anger. Her words twist something sharp in my chest, and I have to swallow before getting out, "But I didn't even know . . ."

"Didn't know what?"

"I thought you worked for a company called Omni . . . I didn't know Omni owned Lux."

"I *do* work for Omni. And help oversee Lux. And your SLEA group is trying to stop the development we're building. You didn't put two and two together?"

"I—I didn't know what you were doing—"

She scoffs again and places her hands on the back of her hips. "Right. Because you don't actually care about anyone but yourself, Gabe. You're trying to tell me you have no idea what my job is?"

My anger rises up at this. "How am I supposed to know what the hell you do? I barely ever see you! We hardly ever talk!"

Her expression turns incredulous. "And whose fault is that?"

Mine. Yours. "I—"

"You realize, Gabe, that if I lose this job you couldn't care less about, your nice little life of luxury wouldn't be possible, right?"

Are you fucking serious right now?

"My life of what?"

"*Luxury.* The one where you don't work and live in a great big house and act like nothing you do impacts anyone else."

I think I hear a small break in her voice, but that sharp thing presses out my words too quickly to stop them.

"*You* realize, Mother, that I don't care about that great big house because it's *empty* and just reminds me of how—"

The next words get stuck in my throat.

Alone I am.

When I don't finish my sentence, because I can't control my stupid bottom lip, there's silence for a few moments.

In the silence, we both hear "Gabe?" and when I look over my mom's shoulder, I see Maya standing next to the SUV, her eyes flitting from the Lux Corp logo to me and my mother.

FORTY-FIVE

Maya

My brain is trying to make sense of the scene in front of me. Gabe, talking to her mom. A sleek, black SUV with *Lux Corp by Omni Industries* on the side, parked in front of Canva's. Gabe with a suitcase beside her.

I don't know what propels my feet forward—curiosity, concern, or something else, but I open Canva's gate and walk down the gravel path to stand next to Karen, who seems irritated and flustered.

Gabe's expression is something similar to when she saw those rapids at Salmon Run—panicked and unsure and wanting to be anywhere but here.

"Maya, what are you doing here?" she asks now. Her voice is gritty, like the gravel beneath our feet.

I glance at Gabe's mom but try to focus on Gabe. "I came to

talk. But I guess . . . ?" I turn my eyes to her suitcase. "Are you leaving?"

Before Gabe can say anything, Karen cuts in. "Maya. I suppose you're part of this eco group, too? Or did my daughter stumble into it all on her own?"

I turn to her. "Pardon?"

"Are you—"

"I *did* stumble into it all on my own, actually," Gabe interrupts. Her panic has turned to something more fiery, but I can still see worry there, too. "I *thought* I was doing something good—something *you'd* see as good. I wasn't trying to mess things up for you, even though I know you think that's all I want to do."

What in the world did I just step into?

Unable to help myself, I wave a hand at the SUV and say, "Hold on . . . do you work for— Are you—"

"The VP of Omni, yes."

"Which owns . . ."

She sighs and flaps an arm in exasperation. "Lux, *yes*."

I momentarily lose sight of what I came here to say, in light of this new information. *Gabe's mom is the VP of Omni Industries, which owns Lux Corporation.* Gabe never mentioned this, right? Before I freak out, I try to collect all the things she *did* say about her parents—one left, one works in Miller's Bay, they're not great, she's not close to either . . . nothing about Lux. I would have remembered.

I freak out.

Ignoring Karen for a moment, I turn to Gabe and say, "Gabe, what is this? Your mom works for Lux? Did you know?"

Her mom scoffs. "Apparently not. Though I find that very convenient."

I flash her mom a frown. I don't really care about what she thinks right now.

"Gabe?" My voice is edged with anger, because I find it hard to believe she had no idea, too. But underneath the anger is disappointment.

She must hear both emotions, or maybe her mom's words land hard, because she lets out a long breath and there's a moment where her entire body seems to sag. It's such a total deflation, I almost feel bad. But then something more familiar must take over—she frowns and steels her jaw. Her eyes seem to empty.

"Yup. Mom's right. Here I am in all my usual glory. Fucking up, left, right, and center." Her arms extend to her sides and smack back against her thighs.

Part of me wants to gather her up, get past the barriers that I can tell she's constructing. But another part of me just wants to understand what's happening here. "But . . . so, what does that mean for SLEA? Are you . . . Will you stop helping?" I ask. *What does this mean for us? For all the work we've put in?*

"I should think so," Karen says. "Right, Gabe? I think that's the *least* you could do, at this point?"

Gabe stares at her mom for a beat, glances at me, but then a soft huff of laughter comes from her lips, and she presses her fingers into her eyes. Her lips are twisted into a kind of smile, but it's one of those smiles that's fighting a sob.

She rubs her face aggressively in the next moment, though,

and both the smile and the sob disappear. She scrapes her fingers through her hair. She looks at her mom, and it's like all the fight's gone out of her.

"Sure, Mom. I'll quit." Her gaze turns to me. "I'm not really cut out for this shit anyway."

Her voice wavers, and a lump forms in my throat, hearing it and her words. But then she just walks away, leaving her bag behind, and leaving both her mom and me confused and speechless.

Fifteen minutes later, I'm at Jellybean Pond, with no memory of even walking here. I guess I just gravitated to where I thought I might find some comfort—in familiarity, the forest, Ruth.

Both Karen and I watched in silence as Gabe left Canva's yard, chose a pathway into the forest, and disappeared down it. Standing there, I could practically feel Gabe's mom vibrating—with anger, I assumed—but when I glanced at her, the fingers of one hand were squeezing the bridge of her nose, her eyes were closed, and her lips pressed tightly together, the bottom one quivering the tiniest bit. She quickly gathered herself, though, stormed to her car, got in, and drove off.

I went into automated mode, wheeling Gabe's suitcase back into her bedroom, then walking here. I guess my brain was having trouble processing everything.

I climb into my hammock, trying to let my affinity with this place take hold, but then I remember that it's not just my place anymore. Gabe found it. And Ruth, Idgie, and the others aren't in the lockbox anymore, either. When I picked up my copy of *Fried*

Green Tomatoes from the couch last night, the bookmark I always keep in it was about twenty pages from the end. I don't know how anyone leaves twenty pages of a story unread. Especially those twenty pages. Who wouldn't want to know what actually happened to Frank Bennett? Or say goodbye to Idgie and Ruth and the others?

But then I guess Gabe didn't have time to finish before leaving. Nor did she probably care how it ends, since she wasn't really invested in any of this anyway—in Spruce Lake, in me, in SLEA, in the friendships she was forming—none of it. She just walked away from it all.

That sense of not being able to trust myself rises up again. All those moments with Gabe—when things felt fun or sweet or close—they *felt* real. But whereas the feelings of love I felt with Rashida were based on our very real care for each other—even if it was a different kind of love than I'd hoped for—maybe any feelings of care I felt with Gabe were just surface level. How else could she just give up on Spruce Lake—on us—like this?

I stare up into the treetops and try to channel some calm, even if *Fried Green Tomatoes* isn't here and the image of Gabe lying in Ruth is. I breathe in the forest air, which is full of cedar and moss and pond water.

The trees are still the trees, the water is still reflecting them back to the sky, the dirt still holds millions of networking roots and fungi, all supporting each other. I'm still surrounded by communal efforts.

My family and Rashida would be so proud of me—for

bringing myself back to what really matters like this, here in the trees. The thought makes me smile, despite the hurt in my chest.

Gabe is a blip, I tell myself. I won't let her ruin this place, or my summer. I still have plenty of people and things I can trust.

FORTY-SIX

Gabe

This was a bad idea. But then, I'm full of those, I guess. So at least I'm consistent.

In my urgency to get the hell away from all the disappointment on my mom's and Maya's faces, I decided to just take any path my feet led me down. I don't even have my phone or bag 'cause I left them back at Canva's. Fuck it. If I get lost, so what? It's not like I have to be anywhere or like anyone's waiting for me.

I hate the self-pity I'm feeling—hate that I'm wallowing in any kind of feelings at all. I frown away these thoughts and try to focus on the trail in front of me.

I pass a tree that has some kind of stained-glass art on it. The path veers off in two directions, and I go left. This path splits and curves around a thick tree in the middle and then I see two sticks someone's made into a little cross and stuck in the ground. A sad little sign next to it says, "Chickapoo the guinea pig lies here." *Because obviously.*

I keep walking, taking another left and hopping over a small stream. I realize I must have been walking for at least twenty minutes, and don't recognize anything around me.

I continue on for another minute or two and come out into a bit of an opening that's less dense with trees, the space half in shadows, half in sunlight. The second I appear, two deer a few feet off to my right raise their heads from where they've been snacking on something. They both chew away and stare at me like I've disrupted their lunch date.

I stare back, staying still, until they both saunter off into the woods. It's not until they've disappeared that I realize the area is dotted with five rowboats, all nestled into the ground a few feet apart. It looks like the bottoms of the boats have been cut away and the boats look super weathered—paint flaking off and covering only about half the hulls. (I only know what a hull is because Jan has been telling me a bunch of stuff about boats that I really don't need to know.)

Someone's filled the boats with a bunch of soil and plants are growing in each. Some plants have fine wiring around them, to protect against the deer, I assume. So much for that, judging by the previous guests. But plenty of stuff seems to be thriving anyway.

Leave it to the people of Spruce Lake to drag some boats into the middle of the woods, haul in a bunch of dirt, and grow a garden. *Weirdos.*

So anyway, I'm lost, I guess, like I knew I would be. But at least it's cooler and pretty in here and no one's around to tell me what a fuckup I am.

I walk in a loop and recognize a few things—tomatoes and some leafy greens. In one boat, some pea pods are growing on a couple of the plants. I glance around me. I don't see any signs or anything saying Private or Keep Out. I also don't see any signs that say Free Veggies, though.

But this has gotta be one of those community gardens, right? Like, for the community? I know I'm technically not part of this community—especially now—but I feel like my two weeks here have earned at least a pea or two.

I pluck a pod, and it's a fat one with the peas inside, like the ones in movies where people are sitting around on their patios shucking or whatever you call it.

I pry this pod open and inside are four perfect little peas. I scoop them out with a finger and pop all four in my mouth. They're sweet as hell. I take two more pods and eat them, too, but then stop myself from taking anymore because, like, *community.*

Not quite ready to leave and deal with whatever's waiting for me on the other side of those trees or on the faces of people I foolishly thought might care about me in some way, I search the area and find an overturned bucket. I go to turn it over, hoping nothing furry with teeth scrambles out from under it, and find a few gardening tools—a spade, a little fork thing, and some gloves.

I shrug. *Might as well be useful.*

I've never gardened before in my life, obviously, and let's face it—I'll probably screw this up somehow, too, but when I think about all the things I've done while I've been here that *haven't* made me feel like shit, most have involved nature or some kind of hard labor. I even kept Jan's "green things" alive for the garage sale. Which is a goddamn miracle.

So I hunch my ass down and start digging out the stuff that looks like weeds. I avoid all the plants that seem like they could turn into something edible. Eventually I abandon the spade because most of the stuff I'm removing is so small I can just pluck it out with my hands.

It's quiet here—just the occasional chirp—and that could be peaceful, but my thoughts are loud. They're telling me what a mess I am. That no matter what I do, I can't make anyone happy, that I've never made anyone proud.

I try to distract myself from those thoughts with my motions—try to focus on cleaning out this little boat and then the next, on making room for the plants to grow.

But by the time I'm finished, I realize I've only half succeeded in dulling the voices in my head, because tears are streaming down my face and I'm embarrassed to all hell even though no one's around to see me.

I try to wipe them away as though I'm just wiping away the sweat that's also damp against my skin. I lift the bottom of my shirt, which is also the top of my shirt because I'm in a crop top, and wipe my face with that, as well. The yellow fabric comes away with smudges of makeup, soil, sweat, and tears on it. *Gross, Gabe.*

But when I step back and check out the five gardens, they look pretty damn good. And then I remember that gardens need water, right?

I grab the bucket and wander back to the stream I crossed earlier, fill the bucket with water, and haul it back to the boat. It takes me six more buckets to fully wet the soil and by then, my arms and legs are tired and sore. I use the last of the water to splash against my neck and face, but the rest of me is too filthy to fix with a few dabs, so I don't bother.

I plunk down next to one boat and lean against it, snacking on a few more peas from my grimy hands. The air is warming up, I'm tired, and closing my eyes seems like the only option right now.

I do and almost doze off when I hear, "Well, well," and "It's Gabe!" in two very different voices—one older and gravelly, and the other young and high-pitched. I don't even have to open my eyes to know who it is, but when I do, Jan is standing in front of me, and Blu is beside her, fake wooden sword in hand. She's smirking, and he's grinning like a little nerd.

"What've we got here, hey, Blu? Looks like someone's been stealing our peas." Jan toes some of the empty pea shells next to me with the tip of her Croc.

Blu marches up to me and peers into my face so his nose is about three inches from mine. His face is mock serious, fists on hips. "Did you eat our peas, Gabe?"

I can't help but smirk at this little hooligan. "What if I did?"

He straightens up and looks at Jan. "What if she did?"

Jan can't hide her smirk, either. "Well, then—she could maybe share something with us, right? But looks like she already did."

Blu looks around, as do I. "What'd she share?"

"Did some of our work for us, didn't she? Lookit those fingernails."

I hold out my hands for Blu to have a look, and he inspects the chipped, soiled nail polish for a half second before getting bored with this conversation, hopping backward, and holding out his sword. "Like my sword, Gabe? I'm defending Spruce Lake from all the stinkers! I'm gonna bring it to the protest, too."

"Wow. Spruce Lake is lucky to have you," I say, but his words just remind me that I won't be at the protest anymore—at least not if I don't want my mom to hate me.

He flits off to fight the stinkers, and Jan eyes up the garden. "You watered, too, huh?"

"Tried to."

She inspects the boat behind me. "Looks like you gave 'em a good douse."

"Should I not have?" I ask, getting up.

She pushes out her lips. "Well," she says, pressing her fingers into the soil, which, I notice now, is more muddy than damp, "you may have drowned a few sprouts, but that's okay."

I look where she's pointing and see now that some of the smaller plants are wilted over in the watery dirt like little green noodles in soup.

Jesus, Gabe.

"Shit. Sorry" is all I say, because my chest is starting to tighten.

"And I guess you decided the herbs had to go with all the weeds, huh?"

"Pardon?"

She stoops and picks at the pile of weeds I pulled from the garden. "Parsley . . . cilantro . . . ope! There's my oregano."

Christ. Strike 682.

"Fuck. Jan, I'm sorry. I thought I was just getting the weeds."

It's just some tiny plants, but for some reason, it feels like my biggest mistake. My goddamn bottom lip starts quivering again, and I bite at it and look away.

"Well, shit, Gabe, you didn't run over a deer or nothin'. We can grow more herbs, ya know. The dirt'll dry up again."

I just nod and stare at Blu, who's using his sword as a broomstick now and riding it like a little wood witch.

After a few more seconds of silence, Jan says, "Well, listen, now that I don't have to weed and water, let's go get some more seeds and replant. Won't take long."

"Okay." My voice comes out in a whimper, and I'm embarrassed all over again.

"Come on." She calls to Blu as we set off on another pathway through the forest to her shop, and I have to will myself to stay on the path behind her instead of just veering off into the trees to get lost again.

FORTY-SEVEN

Maya

I spend a good hour in Ruth, letting the forest calm my body and brain, but by about one o'clock, my stomach rumbles, and I make my way to the pub to eat something. And maybe also to be around people who I can talk to about all of this.

As I walk, I message Rashida to meet me at the pub as soon as she can. She gets back to me instantly and says she can be there in twenty minutes. Despite the empathy she showed for Gabe last night, she's going to lose her shit, especially if Gabe jeopardizes the protest at all. It's less than a week away, and the element of surprise is key.

Everyone else in SLEA will be . . . disappointed, probably, like I am. And confused. And hurt.

"Maya, my love!" Jasper says, smiling, as he sees me enter the pub. "My day just got better." I take a seat at the bar and try my best to smile back. "Coffee? Tea?"

I nod, then realize it wasn't a yes or no question, and reply, "Tea, please."

"Coming right up!"

As he heads back into the kitchen, he and Diamond pass each other, and Jasper gives Diamond a playful poke to the gut.

"Did I hear a Maya is in the house?" Diamond says, smiling at me, as well. He gives my nose a soft pinch. "Good afternoon, beautiful niece. Not too worse for wear, I hope? I heard it was a good romp at Davie and Sean's last night." He winks.

Romp is one word for it.

"It was pretty good, yeah."

I must not be very convincing, because he leans over the counter and his eyebrows rise. "Everything all right?"

My eyes water instantaneously with this bit of concern. I place my elbows on the bar, my chin in my hands. I shake my head. Calming my body and brain in the forest is one thing. It helped to remind me that I'm surrounded by all these people who I *can* trust, who love me in a million different ways. But it didn't manage to strip away the disappointment I feel. Or the fact that I just miss Gabe. Already. I really liked her. I thought she liked me. I was wrong, again.

"Hmm . . . this looks like a job for . . . a milk shake?"

I shake my head.

"Pot pie?"

No, again.

"How about—"

"A massive slice of your strawberry shortcake . . . with a ton of ice cream? Please?" I finally get out.

"You bet." He winks at me.

"And we'll have what she's having!"

I turn to see my parents, dressed in Patagonia everything, descending upon me.

I'm surprised—I thought they were coming back tonight. "How come you're home already?" I ask.

"Hello to you, too," my mom says, squeezing my shoulder as she takes a seat on my right and my dad takes the seat on the left. They're fragrant with the woods and body odor.

"Hi," I say.

"Welcome home, travelers. How was Camp Love?" Diamond asks them.

Ew. That's not the actual name of their favorite getaway spot around here, but it might as well be.

"Stunning, as usual!" Dad boasts. "But Hessy got stung by a wasp on our hike this morning, so we just decided to come home a little early." He turns to me. "Is that all right with you, daughter? Or did you have wild plans for our absence today?" He's smiling like a goof.

I ignore him and turn to my mom. "Are you okay?" She's not allergic to the point of needing an EpiPen or anything, but wasp stings can be super uncomfortable.

"Fine, fine." She pulls her shirt back a bit at the neck to show me the red welt. "Just didn't feel great. But that strawberry shortcake sounds like a perfect balm." She rubs my back and smiles.

"Good timing," Diamond says. "The shortcake does seem like

a balm of sorts." He tilts his head at me and raises his eyebrows expectantly. "I think you were just about to tell me what the sting is?"

All three of them look at me, and I guess I'm sharing now.

Diamond puts our order in with Jasper and then I tell them about Gabe and her mom. Even though I try to leave out the romantic woes, because they think Gabe and I are just friends now anyway, my parents bypass the Lux part to home in on the heartbreak that I must not be hiding very well.

My mom tucks a strand of my hair behind my ear. "Oh, Maya. I'm sorry. You two seemed to hit it off so quickly."

I am not about to tell them the reason we hit it off so quickly is because we were faking it. I can't even begin to deal with their reaction to that particular tidbit.

"And I liked Gabe," Dad adds. "You don't think she'll help with SLEA now?"

I shrug. "I doubt it. Her mom wasn't happy about her involvement. But I don't know. They had a terrible vibe."

"Huh," Diamond says, placing our desserts in front of us. "Sounds complicated."

"Complicated? Or just shitty?" I grumble.

"What's up, team!" Rashida calls out as she enters the pub. She stops behind us and swings her arms around me and my mom, grinning. Then she sees the shortcake and her eyes go wide. "Mmm . . . cake for lunch? Me too, please!" she says to Diamond through a big smile.

Her energy actually makes me smile, too, even though I'm

exhausted. Maybe it's just relief at seeing her and finally not feeling like an enormous weight is hovering over me.

My mom offers Rashida her seat and moves over one. After asking my parents about how their camping trip was, and a quick recap of the stinging incident, Rashida must notice my weird vibe, because she asks what's up.

I tell her and bolster myself for the anger I know is coming.

But she just looks at the strawberry shortcake Diamond's set in front of her and frowns. Then she looks at me. "So she didn't even know her mom worked for Lux?"

"Guess not."

"Wow."

"Wow . . . what?"

"I dunno. She said she and her parents weren't close, but even *I* know what my dad does, you know?"

"So . . . you think she must've known her mom works for Lux and just won't admit it, or . . . ?"

Rashida shakes her head. "No. No way. That was real work she put into the fundraiser, as far as I could see. It just makes me think their relationship is even worse than my dad's and mine."

My mom brings her in for a little squeeze at this, and Rish leans into it thankfully.

I think back to the conversation I witnessed this morning. Karen seemed genuinely surprised—and furious—that Gabe was involved with SLEA. And Gabe seemed so . . . defeated. She'd wanted to fake-date me to impress her mom, after all. Maybe she genuinely thought helping with SLEA would impress her, too? But then, she also seemed to *actually* care about SLEA, as well.

I lean on my elbows and rub my eyes. "I don't get this at all. How do you just give something up if you really care about it?"

"Maybe she just cares a lot about more than one thing," Diamond says. "Which can suck, if those two things are at odds, right?"

"Yeah," Rashida adds. "Honestly, if I didn't have you all, I'd probably try to please my dad a little more, too." She reaches around my neck and digs her chin into my shoulder. "Luckily I do have you. It makes things a lot easier."

I side-eye her, unable to help the smile that forms on my lips. "Yeah, you're lucky."

She pushes at me. "Hey! You're lucky, too, jackass!"

I sit up. "It's true. I am."

"Honey, maybe the real question here is, how much do you care about Gabe?" my mom says.

My eyes water. "I thought a lot."

"You thought?" Diamond asks.

I hunch my shoulders. "I don't know. I feel so all over the place with her. She's not exactly the kind of person I usually hang out with, as you mentioned," I say, giving Rashida a pointed look.

"What the hell do I know?" Rish says, smiling at me. "It was obvious enough to me that you like her, Maya. And that she likes you."

"You never know who you're gonna be drawn to, sweetheart," Mom adds.

"Whatever," I mumble. "You and Dad act like you've known from birth you'd be together."

I can *feel* them giving each other a cutesie, lovey-dovey look down the bar at each other.

"Yeah, love can be like that sometimes," Dad says, and I roll my eyes unabashedly.

"But it can also look like finding someone fruity and gay to work with behind a bar, even though you thought you'd end up with some nice girl, get married, and have six kids." This is Diamond, who aims his thumb behind him toward the kitchen, where Jasper's cooking.

"*Six?*" Rashida shrieks. "On this planet? With these dwindling resources?"

We all can't help but laugh at her focus on the completely wrong thing in this moment.

"*Point being*," my mom interjects, "if you like Gabe, let yourself like her and let *her* know you do. Maybe it ends the way you want it to, maybe it doesn't."

I stare at my shortcake and sigh, unsure if I can handle another rejection this summer, too.

But then, two weeks ago, I would never have believed I'd get over that first rejection, so maybe I can handle more than I thought.

FORTY-EIGHT

Gabe

After leading us back to Need Something? and sending Blu on his way, Jan grabbed her car keys and called for Poppy, Rashida's dog, who was apparently lounging behind the shop this whole time.

Now I'm sitting in her truck, on our way to who knows where to get some more seeds, even though I thought Jan's shop had everything, according to her. Poppy hopped right up onto my lap when we got in, and normally I'd hate this, but when she nestled herself into a curved mass and let out an epic sigh, the weight felt like comfort.

Jan's truck is old and smells a bit like gas and potato chips and the bunch of dried herbs hanging from her rearview mirror. It takes a couple of tries to get started.

"Sure we'll make it there in this thing?" I can't stop myself from asking once we get going, even though I should definitely shut the hell up already.

She pats the steering wheel with a gnarly old hand. "You smack-talk my girl here, and you'll be riding in the back."

I peer behind me to the flatbed, which is filled with disintegrating netting, an oil can, a giant cooler, and more. I pat the dashboard with my own hand, and Poppy grumbles at the movement. "She's a beaut," I say, deadpan.

I may be wrong, but Jan's lips quirk the tiniest bit, and the effect it has on my mood is bigger than it should be.

We drive in silence for a while, and though I'd usually be thankful that an adult isn't forcing me to talk about the newest shitty thing I just did, right now, those voices in my head are already forcing me to think about that shitty thing—*all* the shitty things—and so I break the silence, even though I'm sure I'm just opening myself up to more sarcasm and grunts.

"How long've you owned the shop?" I ask.

"Long enough."

"Did you buy it or start it yourself?"

"Started it."

"Lived in Spruce Lake your whole life?"

"Pretty much."

"So you obviously like it?"

She side-eyes me at this, then brings her gaze back to the road. "Love it. Nowhere better."

"*Nowhere?*" I ask. "Have you *been* anywhere else?" I can appreciate now that Spruce Lake has a lot to offer—way more than I thought it did when I first arrived. But I'm pretty sure I wouldn't choose it over Florence or Kyoto.

"I've probably been to more places than you, ya little shit."

My eyebrows pop up—partly in surprise at her declaration, but also because she somehow makes "little shit" sound like a term of endearment. It brings me a little more out of my funk and encourages me to tease her a bit.

"I mean . . . I know you probably have about sixty or seventy years on me, but I've been a lot of places in my short life." It's true. One of the few perks of my mom's work and Meems's adventurous spirit is we traveled a lot when I was younger and before everything went sideways.

Jan scoffs and looks out the driver's side window, mumbling, "I'll give you sixty or seventy years . . ."

She adjusts in her seat and continues, "Buddy, I've been to every continent and over sixty countries, and none of that all-inclusive shit, either."

I smirk. "Are you counting the 'It's a Small World' ride at Disneyland?"

Jan shakes her head and mumbles, "What a dick." But there's a smile on her lips now—I'm sure of it.

"Okay, I'll bite. What makes Spruce Lake so much better than all those continents and countries?"

"You really askin'? Or just bein' a punk?" She cocks an eyebrow at me.

"Both." I smile.

She grunts again. But amicably, I think. "Every place I've been to has somethin' special about it. Even the smoggy countries and overcrowded cities—there's always somethin' to appreciate. There's always some bit of land to remind me that everything is just dirt and water and roots and air, and some other bit to impress me with how goddamn creative or smart or beautiful humans can be. So I'm not sayin' Spruce Lake is perfect or offers everything those places offer, but it's still perfect for me. Small 'n friendly 'n green, just how I like it."

"But *surely* you've been to other places that are all of those things, too?"

"*Surely*," she teases. "But they don't have my people in them. And I'm not tied to the land there the way I am to this land."

"But can't you find your people anywhere?" I have to hope that you can, otherwise I'm screwed.

She shrugs and leans forward over the steering wheel. "Listen, alls I'm sayin' is I've been a lot of places, met a lot of people, and there've been some good ones, but my people—past, present, future, my friends, my ancestors—they're here, in this place. My roots are here." She pushes her lips out, and if I'm not mistaken, her eyes glisten a little.

I let her have whatever feelings she's feeling and stay silent.

What if no one gets me *any*where I go? So far, I've never met anyone who really got me, even my own mothers. And I sure as hell don't have roots anywhere, whatever that means.

Jan clears her throat and continues. "But here's the thing: None of that comes without a bit of work. I don't have some kinda magical connection with these people and this place just 'cause I'm from here, or 'cause my people are from here. I gotta let people and the place in a little, you get me?"

Now it's my turn to cock an eyebrow. Jan does *not* seem like the type of person who has "let people in."

"Sorry . . . you let people in by . . . ?"

"Yeah, yeah, you think I'm just all frowns and groans, but everyone here knows who I am and where I stand on things. They know they can trust me and that I ask for help when I need it. And give it where needed, too."

Right. Unlike me, who never asks for help and can't be trusted. And who definitely makes things worse instead of helping anything.

When I'm quiet a while, because I'm not sure I can speak without my voice wavering, Jan says, "I wasn't always like that, just for the record. I was an asshole in my youth, too."

"Did you just call me an asshole?"

"Aren't ya?"

I shrug, my chest pinches. "Yeah, guess I am."

"Everyone is, in some way. We make dumb decisions sometimes. What're you gonna do about it, is the question?"

I'm not sure she's actually asking me this, or if it's more of a rhetorical thing. I answer anyway, because I'm practicing *letting people in*: "Sorry's a good start, I guess. I'm just not sure the people I have to say it to are gonna care if I'm sorry or not. I've done a lot of crappy stuff. Like, more than just messing up your garden."

"*More* than that? Christ. You really are screwed."

I scratch at the scruff of Poppy's neck. She's teasing me, but she's right.

Her right hand shoots out and punches me in the arm. It hurts. Poppy barely moves. Not much of a guard dog. "Go on. Tell me why you're just so awful," Jan says.

"First, *ow*. Second, why would I want to *convince* you of how awful I am?"

"Just try, goddammit."

I stare out the front window and sigh, sagging into my seat.

I decide to just say the facts.

"I've been a royal pain in my moms' asses since I hit puberty. So much so that one of my moms decided she'd had it with me and took off. Instead of smartening up, I just kept being an asshole and still manage to disappoint my other mom on a daily basis. And—here's the kicker—I actually *tried* to make my mom happy while I was here. I thought she'd be proud of me for helping with SLEA, surrounding myself with good people. Turns out, she's Lux Corp's VP, and I didn't even know 'cause I'm a shitty, self-absorbed kid, and she is definitely *not* proud of me for helping SLEA. And, oh yeah, I'm also quitting SLEA, because—sorry—I'm not about to risk being disowned by a second mom for the sake of the environment. Maya was real happy about that, too, as you can imagine. Cool, right? Proud of me yet?"

I keep staring straight out at the road in front of us, too scared to see what Jan's face is doing.

But she's silent for a while, happy to make me sweat this out, apparently.

Finally, she says, "So yer quittin' somethin' you care about 'cause you think it'll make your mom happy?"

I roll my eyes and turn to her. "I don't *actually* care about SLEA, Jan. Didn't you hear me? I only joined to impress my mom. Which worked out brilliantly."

"Bullshit."

"Pardon?"

"Yer fulla shit."

I scoff. "I *know*. That's what I'm trying to tell you."

"No, I *mean*, you sure as hell *do* care about SLEA, and you know it."

I frown hard at her, but she continues to stare out the windshield. Something in my chest churns. Caring is not an option.

I look away and say, "I'm not even going to be here for long—what do I care if a resort knocks down some trees or whatever? Maybe it'll make this place bearable for fuck's sake."

The truck swerves right and screeches to a halt on the shoulder. We're on a smaller road, but a car passing us still honks at the abrupt move. Poppy's head perks up and looks around.

"Whoa, what the heck, Jan?" I say, turning to her.

She twists in her seat and leans toward me. I instinctively lean back a little.

"Sounds to me like you've gotten real good at convincing yourself yer a dick who doesn't care about anything or need anyone. I get that. Keeps the hurt away. For a while. But I got news for ya." She peers a little closer. "Ya listening?"

I nod, because she looks serious as hell and I'm not about to mess with her grumpy face or those sinewy arms.

"You haven't convinced me of shit, except that the hurt's finally gettin' to ya and you need good people and this place more than ever."

Before I can stop myself from asking this pathetic question, I say, "But what if you don't have good people around you?" I stare out the passenger side window. "What if everyone sees exactly how disappointing you are?"

"Look at me."

Her voice doesn't leave any room for refusal. I do as I'm told. Her features are stern, but something in her eyes is soft.

"I don't know yer mom or what all's between you two, and I can't speak for Maya and the others, but I can speak for myself, and right now, I'm tellin' you—I'm yer goddamn people, and I'm good as hell." The corner of her mouth twitches before she nods once, puts the car back into gear, and pulls a huge U-turn without even shoulder checking.

I work past the thickness in my throat enough to say, "Wait—I thought we were getting seeds?" I say.

"I got 'em at the shop."

"What? Then why . . . ?" I stop when I see the smirk on her face. "Wow, Jan. Tricky move."

She just keeps on smirking, and for the rest of the drive back to Spruce Lake, we're mostly silent, save for a whole string of curse words when someone cuts Jan off and then the ensuing barks from Poppy. Nothing's silent in my mind, though—but instead of the voices telling me what a mess I am, they're repeating everything Jan just said.

FORTY-NINE

Maya

I leave my parents and Rashida at the pub around four o'clock. I've been enjoying their company and also procrastinating at this next thing I've decided to do—talking to Gabe.

But finally, after a second piece of cake, several of Rashida's French fries, and a game of darts, I "gird up my loins" as my dad said, which is disgusting, and walk to Canva's. I tried texting Gabe first, but she's not responding, and I'm trying not to let that deter me.

When I get to Canva's and enter through the backyard, Blu is in the chicken coop, mid-twirl.

"Hey, Blu. How ya doing?" I say, opening the gate.

He lifts his leg in a semi-ballet move, performing for the chickens, I guess. "Fine!"

I smile at both his energy and his flair for chicken care.

"Canva inside?"

"Yup!"

"Thanks," I say, entering through the screen door. I see Gabe's suitcase sitting inside her bedroom door where I left it, but her room is empty. I turn and call out, "Canva! It's Maya—just walked in," so as not to freak her out when I enter the kitchen.

Canva calls back, "Hello, hello!" and I find her unloading groceries onto her kitchen counter.

"Hi," I say. "Need help?"

"No, no—just a few things. Think Gabe'll like these?" She holds up a pack of Wasa crackers.

I don't have the heart to tell her I doubt very much Gabe will like those, so I just nod and say, "Maybe!" and join her at the counter. "Do you know where she is?"

"I haven't seen her, actually, but I just got home. I did see her suitcase, though. Do you know what that's about?" Worry crinkles her brow.

"Oh, uh. No." Another fib. *Just until I sort things out with Gabe*, I tell myself. And really, I don't *actually* know what Gabe's plans are for staying or leaving. "I've been trying to get ahold of her, but she's not returning my messages."

Canva continues to frown as she puts her chia seeds away. "Strange. Maybe she's busy helping one of the others with SLEA work?"

Doubt it. "Maybe," I say, avoiding Canva's eyes. Before I need to lie any more, I add, "I'm sure I'll find her. I'll tell her to check in with you when I do, okay?"

"That'd be great. I hope she's not planning on checking out

early. I've enjoyed having her around. And I think it's been good for her, too. Don't you?"

That's a tough one, Canva. "Yeah, I think she's enjoyed being here more than she thought she would." I have to hope that some part of this is true.

We say goodbye and I head out, waving to Blu as I cross the yard, where he's now playing some sort of game with a soccer ball and wooden spoon.

I try to think of all the places Gabe could be. Over the next hour, I check spots she already knows about, walking down to the beach and back to Jellybean Pond. I check a couple of spots she might have discovered on one of her accidental detours—I even poke my head into the Spruce Lake Museum, which almost no one goes to.

I decide to check back at the pub and café, because the girl has to *eat* at some point, and as I make my way there, I notice a familiar SUV parked in the museum parking lot, which only has two spots. I stop when I also see Gabe's mom leaning against the back driver's side door, texting violently into her phone.

I'm about to back up slowly and quietly when she looks up and sees me. I feel like a raccoon caught red-handed going through the garbage. Unlike a raccoon, though, I can't just look cute and slink away. Her expression stops me from doing so anyway. Her eyes are red, and her face is drawn.

I swallow and walk toward her. I notice no one's in the driver's seat.

"Maya, right?" she says when I'm a few feet away, her voice tense.

"Yeah."

"Right." She looks at her phone again. Then back up at me. "Have you seen Gabe?"

I shake my head. "No. I've been trying to find her."

She nods, staring somewhere near my chin. "Me too."

This I'm surprised by. I assumed when Karen left Canva's this morning, she went back to Miller's Bay or whatever. Off to get back to work on bringing a resort no one wants to Spruce Lake.

"Have you been here all afternoon?" I ask.

She nods again. "We drove halfway to Miller's Bay, but I had my driver turn back. We've been searching around by car and foot."

I glance at her feet, which are in high heels. *Sounds uncomfortable*, I think, and a small, spiteful part of me also thinks, *Good*.

"She's okay, though, right?" Karen asks—another surprise.

"Do you really care?" As soon as I say the words, I wish I could bite them back. I barely know this woman, and she's clearly upset. But then, from what Gabe's said, she hasn't exactly been mother of the year, so I don't feel *that* bad. Still, I offer a "Sorry."

"It's fine. I can't imagine what she's told you about me," she replies, reading my mind. She's shed the suit blazer she was wearing earlier and unbuttons the top of her blouse now. She must be boiling in that outfit. "But I do care. I'm just shit at showing it." Her eyes find mine now. She shrugs and offers a sad, helpless smile.

I kick at the gravel. "People here genuinely like her, you know. She's been super helpful."

A small huff of laughter leaves Karen's mouth, but it's more gloomy than bitter. "You mean, she's been super helpful trying to ruin everything I'm working for?"

"That depends on how you look at it. Around here, we're working for something else."

"Oh? And what's that?"

I sweep my arm out. "This place. The trees. The water. The land. There are people here who've been taking care of it all forever, you know." I'm thinking about Jan and her water defenders, all the people who came before her, too. "It's worth it to us to challenge what Lux Corp's trying to do here."

She rolls her eyes, and I twitch involuntarily. "That all sounds nice, but it's not exactly how progress works, is it? I mean, you're not exactly living off the land now, are you? This little town of yours came at a cost too, right? There were trees and things before your houses and shops and docks—right? I mean, we're standing in a parking lot, for God's sake."

"Yeah. You're right. We had to change nature to be here. But I like to think we've been pretty responsible about how we interact with the land. I mean, I don't think any of us are trying to go back to a time when there were no towns and cities. But we can work a little better than we are now *with* nature, don't you think?"

"And how—"

"Your resort plans don't seem all that invested in any kind of reciprocal relationship with the environment, do they? You didn't try consulting with anyone here before making those plans?"

Her lips tighten into a straight line. "I'm sure that all sounds simple and straightforward to you, but I don't really have time to explain to you why it isn't. I've already wasted my entire afternoon looking for Gabe."

If I were an animal who growled, I'd growl right now, feeling angry and defensive. Instead, furious words tumble from my mouth. "She's your *kid*! She's not a waste of time. You know she *feels* that, right? That she's not worth your time or care?"

Karen just looks at me, then breathes in and lets out a wavering breath. She looks down and shakes her head. "I do know." Her voice comes out so small. "She just got so hard to deal with. I didn't know how—"

"She can be a pain in the ass," I say, stepping forward. "Even I get that, and I've only known her for two weeks."

Karen looks up at me, and I give her a small smile.

"But I also know it's not how she wants to be. Or that it's all that she is. I don't know everything about what happened in your family, but I do know she's still just your kid, and it's the parents' job to make their kids feel loved." I'm thinking of how Rashida's parents have gotten that so wrong, but I'm also thinking about how my parents and Diamond get it so right.

"Anyway," I say, "I'm going to keep looking. If I find her, I'll tell her you've been looking, too. And that you're worried about her." I turn to leave before Karen can say anything more.

FIFTY

Gabe

Later that evening, I wake up to a cackle blasting me out of sleep. It takes me a second to remember where I am and what I'm doing here.

After replanting the herbs and trying to salvage some of the drowning plants in the boat garden, it was dinnertime, and Jan insisted I join her for a meal at her place because she had "some good medicine" for me. I tried to just trust her and not let my brain jump to all the stuff she might consider "medicine"—the image of Canva's nasty SCOBY in my head.

She let me use her shower, because I was filthy, and then gave me some pajama pants that go to my ankles but are tight around my ass and a T-shirt that has an illustrated slug on the front with the words "Slug Life" across the chest. I had to put my sweaty bra back on, which I hated, but these tits require support. I decided to go commando, though, and threw my underwear, top, and shorts into a paper bag Jan gave me.

In this trendy outfit, I ate a turkey sandwich that Jan fixed for me (she's not vegetarian, thank God). After, she said she was going to have a nap and I should, too, because "it was going to be a late night." She set me up in her sewing room, on an old couch that was comfortable as hell. I must have fallen asleep right away, because I barely remember my head hitting the pillow.

I struggle onto my back now on this very squishy couch and kick off the light blanket that's wrapped around my legs. It's cool in Jan's place, but I run hot, and I feel sweaty. I hear another burst of laughter and realize that it's coming from somewhere outside.

After getting up, folding the blanket, and doing my best in the bathroom to make myself look presentable—it's not easy in the Slug Life T-shirt and ill-fitting pants, with my hair in frizzy chaos—I follow the sound of the laughter and voices.

The kitchen is bathed in dim, warm light, but empty, and it's getting dark outside, but a deck light washes through the windows. I go to pull my phone from my pocket to see what time it is and remember that I left it at Canva's yesterday. I check the microwave instead. Eight thirty-five.

Chatter emanates through the screen door, so I creep over to see what the deal is.

Jan and some women are crowded around a picnic table on the back patio. They all look older, maybe in their fifties and beyond, with hairstyles ranging from buzz cuts to fauxhawks to buns to pigtails, tattoos in abundance, and a range of skin tones.

A couple of them are busy fiddling with . . . dried plants? Or something?

"Quit skulking around and get out here!"

Damn. Not a great skulker, apparently.

I stand up straight and push the door open. The other five women sitting around the table turn to look, grinning or waving at me. I reciprocate with a tentative wave and hello. One of the women at the end of the table is holding on to the ends of what look like long blades of grass, and the other is weaving bunches of the grass together. It smells amazing—like vanilla.

"This here is Gabe," Jan says. She's not braiding but is sorting through a pile of the grass in front of her. "She's been visiting Spruce Lake and helping with SLEA this summer."

It's nice of her not to mention my corporate ties. Or the part where I murdered her herbs and drowned her garden.

There's another round of hellos, and everyone introduces themselves. Jan says these are her "lady defenders," and I have questions about that, but I leave those for later.

"How do you like it here, Gabe?" a woman named Eden, who looks even older than Jan, asks. "Heard you like to garden?" The whole group chuckles at this, and even though I realize Jan *has* relayed my little mishap from earlier and this laughter is one hundred percent at my expense, I can't help the smile growing on my lips.

"Yeah, I might need another lesson or two . . ." I say, climbing onto the bench next to Jan, where she's made room for me.

The women's chatter continues, sometimes punctuated by

more laughter. Some are drinking tea, one is knitting, another is just listening.

Jan elbows me in the ribs and nods toward the others. "Medicine, eh?"

I'm not sure if she's referring to the company, the stuff the women are braiding, or something else. I guess she could mean all of it.

"What is this?" I ask, picking up a long, green blade.

"Sweetgrass," the woman named . . . Robin? says. She's tall with green eyes and a strong jaw. Short, curly hair frames her face, and from her ears hang long, beaded earrings that dangle to her shoulders. She's the one holding the grass at one end.

"Like, it's edible?" I ask.

This sets off another round of chuckles.

Jan nudges me. "You can go ahead and eat it if you want, but Robin and Kate use it for smudging."

I want to ask about the smudging—I've heard of it, but don't really get it—but I'll probably just set off another round of laughter. I scan the piles of grass scattered across the table and instead ask, "Where'd you get it?"

The woman who's braiding—Kate—answers. "Some of us grow it in our gardens. Hard to find it out here on the coast otherwise."

My eyes are drawn to her hands as they come to the end of the braid. Her fingers are thick and wrinkled, but that doesn't limit her dexterity. She loops a piece of grass around the bunch of blades and ties a firm knot. She's peering down through the bottom of her glasses, and her lips push out as she does this, more wrinkles gathering around her mouth.

"You do this?" I ask Jan.

"Sometimes. But these two"—she indicates Robin and Kate—"are Métis and it's part of their cultural traditions. They just make me pick out the brown bits." She indicates the small pile of brown grass in front of her. Robin and Kate chuckle.

"Can I try?" I ask.

"Sure you can, but you gotta come with good intentions. Can you do that?" Kate asks.

I glance at Jan, who's just concentrating on the grass she's picking through. "Uh. Yeah. I think I can do that," I say, even if I'm still sorting out the mess I've made.

They show me how to count out the blades of grass into three groups of seven each, then tie the bottom and get braiding. Kate pairs with me while Robin prepares more bundles. I'm supposed to clear my thoughts as I pull each bundle over the next in the braid.

It all feels a little woo-woo to me. That's what my mom would say, anyway. Me too, maybe. This'd be right up Meems's alley, though. The thought makes my grip tighten around the braids, and a piece of grass frays from the tension.

"Easy, girl," Jan says next to me, eyeing up my braid.

Right. Good vibes. Good vibes. I loosen my grip.

Most of the women keep talking, telling stories and catching up. I gather from their conversation that they've known each other for decades. Robin and Kate are a couple originally from the interior, but they live here now, and Lee, Eden, and Michelle are from here or Miller's Bay—they're Quw'utsun, like Jan. I also get the sense that they've spent a lot of time getting into trouble together—both the fun kind and the protest kind.

"Remember that one cop who tried to lift Briggs up from the armpits and strained his back?" Lee says.

A few of them chuckle.

"Don't know what that guy was thinking, tryna pick up a giant like Briggs," Michelle adds.

"And Briggs just sittin' there like nothing was happening."

I'm getting to the end of my braid and ask, "So, like, are you all some kind of career protesters or something?" I realize as I say it that I'm using my mom's judgy words, and I can feel my cheeks grow hot.

"Protesting is no career, girlie. No one's paying us to do it," Eden says. Usually I'd bristle at being called girlie, but the way she says it sounds like a weird mix of reprimand, endearment, and honor.

"Yeah, we've got no choice," Lee says.

I frown. "What does that mean?"

"We gotta keep Earth safe, right? If we wanna keep her going? If our kids and their kids are gonna have a place to live? What choice do we have if we want them to see a future?" Robin says, emphasizing each of her questions with a wave of the grass she's holding. "The land is us. We're the land."

I nod. I don't get all of what they're saying, but I'm starting to see what Jan said about these being her lady defender friends.

They're gentle with these braids and each other, but I have a feeling they're fierce as hell if they need to be. I hope Jan hasn't told them about anything other than my little gardening incident. I can't imagine they'd take very kindly to my mom working for Lux.

When all the grass is braided, Robin and Kate use their hands to sweep up all the tidbits of grass scattered across the table and place them in a glass jar for who knows what. Jan nudges my shoulder and says, "Come help me make some more tea for these hooligans." The women giggle as Jan and I get up from the table and head to the kitchen.

As we're waiting for the water to boil, Jan asks, "So? What's yer plan?"

"Plan?"

"Yep. How're you gonna sort things out with Maya? Get some mugs out from that cupboard while you talk."

Yes, ma'am. I do as I'm told and open the cupboard. "Um . . ." I think about Maya's partiality to romance. "Maybe I should try some kind of grand gesture?" I line the mugs up evenly on the counter, fidgeting with each until they're perfect.

"Nah."

I wait for her to elaborate. When she just stares at me, I try again. "Okay . . . I guess a conversation or something?"

She nods once and goes to pull a tin box down from a shelf. "Good start," she says, and opens the box on the counter next to me. Inside are just regular, round tea bags. She eyes me up. "Tetley. Orange pekoe. What'd you expect?" She's smirking and I'm embarrassed, because to be honest, I *did* expect the box to have some kind of leaves or bark or whatever in it—maybe even those bits of sweetgrass from before. I can't help but smile back.

As she pours the hot water into a well-used teapot, she asks, "I've got a way to help with SLEA, too, if yer up for it."

"Oh yeah?"

"Yep. Stick around. Medicine's just startin'."

FIFTY-ONE

Maya

Rashida and I are sitting next to each other on my dock, feet over the edge and in the water. I spent all afternoon searching for Gabe, but by dinnertime, she hadn't messaged me back, nor had anyone else seen her. Rashida helped me look for her after dinner, but with no success. Then Canva messaged me. Jan had apparently texted *her* to say that Gabe was fine and with Jan.

I was relieved to hear she was okay and not lost in the woods somewhere, but I was also desperate to talk to her. Rashida stopped me from going over to Jan's, though. She said tonight was her "lady defender time" and warned me *not* to interrupt a water defender gathering unless invited.

I trust her advice, since she's been invited to help with Jan's crew before herself. The fact that Gabe seems to have been included in this group makes me a little proud of her.

Thankfully, Rish was willing to hang out with me, because I think if I had to be alone, my brain would overheat with all the things I want to say, wish I'd said, think Gabe might be feeling or thinking about me, and more.

So we watched a comedy on my laptop on the covered patio while my parents were out, and then came out here to cool off—the water fresh and revitalizing at our feet.

"She probably just needs some time, Maya."

"Yeah, I know," I say, even though my impatience to see and talk to Gabe hasn't diminished at all from before.

"It's good she's hanging out with Jan, at least—right?" She nudges me in the shoulder. "At least she's not by herself somewhere."

That's true. She's safe with Jan, I know. And probably in her element with Jan's crew—those women don't waste time on niceties and bullshit. I do get some pleasure picturing her with them and wonder how she ended up there—if she sought them out or if they gathered her up because they knew she needed it.

And then my heart aches to know she didn't feel she could seek *me* out, and that *I* didn't see she needed to be gathered up.

"Maya?"

I guess I'm crying now, and Rish's face is all twisted up in concern.

"Sorry," I say, swiping at my cheeks. "I think I like her more than I even realized."

"You seemed to really like her—right away, even. I'm not gonna lie, it was weird, to see you meet and date someone so quickly this summer."

"Did you think Gabe was a rebound?"

She side-eyes me and a small smile forms. "I mean . . . I kind of did? It just seemed so unlike you to jump into something like that. Especially . . . you know . . . with last summer and everything."

Man, I need to tell her. After all the messiness of the past couple of days, and the conversations I've been having trying to get to the bottom of that mess, I can't keep letting Rashida think Gabe and I were real from the start, even if the thought makes me nauseous.

"Rashida, I have to tell you something, and I really, really hope you'll let me explain before getting mad at me." Maybe that wasn't the best setup, but I'm nervous and my words aren't perfect.

She looks at me, frowning. "Okay . . . ?"

I kick at the water a bit, take a deep breath, and spit it out. "Gabe and I—at the start at least—might have been . . . kind of . . . pretending." *Pretending* sounds more playful than *fake-dating*, I decide.

Her frown deepens. "Pretending . . . how?"

I wipe a hand over my face and huff out a sigh. I take another breath and launch into a scramble of words.

"I don't know—everything happened so fast when I got here. I was so overwhelmed with seeing you, and my parents and Diamond were on my case about moving on and having a good summer even though it felt like my heart was crumbling, and everyone else just kept reminding me of what a fool I made of myself last summer with you.

"And then I met Gabe, and for some reason, I just unloaded all of that onto her. She came up with the idea to try and make you jealous, and I thought it was a terrible idea at first, but then karaoke happened and you *did* seem a little jealous—or maybe just worried?—and Gabe was so . . . *persuasive*? And everyone else seemed to be so excited for me and stopped giving me weepy looks, and I felt just a tiny bit less embarrassed and pathetic, so I agreed to pretend we were dating."

I realize I've said all of this to my lap, so I look up now to see what Rashida's reaction is.

She's staring at me, eyes wide open. "Holy shit."

"Yeah . . ." I'm trying to read her face, and it doesn't seem angry . . . yet.

"So . . . your 'dates' weren't real?"

"Well . . . we went on them, so they were real, but we weren't really *dating*. Just pretending."

"But you were holding hands and stuff? Did you . . . ?"

"That's all we've done—hold hands, a kiss on the cheek here and there."

"And then . . . you caught real feelings for her?"

I nod, eyes back on my lap again. I press my hands into the cool dock beneath us. "I did. I'm not exactly sure when, but things definitely didn't feel fake these past few days."

She's quiet for a few moments, and I can't help but ask, "Are you pissed? I'd obviously understand if you are."

"Maya . . . I think I'm actually kind of proud of you. I mean, I'm *also* a little mad at you for trying to make me jealous like some kind of *brat*—" She cuts her eyes at me and purses her lips at this. "But the fact that you did this completely over-the-top thing also impresses me? Like, you've *never* been the kind of person who would do something like this. Spontaneous fake-dating shenanigans with someone like *Gabe*? Who even *are* you?"

She pushes at my shoulder and then wraps an arm around me, bringing me in. "It's like you're all grown up, but via the most ridiculous, immature thing possible." She grins and laughs at me.

I can't help but laugh along with her, because this is all just so absurd—the "shenanigans" themselves *and* her reaction to them.

"I haven't told my parents about that part yet, just FYI," I say, once we've had our laugh.

"Maybe you won't need to."

"Really?"

"Well, if you and Gabe actually end up dating, why would it matter?" Rashida says, surprising me a little.

"That's a big 'if,'" I say.

She shrugs, a smarmy look on her face. "Make it work, bish."

I scoff and whack her arm. But that's exactly what I'm set on doing. Only this time, I plan on leaving the boat, twinkly lights, and flowers out of it.

FIFTY-TWO

Gabe

It's almost ten thirty by the time I leave Jan's. I spent the rest of the evening listening to her and the others plan for the protest, finally getting some insight into who exactly this group of "lady defenders" is and what they do. I know by the end of the night that being included at all in this conversation isn't something I should take for granted. Jan letting me stay makes me feel a little less hopeless, too.

But as much as she trusts me with their planning, she doesn't trust me to make it back to Canva's on my own without getting lost. She offers me her couch again after everyone else is gone, but I tell her I know exactly where I'm going, and I do.

Except I'm not going to Canva's. I walk to Maya's instead. When I get there, light glows from the cabin, but I don't want to disturb her parents if they're home. I should have just picked up my phone from Canva's, but was avoiding getting caught up with her or Blu.

Making my way down the side of the cabin to check the lakeside, I hear low murmurs. When the dock becomes visible, I see Maya and Rashida sitting on the end of it, their feet in the water. They're laughing and having a jolly old time.

Dammit. I have to fight that shitty little spike in my chest from reemerging when I see the two of them together, but I keep moving my feet down the stairs, one by one.

They both look back at me when they hear the dock creak out of rhythm with its usual squeaks and groans. Maya scrambles to her feet immediately. Rashida follows after her.

I pause, uncertain. "Uh. Hi."

"Gabe. Hi." The outdoor deck lights that are strung around the canopy are on, and I can see relief on her face. That's encouraging, at least.

"Sorry. I can go if I'm interrupting—"

"You're not," Rashida says. "At all. I was just leaving."

She doesn't even look at Maya as she walks up the dock and past me, but gives me a small smile and a light touch to my arm with her knuckles as she does. I wonder if she knows who my mom is by now. She can't possibly, given that smile, right?

When she disappears around the side of the cabin, Maya says, "Come sit?" and I close the gap between us. I'm still in the most ridiculous outfit—slugs and pj pants—but I don't even care. I'm actually a little glad when it causes Maya to give me a once-over and ask, with a tiny smile on her face, "All about that slug life now?"

"It's a long story," I say as I pull up my pant legs and we sit down on the dock.

Being this close to her makes me want to touch her, but I keep the few inches between us.

"I looked all over for you today," she says. "You were at Jan's tonight, though?"

I face her. "You were looking for me?"

She nods. "Yes. I was worried."

"Oh." I look down at the lake and press my hands into the edge of the dock, swish my feet around in the water. It's refreshing. "I was on an impromptu tour of Spruce Lake. You would have been proud of me." I allow myself a half smile but keep my face forward.

"Oh? How was that?" she asks.

"Uh . . . well, it started out with a bit of a fail. Then it got better." I look at her again.

She's smiling. "And?"

"And I'll save the rest for later."

"Okay . . ."

"Because now, I have other things I want to say."

"Oh. Me too."

"Can I go first?"

She nods. "Sure."

I turn my body toward her, bending one leg between us and keeping the other hanging in the water. She does the same. Our knees touch, just barely.

"I wanted to say, I'm sorry for pretending like I actually cared about SLEA, at the beginning anyway—and about letting it go so easily to make my mom happy. *And* I'm sorry for getting weird about you and Rashida and then leaving last night. It wasn't my right to resent you for going with her."

She places a hand on my knee and says, "You were scared."

Her words are blunt, and I automatically bristle, but they also hit a truth I've been unwilling to admit. "I was . . . scared. Yeah. I guess?" My voice is starting to waver, and my eyes sting. "Because I'm not . . . I don't really have . . ." I shake my head a little, all the words I'd worked through in my head getting lost somewhere between my thudding heart and the tightness in my throat.

"Gabe"—Maya's hand presses into my knee—"I *really* like being with you."

"Because I'm a good time, I know."

"Yes. That. Definitely." She gives me a smile. "But also more than that."

I frown, a little confused, a little disbelieving.

Maya swallows and seems to think about her next words. "You brought out something in me that I didn't even realize I could be here. Like . . . I felt more confident with you, more daring. It's been unpredictable and a little scary, but also . . . refreshing?"

My eyebrows rise, and I can't help the small smile that lifts my lips.

Before I can respond, she adds, "You also helped me realize I could move on from Rashida."

I tilt my head and the frown is back, because this is hard to believe. "You and her seem so tight," I say.

I nod. "We are. And we probably always will be. But that doesn't have to stop me and you from being something good, too." She shuffles a smidge closer so our knees are pressed into one another now, her hand moving an inch up my leg.

I place a hand on hers because as much as I want to continue this forward movement, I still have things to say. "Jan said I have to 'let people in,'" I blurt.

Her eyebrows pop up, and an amused smile appears on her lips. "Did she?"

"Are you laughing at me?" I say, but I'm smiling, too.

"Not at all."

I narrow my eyes and squeeze her hand. "Better not be." She grins in response. "I guess I'm just trying to figure out how to be around people who might actually care about me." Then I smile slyly at her and add, "I'm taking a look at myself and making a change, you see. I'm starting with the man in the mirror. I'm asking him to change his—"

"Stop."

I laugh. "But for real." I let my smile drop. "I think it's hard for me to trust that people will actually want to be around me. Or stay. Or care about me at all. No one really has, so far." I swallow, but when I blink, my eyes blur with tears.

"Gabe, I'm so sorry. I'm not pretending to understand what that's like—you've seen how ridiculous my parents are—but I hope you know that people here *do* care about you. Genuinely.

And fully. Even after just two weeks—you've made us care about you so much."

I try hard to let her words sink in, but it's not easy to believe them.

"*And* you might not want to hear this, but your mom spent all afternoon looking for you, too. I saw her, and we talked. She was genuinely worried about you, Gabe. I could see a bit of what you must see—she's got some serious defenses up, too—but I think she was actually so scared."

My defenses rise right now. I scoff before I can help it.

"You don't have to believe me, and obviously you know more about your relationship with your mom than I do, but I just wanted you to know—she was here, sweaty and hot and in heels, hoping to find you."

She gives me the softest smile, and it lowers my defenses again.

"Noted" is all I say. We stare at each other for a few seconds, and I wonder if it'd be okay to hug her now, but before I can ask, another light in her cabin goes on.

We both look up.

"My parents are home," says Maya.

Damn.

"But . . ."

"But what?" I ask, searching her face, which looks a little mischievous.

"But we could get in the water? Hide from any prying eyes?"

My eyebrow peaks and I smirk. "And why would we want to do that?"

"No reason." But her eyes definitely drop to my lips.

"I'm in," I say. But then I realize I don't have underpants on underneath these pajama pants. "Oh, shit. I'm commando right now." When she gives me a questioning look, I add, "Don't ask."

To my surprise, Maya shrugs at this. "Gabe, skinny-dipping in the lake is, like, a rite of passage here. Consider it the next stop on our string of Spruce Lake dates."

Holy shit. I did not think Maya had *this* in her, but I'm not complaining.

The next couple of minutes involve a whole lot of giggling and trying not to be heard giggling and hopping out of clothes and trying not to stare at each other while naked.

Finally, we're in the water, and it's chilly as heck but also feels so smooth and almost *silky* without clothes on. Maya whispers, "Come on," and she starts wading to the small floating dock that's a couple cabins down. I follow, but by the time we get there, I'm winded, and it takes a minute for me to catch my breath.

"Christ, you could have at least offered me a pool noodle," I say, grinning. We're around the lake-facing side of the dock, hidden from the cabins. We're holding on to the ladder with one hand and facing each other, our other arms sweeping back and forth beneath the water.

She grins back. "You're a better swimmer than you think."

It's very difficult not to be aware of our naked bodies below the water's surface, but the water is so dark that we're just shadows down there. If I move just a little closer, though . . .

Maya beats me to it, and in the next second, her arm slips around my waist and our stomachs and chests are pressed against each other. My body is instantly on fire, despite the cool water.

I wrap an arm around her, too, because Lord knows she's going to have to keep me afloat during this.

Our faces are so close, and we just look at each other for a few moments.

Then I say, my voice lowered, "It took way too fucking long to get here, you know."

"Gabe, it's only been two weeks."

"Too. Fucking. Long."

We grin until the last second, when our lips meet, and as they do, I finally get what some of the fuss is about, because along with the very familiar, very hot feeling between my legs is a new mix of ache and pleasure in my chest.

She parts her lips a little, and I waste no time finding her tongue with mine. She lets out the softest, sexiest sigh into my mouth. With her arm holding me tight, I'm able to let go of her waist and bring my hand to her face, to the back of her neck, pulling her farther into me as our kiss deepens.

Even though I have to hold on tighter to the dock when her own arm loosens around my waist, I am *more* than delighted when I feel her hand move up the side of my torso toward my chest. She pulls her mouth away from mine for a second to ask, "Can I?" and I nod in the dark, but she sees it, because the next thing I know, our lips are together and her hand is on my breast and she's so gentle I have to stop kissing her again to just enjoy her touch.

Our foreheads meet, and I sigh into the space between us as the water shifts around us.

Her skin and the water, the warmer air around us—even my fingers curled around the rung of the ladder—feel like a refuge.

"Is this okay?"

"It's perfect," I say, and lean in for another kiss.

FIFTY-THREE

Maya

The next two weeks are a flurry of protest planning and *real* dates with Gabe.

I take her to the wishing well, where, instead of throwing coins into the crumbling structure, people leave painted rocks with wishes for others—including for animals, the water, trees, and the earth. Gabe and I painted rocks ahead of time and brought them with us—mine is a green tomato and I tell Gabe my wish is for her to finish the damn book so we can talk about it. Gabe paints four little canoes, but won't tell me what she wishes for.

Fine.

We see the fairy home co-op in the forest where people build affordable housing for fairies and picnic with them all summer long. And we go to the pub for karaoke again and finally sing that duet of "Islands in the Stream" that I dodged before. On Gabe's urging, we head back to Salmon Run for more tubing, too, and enjoy a few meals with my parents at the pub . . . a couple of those times *with* Rashida, even.

And there's been plenty more kissing and exploring that side of us, as well, which, I'll admit, has been my favorite part.

Things aren't always smooth and easy. I still have moments where I miss the history and predictability of what I had—*have*—with Rashida. Familiarity can be so comforting, after all—both in people and places—and I get hit with pangs of wishing I could just jump ahead in time and know Gabe as well as I know Rashida. Gabe's edge, her defenses, her continued resistance to hiking or camping—all of that throws me for a little loop sometimes.

But then I catch myself responding to her in a wholly different way than I've ever responded to Rish—ways that I *like.* She makes me more . . . unpredictable, I guess. Spending time with her is a kind of change I could get used to.

Gabe was also busy doing her own thing this week, though.

I discovered over these past few days that she's kind of been adopted by Jan's water defenders, which I think shocked all of us who know both Gabe *and* Jan. Jan's "lady defenders" are a tight group, and they must see something in Gabe to take her under their wings, which just makes me like Gabe even more.

Gabe has been spending time with them when she isn't with SLEA, planning their own approach to Lux, and I wonder if that has anything to do with her little painted canoes, but mostly I'm just impressed with her—she's almost as committed to the protest as Rashida, and that's saying something, especially since I know it means her mom won't be happy.

When I asked her about this last part, she chewed on her lower lip and took a few moments to respond. "I guess I'm trying not to worry about it? Like, Jan said to get centered on what makes me feel most grounded right now. And that's this protest. And you." She shrugged and gave me the sweetest smile and—though I don't think I'll ever get tired of her smirk—that smile dissolved every bone in my body.

While she was off doing whatever she was doing with Jan, I helped Rashida and the others with our own protest planning, and all that planning seems to have paid off, because I'm standing in a crowd of hundreds right now.

Lux is supposed to break ground in Tipper Park today, and we've descended upon the site. Turnout is amazing. The whole space in front of Lux Corp's intended worksite—every inch of grass and dirt and sand—is covered with towels, yoga mats, and blankets. And on top of those are people dressed for the beach. Bikinis, Speedos, board shorts, one-pieces, swim trunks—some people are wearing as little as they can get away with. People have set up umbrellas and small tents, brought coolers for their cold drinks, books to read, cards to play games. Someone even brought a giant Jenga set.

And then of course there are signs. Lots and lots of signs. Each one with a different fact about the impact of Lux Corp's actions on the forest, land, and water, or with slogans like "Let the land lead you" and "Planet over profits" on them. And we're getting plenty of attention. Two local news crews are already here, and more folks are arriving every minute.

"Lux Corp's construction crew is coming!" someone shouts.

I'm standing next to Rashida and my parents, while Diamond chats up the news people. We look over and sure enough, several trucks and machinery are approaching like angry bulls, blowing dirty air from their exhaust pipes.

I look around, searching for Gabe. She was supposed to be here by now. But I haven't seen or heard from her all morning. An annoying pinching sensation settles in my chest, and I have to will it away. *I can trust Gabe. I can trust my own trust in her and how she feels about me, and how she feels about all of this around me.*

But I really hope she arrives soon.

FIFTY-FOUR

Gabe

I'm standing at the four-way stop in town, where my mom will pass through soon on her way to the construction site. I could have messaged her and asked her to meet me, but I need the element of surprise here.

The night after Maya and I went for the best skinny-dip of my life, I arrived back to Canva's to find four messages from my mom.

Mother-Figure: Gabe, where are you?

Mother-Figure: I need to talk to you.

Mother-Figure: Can we talk?

Mother-Figure: Are you okay?

That last one made my eyes sting, but mainly because I *did* feel okay. After spending time with Jan and all her friends, making the decision to keep helping with the protest, and figuring things out with Maya . . . I felt okay. Not completely good, not necessarily new and improved, but okay enough to text back: Yes, I'm okay. Talk soon.

And I meant it. I wanted to talk to her. But I couldn't until today. She'd want to know more about SLEA, so it just felt right to hold off. I was actually surprised she didn't push me for more information, but she must have been so busy with the ground-breaking that she just messaged back I hope so. Text me when you can talk.

But now I'm in charge of running interference, so here I am, standing next to a stop sign kitty-corner from the pub, waiting for my mom's SUV to drive up. I'm wearing my kicks, jean shorts, and my bright red cropped shirt that you can't miss.

The village is quiet right now. Most people are already at the protest. I was supposed to be there by now, too, but my mom is running late, which is actually a good thing because my whole role is to delay her arrival anyway. I can't text Maya to let her know I'll be late, though, because she'll want to know where I am and what I'm doing, and Jan made me swear to keep this plan to myself, "on penalty of death" if I don't. LOL.

Jan and her defenders should be on their way to the site at this point. The timing was important. They wanted to get there when the protest was in full swing, but also before my mom arrives, because rest assured, my mom is going to try to put a stop to things as soon as she can. I'm here to give Jan some buffer time before that happens.

I'm sure my mom already knows about the protest by now, but she's the type who likes to survey the scene in person before making decisions.

I see a couple of black SUVs approaching, and it's gotta be them. Not a lot of slick gas guzzlers like those around Spruce Lake. As they get closer, I can see the Lux logo on the sides of both, too.

I start waving like a weirdo.

My mom must see me, because the first car pulls up, the second behind it. The rear window lowers and my mom's head appears.

"Gabe? What in the world? Are you okay?"

Even though I have an objective here, I can't help but feel that little twinge again at her last question. Not "What are you up to now?" or "Is this a ploy?" (which it is), but "Are you okay?"

I can't get distracted with that twinge right now, though.

"Hey. Yes. But I need to talk to you?" I say, approaching the open window.

"Oh. Now?" She looks down quickly, and I can tell she's checking the time on her phone. "It's—this is tricky timing, Gabe. I'm on my way—"

"To the ground-breaking, I know. But this is important, I promise."

She gazes at me for a few seconds, then sighs, her eyes closing. "Yes. Of course. I'll just let the others know . . ." She opens the door and steps out of the car. She doesn't make a move to hug me or anything, and I have to close my own eyes for a moment to picture the gruff, tight hug Jan gave me just this morning, and the warm, close hug Maya and I shared last night when I left her place.

My mom heads to the other SUV. She's in her predictable uniform of black business suit, white collared shirt, and chignon—although I notice she's in flats today. When she returns, she asks, "Can we step into the shade somewhere? Or sit in the car?"

I don't particularly want my mom's driver to hear our entire conversation, so I glance around and see the nearest bit of shade is under the pub's patio. "Sure. Yeah. We can go over here if you want?"

She nods and we walk the several steps together in silence.

When we're under shade, she asks, "So what's this about, Gabe?"

I try not to let the impatience I hear in her voice deter me, but my hands instantly move to a heavy flowerpot sitting on the patio railing. It has spiky scarlet flowers bursting out of it. My thumb and pointer finger press at a soft, green leaf.

A long moment passes, my throat getting tighter and tighter. *Fuck. Come on, Gabe.* My mom moves to the railing next to me and leans over it. I'm sure I don't have long before she loses her patience entirely.

"That's wild bergamot," she says.

My eyebrows lift, my eyes shifting to the deep red flowers instead of the green leaf in my fingers.

"The flowers can be used to make tea."

How the hell does she know that?

"Your mother brought me a big, chaotic bouquet of them to our first date."

Oh. This can't be good.

"I thought it was so old-fashioned and a little cheesy, but it was also the first time someone brought me flowers on a date."

Her arm brushes up against mine and I realize she's right beside me. My fingers instinctively move away from the plant and slip into my pocket instead, where the small braid of sweetgrass that Jan's buddy Eden gave me is hiding away, just to help keep my thoughts clear. My mom's fingers take my place on the plant.

"If you rub the leaves, you can smell a little spiciness and mint. See?" She holds her fingers out for me to sniff. I hesitate, because this isn't how we do things. She must be embarrassed, too, because her cheeks turn a little pink and she retracts her hand, but holds them to her own nose instead. She breathes in and says, "Tracy told me that within two minutes of meeting her. She thought it would impress me—which it did. I definitely wasn't used to dating the gardening type."

I pick a fallen, dried leaf out of the soil in the pot and flick it to the side. "What made you date her, then?"

She rubs her fingers against her dress pants and folds them in front of her again on the railing. "Honestly, she was refreshing. Outgoing and a little silly. Down-to-earth. Optimistic."

So not you at all, then. Me and her, mixed together. And so many things you hate now.

"Gabe, our project is going to bring a lot of good things to this town—you know that, right?"

Her eyes are on me and my skin bristles. Maybe it's my spidey senses telling me I should be worried, or maybe it's just my brain telling my skin it wants the sun.

"I'm still helping SLEA," I blurt. She opens her mouth to speak, but I keep going before she can. "And I know that pisses you off. But I need you to know I'm not just doing it to piss you off. I'm doing it because it feels right to me."

"It feels right to make my job harder, Gabe? Really?" Her voice has frustration in it, but there's also something like sadness, too, I think.

"That's just it—it's not about you and me. It's about . . . this place. About what's best for the people and . . . land here?"

I'm nowhere near as good at talking about this stuff as Rashida or Maya is. I don't know all the lingo or have all the stats. Jan just said to say whatever I knew to be true for me, so even though my stomach is churning, I open my mouth to continue, but my mom beats me to it this time.

"Gabe, you've been here less than a month and all of a sudden you're concerned with the *land*? About *nature*? You've never in your life cared about any of this. What's really going on?"

"I know. I know it seems weird. I know you don't trust me, and I understand why. I haven't given you any reason to. But I swear I'm telling you the truth now." Her expression remains skeptical, but I try to keep going. "I *care* about the people here, and I guess I'm learning from them what else is important to care about? Like . . . um . . ."

God, I'm so bad at this. Why am I so bad at this? I can feel my eyes sting, and I hate it. I'm supposed to be delaying her, but I also wanted to make her see a little of what I see. And I'm failing miserably at it. I have to close my eyes again for a moment. I have to get it together.

I feel my mom's hand on my arm. I open my eyes to find her closer, the skepticism gone, replaced by . . . worry? Or—more likely—confusion?

"Gabe. What is going on with you?"

And then I realize. It's concern in her face. For me.

My own face crumples, and there's nothing I can do to stop it. Her hand squeezes around my bicep, and that just makes things worse. I can't actually remember the last time she touched me like this—steady and firm, skin to skin. I'm moving before I can even stop myself—like there's no other option than what I'm about to do.

I fold myself into her, my arms wrapping around her waist and my head collapsing against her shoulder, probably ruining her fancy suit with my blubbering.

She's startled. I can tell. Her body goes stiff for a second, and I almost pull back, but then her arm is around me and one hand is against the back of my head, holding me against her shoulder.

"Gabe."

Her voice breaks at the end of my name, and her chest hitches against mine.

"Gabe, I'm so sorry."

Genuinely confused, I mumble, "For what? I'm the one who messed everything up."

She pulls back at this and holds my face in her hands, frowning at me.

I'm a little embarrassed about how snotty I am, and I wipe my face with my shirt, which is disgusting, but I didn't think I'd need tissues with me today.

She pushes my wild mane of hair back behind my ears and it feels so good I almost start blubbering again. She says, "You haven't been easy—that's for sure. But that's on me and your mom, too. We didn't—I didn't . . ." She gives her head a little shake, and I guess she sucks at this, too.

"We didn't pay enough attention to each other," I say.

She tilts her head and gazes at me. Her eyes are watery now, too. "Yes. Except—we're the adults. We needed to make sure you know how much we love you." She smiles a little. "Your friend, Maya, gave me a good talking to about that."

"She did?"

"Oh, yes. She wasn't mincing words."

I smile at this. Tough little bish, that one.

I think of her and the others at the protest right now and blurt, "What about everyone else?"

She frowns. "Pardon?"

"I mean . . . this development you're doing here in Spruce Lake—it's going to have an impact on the people here, and the land around it. Shouldn't it be your job to care about that, as well?"

"Gabe, come on. One thing does not have to do with the other—"

"They do, though! I'm just asking you to think about it."

“Think about what? Stopping the development? You know that’s not—”

“No—I mean, maybe. But if that won’t work, then can’t you at least think about—I don’t know—talking with some of the people here and seeing if there’s a way to work together or something? Like, there’re some really smart people here who know a lot about sustainability and stuff. Maybe your project could be built in a good way?”

An eyebrow peaks. I only realize now, though, that neither of us have pulled back from each other. Her hands are still on my shoulders, mine are around her waist. She absentmindedly plays with strands of my hair as she contemplates me now.

Finally, she says, “I don’t know, Gabe. You’re making it sound very simple, but it’s not at all. You have no idea all the complexities involved in land development—the people involved, the money side of things, the consultations that already do take place.”

“But nothing’s *impossible*, right?”

“Not impossible, no. But I’m just one person. And I’m not even the *top* person.”

“You’re not just one person. I can introduce you to a bunch of people who’d be happy to help. And you’re *a* top person. You’re clearly a power player. I mean, look at this suit.” I glance down at her fancy outfit and smirk.

She laughs lightly into her chest and shakes her head again. When she looks up at me, though, her gaze is soft, almost curious. “Where’d you come from, Gabe Martin?” she asks, head tilting.

I shrug and give her a half smile. “You. Meems.”

She smiles a sad smile and nods once.

"So . . . you'll at least think about things?"

She sucks in a big breath and lets it out slowly. I can tell she's not completely on board with all of this. But she says, "I'll think about it. I'm not promising anything, and please don't go back to your protester friends and tell them that I *did* promise anything, okay? This is still my *job* Gabe. I need you to understand that."

I nod. "I understand. But I *am* going to ask them to stay open to talking to you . . . in case you decide to reach out. Okay?"

Another big breath. "Fine."

"Fine."

She continues to gaze at me, a small crinkle on her brow.

"What?"

Her hand moves back to the plant beside us. She takes another leaf in her fingers. "You're really into all of this? It's not just to needle me? Or for Maya?"

I turn to the plant, as well. "I'm really into this, Mom." I side-eye her and smirk. "Like, did you know this is bergamot? You can make tea with it."

FIFTY-FIVE

Maya

I watch as four canoes move through the water like paintings slipping across the surface.

Shortly after the construction machines arrived, stopping at least momentarily before the horde of cyclists chained together across the entryway to the site, a few people started looking out across the lake and drawing everyone's attention to what they were seeing.

Four slivers in the distance, moving toward us.

As the slivers grew bigger, Diamond said with both surprise and maybe a little pride in his voice, "That's Jan. And she's got her water defenders with her."

The canoes are red and black, some with the warm cedarwood showing through, and each one carries six people in it. I can make out Jan at the bow of one, her arms working in time with the other paddlers in her canoe, plunging into the water and stroking backward, the canoe cutting through the water smooth and quick.

The women paddling don't even look tired, though they must have been paddling for at least twenty minutes straight from the closest launching area.

When the news crews—three of them are here now—notice the canoes, they immediately move to the edge of the water to start filming. I'm sure it will make for a great shot—these four traditional canoes helmed by women in cedar hats and kerchiefs and baseball caps, slicing through the water like it's nothing. The canoes are art themselves, but the actual art painted across them is also striking and bold. The news coverage will certainly help our cause—hard to ignore this show of solidarity from local First Nations and Métis water defenders and so many others.

But the rest of us know Jan's not just bringing good optics for the cameras—I've heard her talk about what canoeing brings her and the community when she gets out there.

"Every time my paddle hits the water is a prayer, ya see? And that prayer goes out to all of ya. All those ripples comin' off our canoes are ripples into the community. There's healing in that, right? We got some ancestors pulling with us, each stroke. Can't beat that with a damn motor."

Jan has a motorboat, too. And a gassy old truck. But she's pretty careful about how she uses the things she knows aren't great for the environment. We all try to do that, I guess.

I watch the four canoes now as they glide up to the beach, lining up diagonally so we can see the curve of the bows and the salmon, eagle, orca, and bear designs traveling up the hulls.

The women climb out of their canoes and move together through the crowd, across the beach and grassy area. They're a stark contrast to the bubblegum aesthetic of the protest, with all its bathing suits, bright umbrellas, and such. But then, a few of the defenders, I notice, are also in pretty snazzy bathing suits, as well, along with some in shirts with their nation printed on the back, and those who are in just plain shorts and tank tops. A few of the women carry drums with them.

They come to a stop in front of the row of chained bikes, and a number of protesters scramble to bring them chairs, which some accept and some scoff at (including Jan, of course). Then they just remain there, facing off against the construction crew.

As I watch along with the rest of the crowd, my phone buzzes. With relief, I see it's from Gabe.

Gabe: On my way! Sorry for being late. Will explain soon.

Maya: Get here fast—you'll never guess who showed up.

Gabe: Oh, I can guess. 😉

Things click into place. The four little canoes on her wishing rock. Of course she knew about this. But that doesn't explain why she's late.

What *does* partially explain her tardiness, though, is when she rolls up with her mom in a big black SUV.

My stomach dips. Is she in trouble? Or is this somehow part of the plan?

I make my way through the crowd toward her as she leaves her mom behind and waves at Jan. But then her eyes search past the blockade of bikes and paddlers to find me. She grins and waves, almost jogging toward me (but not actually jogging, because she's still Gabe).

When we meet among the crowd, she wraps me up in a big hug. "Sorry I'm late," she says into my neck, sending a little shiver across it. "I was on distraction duty." She pulls back but doesn't let me go. "Looks like it worked?" she says, glancing back at Jan and the others.

"You were keeping your mom away somehow?" I ask, still trying to put everything together.

"I stalled her at the four-way stop. We talked for even longer than I planned."

I study her face. The last time I saw her talk to her mom, the whole interaction was brutal. "And? Are you okay?"

She nods immediately. "I am. It was a good talk. I'll tell you more later. But I think we should stand up front, don't you?" she says as she grabs my hand and pulls me toward the blockade, where some of the defenders have begun drumming and singing.

The next half an hour gets testy and chaotic. Someone from Lux finally called the police—Gabe doesn't think it was her mom, but I'm not so sure—and when they arrive, tense conversations, glowering stares, and a lot of close-ups from the camera crews ensue.

Gabe and I watch, now alongside Rashida, my parents, and Diamond, who have gathered next to the water defenders, as Gabe's mom spends a lot of time on her cell phone, having very intense conversations with someone or another.

Gabe leans in and whispers to me, "I think she's gonna call off the cops."

I look at her, surprised. "You do?"

She nods, but then her face falls as the police start to make a move toward the blockade, and everyone around us immediately tenses.

FIFTY-SIX

Gabe

As the police advance, I'm momentarily frozen.

"Fuck," I whisper under my breath.

"Gabe," Rashida says, and looks at me. She's standing next me and takes my hand, which is a bit weird to me, but I go along with it. Then she says, "It's okay if you want to step aside—this is a lot for someone's first protest."

A couple of weeks ago, I would have thought she was just trying to get rid of me, but I know that's not true at this moment. "It's not that." Although it kind of is that, too, because the thought of getting arrested is scary as hell. "I'm just trying to figure out how to get my mom to stop this shit."

"Will she listen to you?" Rashida asks.

Before our conversation today, I would have said no. But . . .

"Maybe?"

"Can't hurt to try?" Maya says, from beside me. "But only if you feel okay with this, Gabe." She squeezes the hand she's holding.

"Yeah—there's no pressure, I promise," Rashida adds, squeezing my other hand. "Everyone here is ready to hold the line if they have to."

I look over at my mom, but she's still on the phone, not looking at me. I let go of Rashida's and Maya's hands, and my feet start moving, even though my stomach is freaking out.

I pull up beside my mom and touch her elbow, warning away with a glare the guy in a suit who moves toward me. "She's my mom, so get lost," I say, and he slinks back.

My mom looks at me and says, "Just a minute," to whoever's on the phone. "Gabe, don't. I know you're doing your thing, but I also need to do my thing."

"And your thing is to call the cops on a bunch of people just trying to defend their home?"

"I didn't call the police. My boss did. And now I'm trying to deal with it. You're making that harder."

Her voice is rising, and I take a step back. She swallows and her face softens.

"Gabe, you asked me to think about things. I haven't even had a chance to do that yet. But I'm trying to manage this as best I can. You're just going to have to trust me. Or not." She holds the phone farther away from us and glances at the other suits around her. Leaning in, she whispers, "I promise I'm not trying to get anyone arrested today."

I look back at where Maya and the others are standing, the cops only a few feet away.

I turn back to my mom, unsure of my next move. *Do* I trust her? What else can I say to her that will actually change anything? "Okay" is all I manage at first. But then: "Just know that if anyone does get arrested, it might be me."

Her mouth falls open, and I turn to walk back to Maya. I give her a small smile and take her hand, and we wait for whatever comes.

Thank fuck no one actually gets arrested. I talked some big game with my mom, but I'm not sure I'd last a minute in a jail cell or whatever. From what I've seen on TV, that shit just looks like concrete camping to me, minus the cute deer and soothing sounds, and, oh yeah, any means of escape.

Unfortunately, it wasn't my mom who managed to keep the police from hauling people off. Maybe she did try her best, maybe she was just putting on a show for me, but either way, while she was still on the phone with whoever, some of the cops started to move in with bolt cutters to remove locks from the bikes, and others began pulling people away from their spots.

Hesara, Jack, and Diamond got out in front of the bikes and water defenders to try slowing the cops down by talking to them, while Casey brought over their friends from the press to get in nice and close to capture any sketchy business.

I definitely started to panic, my hand tightening around Maya's, but she assured me that SLEA was prepared for this. Somehow I managed to keep my feet rooted to the ground. It helped to have both Maya and Rashida with me, and see Jan standing her own ground—in her pj pants and Crocs, nonetheless.

Eventually, even the mayor from Miller's Bay arrived and got in on the action, negotiating with my mom and the other Lux reps as the standoff between cops and protesters continued.

This messy business went on for another three hours—late enough in the day that any ground-breaking will have to wait at least until Monday. And that leaves time for the press to get out, which is going to make things even harder for Lux. I just have to hope that my mom knows that SLEA won't stop what it's doing, and that the press we got from this one protest is about to bring Lux a whole bunch of attention it doesn't want.

I also just hope she can see there might be a better way of going about this whole project, even if she couldn't—or wouldn't—come through for me today.

As my mom is getting into her car to leave, I catch up to her and place my hand on the door to keep it open. She turns to me and says, "Yes, Gabe?" Her hair is starting to unravel, and her face looks drawn. I'm sorry she's stressed, but I'm not sorry things went the way they did—not at all.

"I just wanted to say bye and . . ." *What?* "I hope you can see I'm just trying to do the right thing."

She gazes at me, then sighs and brings her hands to the back of her hips. "Yes. I think I can see that. I'm just not sure what to do about all this."

She probably means the protest and building site, but on some level, I feel like she's talking about us, too. "We can figure it out, though, right?" I say, tentative. I'm not used to talking like this—least of all to my mother.

She sighs again and puts a hand on my arm. Gives it a squeeze. I think we're both unsure about this new ground between us—knowing when the other is open to physical touch or honesty or what. But I decide to just follow my gut right now, and I lean in to give her another hug, because that last one felt really fucking good.

She receives it, and I don't even care what the others think—I know I'll have to explain to a bunch of people why I'm hugging this Lux exec, but that's fine. I know who thinks I'm a pretty decent person around here and who will understand. My mom gets into the back seat, and I close the door behind her.

When I head back to Maya, she takes my hand but doesn't ask about my mom, which I appreciate. I'll tell her about it later, I'm sure, because, like, I'm doing that sort of thing now. But this moment is for joining the others and celebrating our small win.

FIFTY-SEVEN

Maya

"The old woman stood on the side of the road and waved back until the car was out of sight."

I have to control the wobble in my voice before saying, "*The end.*"

I pause, looking up through the trees. It's probably the thirtieth time I've read the ending to *Fried Green Tomatoes*, but I get that choky feeling in my throat every time. I realize Gabe hasn't made a sound next to me for a while, and I turn to her now, hoping she didn't fall asleep. But when I look, her face is all crumpled and red.

"Don't look at me!" she says, and covers her face with her hands.

An "Awww!" is out of my mouth before I can stop myself.

She yells, "Ugh! Stop! I hate books!"

This just causes another laugh and makes my heart swell. This girl is too much. But just the right amount of too much.

"Gabe"—I tug at her hands—"crying at the end of books is the best thing ever. Just embrace it."

She lets me remove her hands but turns away. "I will *not*!"

I place the book behind me and keep laughing as I wrap my arm around her and fling a leg over hers, setting us rocking back and forth a bit. We're cuddled in Ruth, fittingly, and the afternoon sun is marbled across our skin. "Look—it's like Ruth's spirit is here, rocking us gently."

She finally turns her head toward me, the tears replaced by an incredulous look. "That's fucked, Maya."

I laugh again, and so does she this time. She wiggles her body so we're facing each other, setting Ruth swinging again. Her leg slips between mine so we can get close and our arms wrap around each other. Our laughter dies down as our foreheads meet. We close our eyes and breathe a little as the hammock stills.

"I can't believe I like this," Gabe says, with a sigh.

My eyes open to find her looking at me. "Like . . . ?"

"Lying in a hammock in the forest without a drink in my hand."

I smile. "I knew you had it in you."

"No, you didn't."

"No, I didn't."

We snicker into the space between us.

"I definitely didn't know you had it in you to try to stop your high-powered exec mom from arresting all of us and building a crappy resort in Spruce Lake."

"I'll get it right next time, no doubt." She smirks, cocky as ever.

Since the protest, Lux Corp's been mired in a publicity nightmare, as we'd all hoped. Social media picked up Jan's water defenders with utter zeal, spurring a letter campaign that already has thousands of signatures. The news outlets who were here that day definitely did not make Lux look good, either.

Now, a week later, Gabe has updated SLEA that her mom is trying to convince her boss and the Lux board it's in their best interests to consult with SLEA and the Quw'utsun Tribe if they want to move forward with their project in any way.

It's not the definitive win we were hoping for, but then it almost never is with these things. One thing at a time, though, as Diamond would say.

"But I should probably stick around for a while, just to keep my mom on her toes, don't you think?"

I smile at her. We haven't really looked past this summer—why would we, given I'll be going back to Greenview and Gabe will be either back in Piedmont or in Miller's Bay with her mom? I can't imagine Gabe jumping into some kind of long-distance thing with me. I'm just trying to be okay with that, even though I know it won't be easy saying goodbye at the end of the summer.

"You think you'll stay in Miller's Bay with your mom? She'll let you?" I ask.

Gabe keeps her eyes on me. "Yeah. She's warming up to the idea, I think. We're warming up to each other."

I stroke her back. "That's great, Gabe. I guess it'll take a bit of work for both of you."

"That's fer damn sure. I'm exhausted just thinking about it." She smiles.

I shake my head at her. "Worth it, though, right?"

She lets her smile disappear. "Yeah. Totally worth it."

I squeeze her leg between mine. "I'm proud of you, Gabe Martin."

"I'm proud of me, too, Maya Brady . . . um . . ."

My eyes open wide at her, and I scoff.

"Kidding! Jayasinghe . . . Jayasinghe . . . Jayasinghe!"

We tussle with each other and then our playfulness turns into kissing and more. But eventually, we just curl up together, letting the evening light find its way through the trees to our skin, breathing in leaves and earth, and listening to the hum of busy, living things working their magic around us like they've always done.

ACKNOWLEDGMENTS

To Jim McCarthy, my ever-supportive agent, thank you for always championing my ideas and stories and being there when I need your wise advice. And to Jennifer Ung, my editor—our fourth book together! How wild. Thank you for guiding me through all the sticky, frustrating bits of the writing process and for caring so deeply about my characters.

To all the folks at HarperCollins and Quill Tree who contributed to this book—eagle-eye copy editors Ana Deboo, Erin DeWitt, and Mikayla Lawrence, as well as everyone else behind the scenes who help to make books better!

And for this stunning cover, huge thanks to designer David DeWitt and artist Jeff Ostberg, who have now given me two book covers I adore. This one captures the beauty of the West Coast setting and the playful "heart" of the story so perfectly.

Huge thanks to my expert reader, Jackie Lever, for her insights and guidance around Indigeneity in this story. And to the trusted folks who gave me their time and feedback when I sought out added perspectives—Katherena Vermette, Kim Spencer, Meredith McInnis, Zosia Dorcey, and Ly Hoang.

To my beta readers, I am also so thankful. Ruby Harris, my "young adult" reader who is also an excellent writer in her own right, thank you for keeping my young characters consistent, and for offering some wonderful thoughts on their development. To Katie Marti, my "chicken consultant" first and foremost, but also an exceptionally good source of outdoorsy info and writing know-how. Thank you for your impeccable insights. I can't wait to see more writing from both of you in the world!

To my most consistent of beta readers—Joanne Darrell Herbert and Ly Hoang—who continue to lend their compassionate, wise eyes to my work and share their enthusiastic support for my writing life. I'm so grateful for both of you.

Gratitude to my big sis, Karen, and her family, whose cabin in Shawnigan Lake, the traditional territory of the Malahat, Quw'utsun, and W̱SÁNEĆ Nations, inspired so much of this story. Thank you for letting me spend so much time there over the years. Thanks, Dennis, for the boating information! And thank you, Akki, for always reading my books the minute they come out and for being so supportive of my writing.

To readers who keep reading and listening to books, and to booksellers and librarians who keep bringing stories to the people, I appreciate you all so much. Truly. What are we without a love for stories?

And finally, to my Jennifer, who said, "Write me a story set at a cabin!" which started this whole thing off. I'm always thankful for your story ideas, even when I don't use them and you pout about it. And thank you for building a cabin for me so I can write my stories in peace and so we can fill it together with our own silly and beautiful rom-com of a life.